I0547095

April's Reign
By Mark Martínez

©2018 Mark Martínez

ALL RIGHTS RESERVED

No part of this publication may be stored in retrieval system or transmitted in any form- written, electronically, mechanically; digital or recording. For information about permission to reproduce selections from this book, write to J3National@gmail.com, Attention: Latisa Martinez

Edited by Latisa Martinez

ISBN: 978-0-692-08458-8
Library of Congress Control Number:

J³ National Publishing, LLC.
MarkJMartinez.com

DEDICATION

Black and Brown girls across the world: You come from royalty. You descend from the very first queens of this earth- queens who gave us beauty that is still imitated today in the music you hear, the movies that you watch and the books that you read.

But you, beautiful sisters, you are not the imitation. You are the real descendants. Take pride in this gift that you have, for you will carry it through your life. And while this gift may feel like a burden at times; always remember how far your gift has come and how far through time it has traveled to get to you.

Use your gift wisely. Use your gift regally.

Asé

Jazmin

Juliana

Jayla

Contents

April's Reign

Prologue

She was awakened by a refreshing wind that energized her body with a feeling stronger than any feeling she had ever felt. She stood up looking towards a figure in the distance, hearing a crackling behind her. Yet, far ahead, there was a sight of beauty.

Standing in the middle of a dry, sandy desert plain, she was captivated by the distant city surrounded by buildings and statues. As she walked closer, she noticed the sun reflecting off the body of water that surrounded the city. At her feet, she noticed a shadow of smoke that towered above her head; just yards behind her. She felt a stinging on the right side of her head and wetness above her brow. She felt dizzy as she brushed her braid aside and wiped her forehead and noticed that the wetness above her brow was not sweat but blood. Still, captivated by the distant beauty and refreshed by the freshest breeze she had ever felt, she did not pay much attention to the blood. Nevertheless, the blood made her wonder what had happened.

She looked back and noticed wreckage. She saw what appeared to be an airplane engulfed in flames. She became confused and she had no idea what had just happened. Everything around her became distorted. The fear of not knowing; pain, sadness and anger set in. Suddenly, the figure in the distance, which appeared to look like a giant sphinx standing at the entrance to the city, appeared to walk toward her. Then, with all of the confusion, fear and pain reaching their peak, she screamed as loud as she could and fainted. Before completely blacking out, thinking she may be hallucinating, she looked up and saw the shadow of a giant lion leaning over her.

"Please... Please, don't eat me," she pleaded breathlessly.

Then, as if coming from the depths of the sky, a deep echo-like voice whispered, "Do not worry, princess. I will not harm you."

▲

In what appeared to be a futuristic room with lights and colors that she had never seen before, the young girl awoke.

Releasing an enormous shout, she quickly sat up.

"No. Don't eat me!" she yelled.

"Relax child! No one is going to eat you,"

An older man said to the young girl with an accent she had never heard.

"There was a lion. A... A giant lion," she stuttered.

"You are fine, young one." The older man assured her. "What is your name?"

"April, my name is April," she answered. "Where am I? What happened? Who are you?"

"Relax. Answers will come." The older man said calmly as he sprayed a gentle mist in the girl's face.

April yawned and gently fell to sleep.

As April slept, she visualized her life at home. In North Philadelphia, she lived in a foster home and was mistreated by the family with which she had lived. In her stressful dream, she experienced pain and hurt; sadness and anger.

"April. April." A deep voice echoed.

Her eyes slowly open. She was calmer and relaxed in what appeared to be another room. This time, the room where she awoke looked more like a typical bedroom in a home, except that the ceiling was higher than two stories and shaped like a dome.

The voice became clearer. She looked over to a chair in the corner of the room from which the voice was coming. It was another older man.

Without realizing that the voice was not coming from the old man, she said to him, "Please. Can you tell me where I am?"

The man stared at April for a moment.

Then, he looked up and said, in a different voice than what she had heard, "Balhib, May I?"

April looked up and saw something so amazing; something she had never seen but had only read about. She felt cold and shaken. She felt a tingling sensation all over her body.

Starting with what appeared to be giant paws behind the old man; April slowly looked and examined the being that, by this point, she realized was what she had seen in the desert. There were paws- giant lion paws. They were thick and muscular and each the height of a full grown man. The body was massive and muscular with fur as golden as the desert sand at high noon. His mane was full, silky and brown. His body was that of an immense, great and graceful lion. But when she looked at his face, she realized that she was in a world of wonder; a world not of her own. The face of this being was that of a man. His facial structure was strong and serious- like the face of royalty. His face was dark brown with dark brown eyes. When April saw this amazing being, she felt weak, confused, amazed, scared and excited all at the same time. April became dizzy.

Balhib, the giant being, looked at the old man and said in a deep voice, the voice April originally heard, "I think we will have to wait until she awakens again."

April then fainted.

that the ceiling was higher than two stories and shaped like a dome.

The voice became clearer. She looked over to a chair in the corner of the room from which the voice was coming. It was another older man.

Without realizing that the voice was not coming from the old man, she said to him, "Please. Can you tell me where I am?"

The man stared at April for a moment.

Then, he looked up and said, in a different voice than what she had heard, "Balhib, May I?"

April looked up and saw something so amazing; something she had never seen but had only read about. She felt cold and shaken. She felt a tingling sensation all over her body.

Starting with what appeared to be giant paws behind the old man; April slowly looked and examined the being that, by this point, she realized was what she had seen in the desert. There were paws- giant lion paws. They were thick and muscular and each the height of a full grown man. The body was massive and muscular with fur as golden as the desert sand at high noon. His mane was full, silky and brown. His body was that of an immense, great and graceful lion. But when she looked at his face, she realized that she was in a world of wonder; a world not of her own. The face of this being was that of a man. His facial structure was strong and serious- like the face of royalty. His ___ ___brown with dark brown eyes. When April saw this ___ onfused, amazed, scared and ___ ril became dizzy. ___ ked at the old man and said in a ___ iginally heard, "I think we will have ___ n."

Part ONE

▲ Chapter 1

April slept for days, dreaming about her life at home. She lived in a rough neighborhood, full of drugs and violence.

Her mother raised her on her own. She was a loving mother. April's mother was young but determined to make sure that April was safe. She loved April very much. Sadly, she passed away when April was 8 years old. Since then, the young girl lived in several foster homes where she was mistreated and neglected. Now, at the age of 14, April had little trust in anyone.

After three days of restless sleep, April awoke in the same room. She was alone. She was scared and confused. April lay on the comfortable bed, afraid to sit up. She examined the room as she lay. Looking to her left, she saw a neatly folded white robe with slippers. To her right, she saw fruit, bread and a glass with white liquid.

Behind the food, there was a great orange curtain with a bit of blue light shining through. Hesitant, April sat up, walked over to the fruit, and grabbed what appeared to be an apple. It was big and shiny. She smelled it. It smelled delicious. She took one bite out of the fruit and, with a look on her face as if she had never tasted anything so good in her life she said, "Oh, my goodness!"

April continued eating the fruit to the core, while looking at the white liquid in a glass next to the fruit. As she examined what appeared to be white juice, she couldn't help being curious about what was behind the curtain. Still, she was very thirsty and wondered about the juice. She cautiously grabbed the glass.

Slowly, bringing the glass to her nose, she sniffed it. She couldn't decipher the smell. She sniffed again, put the glass to her mouth, tilted the glass and let the juice splash against her lips. After licking her lips, she felt comfortable taking a sip. She went for a sip and, after one gulp, she could not stop. Her eyes lit up and then closed to savor the delicious juice as it quenched her thirst.

After she drank, April walked over to the curtains. She heard voices outside the room and ran to the bed. When the voices passed, April slowly sat up and made her way to the curtain again. Again, outside the room, she heard voices and ran back to the bed. This time, the young girl stayed on the bed, afraid that someone would surely come in. After a few moments, April realized that no one was coming and she sat up. She sat up on the bed staring around the room, wondering where she was and what was going on. She looked at the folded robe and slippers on the table next to the bed. She decided to put them on.

April felt very clean and comfortable. Suddenly, she remembered the curtain. She rushed over without a care, grabbed the curtain, pulled it back and gasped. It was the most beautiful sight she had ever seen. She was so taken by the sight that she reached out and placed her hand on the giant window in front of her. April saw beautiful, huge glass pyramids, circular buildings that looked like giant spheres, palm trees and water fountains on roads of golden colored brick. Buildings with arches, domes and triangular roofs that spread out for miles. Beautiful dark skinned people in the cleanest robes and head dresses walked with grace and tranquility. Vehicles hovered over the land with gentleness. April stepped back with surprise as she saw children playing with large cats that looked like cheetahs and leopards. However, it was the next site that sent chills through April's body.

Walking down the road, was the great creature she saw some days earlier. She quickly closed the curtain and ran to the other side of the room. Still, curious, she slowly walked to the curtain and peaked through. She stared as the great lion with a man's face walked towards the building where she was.

Apprehensive, as April typically was, she stared with a suspicious eye. Suddenly, something caught April by surprise. Something that she did not expect happened. April saw the children outside become joyful and excited. They began running towards the majestic beast. They waved with enthusiasm. They jumped on his paws and hugged his legs as he saluted everyone. The scene amazed April. She stared with her eyes wide open.

Suddenly, there was a knock at the door. It startled April so much, that when she turned, she knocked the tray of fruit over. The door slid open and what appeared to be a young child that looked a bit younger than April walked in. April just stared. As the girl came closer, April noticed a sense of maturity about the young girl. April continued to stare.

"April, are you ok?" the young girl asked in the most mature manner. "Allow me to get that for you," she said to April as she reached for the fallen fruit.

April continued to stare.

"You must feel restless," the young girl said with a strange accent. "Where are my manners? My name is Amisi. I am here to help you dress and take you to Saini, then to Khai. But I see that you are already dressed. Is there anything I can get for you before we go?" The small and apparently wise one asked.

April stared speechlessly.

"Well, child, speak." The girl stated with a smile.

"I ain't no child, little girl!" April exclaimed.

"I see," Amisi said. "Well, you are not an adult, are you?"

Before April had a chance to respond, Amisi quickly interrupted, saying, "Quickly, April, we must go."

Amisi grabbed April's hand.

April pulled her hand away and said, "Wait!"

"My apologies, April, you must be so confused," Amisi sympathetically said.

"Yeah, I am," April responded. She then began crying. "Where am I?" April wept. "What is going on?"

Gently, Amisi took April in her little arms and hugged her. "You are going to get your answers soon April... Very soon."

▲

On their way to see Saini, April did not say a word. Although she was typically loquacious and asked many questions, by this point, she was speechless. April did not know what else to say much less think.

Amisi walked April through majestic hallways. As they walked, April just stared at the people dressed in beautiful colorful robes and head dresses. There were a lot of children. And, although they were small like children, they walked and carried themselves as if they were mature adults.

April looked at the ground and noticed that it was golden. She stared at her reflection on the floor as she walked.

Suddenly, a deep voice echoed, "I see the young princess is awake. On your way to see Saini?" April looked up. It was Balhib, the majestic sphinx-like creature speaking to her.

"Yes. Hotep, your grace! I am taking her now," said Amisi.

With a graceful smile, Balhib bowed his head with contentment and said, "Shem hotep. Very well. Be well, princesses. I will see you at the Opet."

"Opet?" asked April.

"It's a festival," Amisi answered. "It's an ancient festival our ancestors had long ago. We brought it back into existence in recent years."

"Who are your ancestors?" April asked.

"You will learn everything soon. Let us just focus on your well-being first," Amisi answered as they approached giant doors.

As the doors slid open, brightness came toward the young ladies like a gentle breeze. On the other side of the doors, April saw grass and trees. She smelled the freshness of the air and was at ease. It appeared as if they were outside. However, they were actually inside a glass dome. Before they entered the dome, Amisi asked April to remove her slippers. Completely at ease, April complied. When they entered the dome, Amisi walked April towards a white table. While walking, April felt a very comforting sensation on her feet. The air, scent and sun light in the dome combined with the comfortable grass like material on the ground was so stimulating to April, she felt like she was under a spell or under the influence of a sedative. April was completely at ease. Her eyes were so relaxed and overwhelmed by the light that she could barely see. When they reached the table, a voice asked April to lay on the table.

Calmly, April asked, "Who said that?"

"I am Saini," the voice replied. "We met when you first arrived. How are you feeling?"

"Real chiiiilll!" April replied serenely. "What did ya'll give me?" She asked.

"We did not give you anything," Saini answered. "This room is a tranquil room. It has a calming effect on everyone who enters it. It has a very strong effect on you because it is your first time in here." Saini explained. "Do not worry, you will be alright."

Calmly, April responded, "Oh, I'm not worried. I told you. I'm chill."

Placing his hand on April's head, Saini closed his eyes and said, "This will only take a moment."

April then closed her eyes. Once April closed her eyes, Saini's voice became a faint echo. A moment later, April awoke in her room. She was calmer than she had ever been.

On the table to her left was a neatly folded peach colored robe with golden trim and peach colored slippers with gold colored straps. Next to the robe, there was a golden object. It was circular with flower shapes engraved. On the back was a comb-like piece. It looked as if it is a decorative hair piece.

On the table to April's right was a glass of the white juice she drank earlier that day. April remembered how good the juice was and quickly reached for it and drank it. She then walked to the giant window; pulled back the curtain and saw that it was nighttime.

April felt very comfortable and at ease. She also felt very clean. April smelled herself and her hair. She smelled good and fresh.

"Did somebody bathe me?" She asked herself. "I've never felt so clean in my life."

She put the robe and the slippers on. She pulled her clean, braided hair back, tied it with a gold colored ribbon that was on the table and placed the gold hairpiece in her hair.

April walked towards the door as if she knew where she was going. The doors slid open. As she walked out of the room, Amisi was there waiting for her.

Amisi was looking radiant. Her gown was white and gold. She was wearing a white headdress and golden sandals. Her eyes were shadowed with golden make-up and black liner. April barely recognized her.

"What are you doin'?" April asked Amisi, surprised that she is outside her door. "Are you spying on me or are you my bodyguard?"

"I was just waiting for you my dear; to accompany you to the festival," Amisi answered.

"I don't need you to wait for me or accompany me," April said rudely.

"Do you know where you are going? Do you know where the festival is?" Amisi asked.

"No." April answered.

"Exactly," Amisi responded in a snobbish tone with a slight smile.

After a brief silence, they both giggled.

They walked silently for a moment; April appeared to ponder. She then asked, "Why do you put up with me? Are you being paid to deal with me until they figure out...?"

"Being paid?" Amisi inquired. "Put up with you? I do not understand."

"I mean, I'm not exactly the nicest person here. I know it. I can have an attitude. I've been that way since... Well, I've been like that for a while." April explained.

"April, you are a child. It is understandable for someone so young, when confused and in a strange place to act defensive and defiant." Amisi said frankly.

April took a deep breath as if to have seemed frustrated.

"There you go with the whole child thing..."

"April, relax, relax. Things are not what they seem... Amisi was interrupted.

"I..."

"Let me explain," Amisi continued. "What is your age; April?"

"I am not a child." April said insolently

"April, I apologize for insulting you. However, you need to understand something. Please let me explain." Amisi said calmly.

April bit her bottom lip in a stubborn manner.

"What is your age?" Amisi asked.

"I'm 14 years old," April answered.

"You see, April," Amisi began to explain. "Here, people age differently."

"What do you mean? The years are shorter?" April asked.

"Well, I am not sure how different our two worlds are. I mean, it is obvious to me that we are from two different worlds. Saini and Khai however, have so much knowledge about you. I heard them say things; comparisons of our societies." Amisi told.

"What? What do they know about me? Who's Khai? I mean, I know that this…"

Confused, April didn't know what words to say or questions to ask.

"I do know that time in both our societies are measured the same. I also know that your mind and maturity is, well…"

"Are you sayin' I'm immature?" April asked defensively.

"April, I know that you are a normal child where you come from. However, here… Things are just different," Amisi states. "You will understand eventually"

"Whatever," April said silently with a stubborn tone.

Amisi looked at April disappointed that she did not have any more answers.

April laughed in disbelief and slight antagonism.

"You know what…" April said.

"Answers will come April. I promise." Amisi said silently.

Just then, they walked outside and began to walk towards a building that appeared to look like a four story glass pyramid with a glass dome built around it; the tip of the pyramid pierced through the top of the dome.

"Wow." April whispered as she reached for Amisi's hand.

As they walked through the fields lit by small fiery light, tamed and friendly large cats and dogs gracefully strolled past. Birds that April had never seen before flew from tree to tree, singing beautiful songs. April looked at Amisi and saw how un-phased she was. April then looked ahead, continuing to hold Amisi's hand like a child holding the hand of their parent. They walked through silently.

As they approached the magnificent structure, the sounds and vibrations of majestic music and drums became stronger. Suddenly, the doors slid open and April and Amisi were welcomed with overwhelming festivities.

As they entered, April was overwhelmed by the energy, colors and happiness. April's eyes were wide open as she looked around at the people in their magnificent attire.

Wardrobe and hair appeared regal and magnificent. Many were wearing masks of hippos, crocodiles and birds. The room was dark yet lit with golden lights. The high ceiling looked like the evening sky with golden stars lighting the room. Every few seconds, birdlike objects or creatures flew by with sparks streaming from their tails, sprinkling down.

Drums and horns played in the background, Amisi held April's hand guiding her through the crowd. As they walked through the crowd, people looked at April with a curious yet respectful eye. All bowed their heads as April and Amisi walked by. Then, as they reached what appeared to be a stage area, the music suddenly stopped.

"Wait here," Amisi said to April.

April happily complied.

As silence filled the room, Amisi walked onto the stage with elegance. With every step Amisi took towards the center of the stage, she appeared to be transformed into a royal figure of this world. April stared in awe and admiration.

When Amisi reached the center of the stage, everyone bowed their heads. Amisi then began to speak a language April had never heard. The audience gazed at Amisi with admiration and reverence. Amisi's voice was high, strong, assertive, happy and regal all at the same time. Finally, Amisi said one final thing and the crowd began to cheer with much enthusiasm.

Suddenly, everyone's attention turned to a giant circular door on the side of the great room. When the door rolled open, Balhib stepped in. As he entered, a silent and respectful excitement filled the room. Everyone bowed their heads. Some even walked up to Balhib and kissed his giant paw. He gently and gracefully walked through the crowd.

With so much magnificence in this world, none of it really hit April until this point. April began to look around. The magic, energy, creatures, colors, dream-like structures, food, clothes, people and all were too overwhelming as it all registered in her mind. Suddenly, everything went dark, and April fainted.

When April awoke, she was surrounded by everyone in the room. Amisi was kneeling next to her.

With a smile, Amisi said, "Child, you must stop doing this."

Then, a voice from behind the people echoed across the crowd in the same language that Amisi was speaking earlier. The crowd parted. A gasp whispered throughout the mob. April looked over and saw the crowd part slowly as an older man walked through.

"Child, are you alright?" He gently asked April.

In a weak voice, April asked, "Who are you?"

Replying with a deep gentle voice, he answered, "I am Khai."

▲

"Tell me about your mother, April," Khai said softly as April awoke in her room.

"My mother passed away when I was younger," April calmly whispered as she slowly opened her eyes.

"Tell me about her."

"She was the most beautiful person I have ever known," April described in a tone and manner she had not spoken in yet since she had arrived.

She lay still on her bed. She was calm and focused; almost as if she were in a trance.

"My mother loved me. She loved me so much," April said as her eyes became watery. "I was so young when she died, but I remember so much. There was always so much going on outside our home. I would be so scared. To put me to sleep, I remember she would cradle me on her lap while sitting on the floor and rock me to sleep singing, (with the 'This Old Man' melody) *'April rains, April rains, wash the troubles all away. With your loving grace and magnificent beauty, you will set your people free.'"*

Khai slowly slid his chair closer to April's bed side and asked, "What does that mean to you, April?"

April slowly turned her head towards Khai and asks, "Why am I here?"

Khai responded, "To grow, April; to learn; to become what your mother wanted you to become."

"What?" April whispered.

Khai moved closer and said, "The rain."

April turned her head and stared at the ceiling for a brief moment as if to contemplate and said, "Oh."

She then closed her eyes.

▲

"BOOM!" Loud thunder rolled as April reawakened.

The thunder was so great that she felt the ground shake. As she opened her eyes she noticed that the room she was in was very dark and damp. She quickly sat up and noticed that she was not in the room she had slept in just before she met Khai. April became frightened.

Suddenly, there was another loud explosion. April screamed.

"Where am I," she yelled. "Amisi!" she called.

No one answered.

"Amisi!" louder, she yelled, "Anybody!"

Anxiously, she examined the room where she was. April did not recognize where she was. The room's walls looked like they were made of old copper and there were no windows. She saw an old odd shaped door. As the ground continued to quake, April ran towards the door and pushed it open. Breathing heavily and trembling, April was confused. She entered another room similar to the one she was just in. She ran towards another door and pushed it open. When April pushed the door open, she tripped down a step onto hard ground. April scraped her knee and the back of her right hand as she tried to break her fall. Her knee was not too badly hurt. However, her hand was bleeding profusely. She looked at her hand in pain. But, what she saw in front of her took her attention away.

April stood up and stared. In front of her was a grey-sand desert with grey skies. She looked to see where the explosion came from.

Suddenly, lightning struck a lone dried up tree about 30 meters away. As the explosion shook the ground, April jumped backwards and tripped over the step and through the door behind her. Confused, shaking and with tears in her eyes, April sat on the step and stared.

Far away, April noticed smoke. She also noticed that the lighting had died down and she began to walk. She looked back and saw that the place from which she came was a small triangle-shaped structure. It was no bigger than a shack.

April continued to walk toward the smoke not noticing the blood dripping from her hand. Leaving a trail of blood as she continued to walk, April continued to tremble and breathe heavily. All she wanted was to find someone. April was scared. Her experiences made no sense to her. She experienced things that no one her age where she was from had ever experienced. She did not realize it, but April was stronger this day than she had ever been in the past. Through her recent experiences, she was becoming stronger and more tolerant to the unexpected.

All of a sudden, four wild dogs appeared from behind the triangle-shaped shack behind April in the distance. April did not notice them. She was too focused on what was in front of her. In the distance, April began to see flashing lights over the horizon. As the lights flashed in the eerie grey sky, the ground trembled softly. Behind her, the dogs followed. The dogs growled. April, almost in a daze, continued walking without noticing.

Over the horizon, appeared trees. The trees were odd. As April walked closer, the trees looked more like giant bushes with purple leaves. They were spread out with a few feet in between each of them. The giant bushes ran for miles from both the right and the left as if to fence the other side of them off.

Afraid, April walked closer to the odd shrubbery as the dogs ran faster towards her. By this point, it appeared as if the wild dogs were intending to harm April.

Exhausted and ready to submit to the pain in body, heart and mind, April stumbled to the ground. When April fell, she noticed the dogs behind her. They were growling and running fast towards her. April gasped. She gathered all the energy she had left in her, pushed herself up off the ground and, confused, she began to run. April ran with fury in her eyes. After passing the row of bushes, April stumbled and fell to the ground. Suddenly, just as the dogs were about to pounce on April, a giant creature leaped out of the giant bushes. It was Balhib.

Letting out a giant roar, Balhib swatted one dog, stepped on another and roared loudly at the other two.

In fear, the dogs bowed as if they were pleading for their lives.

"Leave these grounds!" Balhib yelled with a roaring voice.

The dogs continued to bow. They howled and then walked off.

The ground continued to quake.

Balhib then turned to April and softly asked, "April, are you alright? Your hand…"

Balhib rubbed his mane on the scrape, wiping the blood away. He then had April climb onto his back.

"Where are we? What happened? Why was I…?" April asked exhaustedly.

"Things are no longer the way they were April." Balhib answered. "The war has begun."

He then began to walk quickly towards the light over the horizon.

"War? What war?" April asked breathlessly. "Things were perfect. I don't understand."

"Worlds change, April," Balhib replies.

"Over night? So quickly?" April asks as tears fell from her eyes from fear and confusion.

"April, you have been gone for some time."

"Gone?" April cried, gasping from exhaustion. "How long? Where did I go? I don't understand? I don't remem…"

Suddenly, April remembered being in a hospital…

"…What is your name?" a strange voice echoes.

"There are no records of her on this flight," said another voice.

April is taken back to what she has forgotten.

"What is your name?" the strange voice echoed again. "Do you know where you are?"

The voices then faded out. April opened her eyes and took a deep breath. April heard beeping and people talking in different languages. When she looked around, she noticed that she was in a hospital.

As she quickly sat up, April screamed.

A nurse ran into the room. The nurse said nothing to April. She simply took April by the shoulders and gently laid her back down.

"Where am I," April asked.

Suddenly, a doctor walked in the room. "You are in a hospital far from home, Miss," the doctor answered. "The question is how did you get here?"

"Where is here?" April asked.

The doctor examined April's eyes, checked the monitors and began to write on the chart at the end of April's bed. "You are in Puerto Rico.," he said perfectly switching from fluent English to perfect Spanish to April.

"Puerto Rico?" April asked with much confusion and attitude.

"Yes, young lady." The doctor said. "My name is Dr. Dupri. What is your name?"

"April." She answered calmly and in deep thought.

"Well, April, when you came to us, we didn't know who you were so we needed to take blood and finger prints. I hope you don't mind."

In deeper thought, April responded with a simple, "uh huh."

"April, how do you feel? Does anything hurt?" Dr. Dupri asked.

The nurse was still in the room. She looked very familiar to April. She looked very young; with a dark brown complexion and very light green eyes.

April stared at her as if she knew her from somewhere. Still, April did not know from where.

The conversation became a blur to April. All of the events; traveling from one world to another was too overwhelming for her. She did not want to be there anymore. She did not want to speak anymore.

"Doctor?" April said.

"Yes April," he replied.

"I have a terrible headache. Would you mind if I took a nap? I just want to take a nap. Do you mind?" she asked calmly.

The doctor paused for a moment then said, "Of course not April. Get some rest."

"Thank you," she said.

As the doctor and nurse left the room, April turned her head towards the window and stared. It was cloudy and rainy out and palm trees were blowing. April wanted to think. She wanted to figure out what was going on. She was just too overwhelmed. She really needed rest. April closed her eyes and fell asleep.

Suddenly, April was face to face with her mother. In a sandy, bright dessert, April was calmed by the dry breeze. Her mother stared at her with a smile.

April's mother was young-looking with clear, beautiful dark skin. Before she passed away, she had straight, shoulder length hair. But, here, with April, she wore thin dread locks wrapped in a white cloth. April's mother wore a bright white gown. Her eyes were brown, bright and elegant.

"Mommy!?" April said with her arms extended towards her mother.

"Anok me ba," April's mother whispered with a smile.

April stared at her mother with a slight smile and confusion. "What, Mommy?" she asked.

Her mother smiled as a tear fell from her eye. She continued to speak a language that April did not understand—a language that sounded like the one Amisi spoke. She began to walk towards April with her arms extended as April began to cry.

"Mommy," April said.

April and her mother embraced one another. April cried; her mother smiled.

"Rain," April's mother whispered, "Rain."

April looked up to the sky with tears in her eyes. "Huh?" She responded.

"Rain, April." She repeated in a faded whisper.

"Mommy, I don't understand." April said as her mother and the dessert began to fade away.

"Mommy, I need you. I need you," April cried.

April then opened her eyes. She was laying in the hospital bed staring out the window. It was late in the afternoon and it was getting dark outside. The rain continued. April continued to stare out the window throughout the night; pondering.

Later that evening the nurse from earlier walked into April's room. April continued to stare out the window. But, the thought that the nurse looked familiar stayed in her mind. The nurse placed a tray of food on the high table next to April.

Realizing that it was late, April asked "Isn't it a little late for food?"

With a thick accent, the nurse replied, "Sorry Miss, no English."

"Of course, I forgot that I was in Puerto Rico," April said quietly to herself.

At that moment, April thought that she could not have known the nurse. April smirked at the nurse, said, "It's ok." She then got out of the bed and went into the restroom.

When April finished in the restroom, she came out to find the doctor and two other men in her room.

"April, we have someone here that needs to ask you some questions," the doctor said. "How are you feeling?"

▲

April was suddenly awakened by drops of rain on her head and a chill. Being carried on Balhib's back, she was asleep for some time, dreaming and remembering some moments of the past few years that had escaped her memory.

In a weak and exhausted whisper, April asks, "Why was I alone in that… That shack? Where was that place? Where are we…?

"You were safe April," Balhib said. He then became silent for a moment. Then he said,

"Unfortunately, many are perishing April."

"What?" April became surprised. "Why?"

Balhib did not answer.

"Who were those dogs?" April asked. "And why were they trying to kill me?"

"They were confused. They did not know who you were," Balhib said.

"I don't understand. Who I am? What do you mean?" April responded.

"Humans have always been protected. Throughout time, for thousands of years humans have always been watched, served and protected. And for much of that time they did not even know it.

"Protected?" April asked. "From who?"

"From many things... Mainly from themselves." Balhib answered. "And now, they need to be protected from themselves more than ever," Balhib explained.

"What are you talkin' about?" April asked with an belligerent tone.

"April, in history, humans have always been divided. Then, a time came when humans and animals became one. Sadly, they became enemies. Many humans are good. But for a very long time it was difficult for the good to determine who is evil, who truly is evil" Balhib explained.

With a confused look on her face, April stared blankly and pondered.

"I..."

"April, you will come to understand your fate. But you must be patient," Balhib.

April just stared. "My fate?" she asked.

Balhib became silent and continued walking.

April eventually laid her head on his back as they continued their journey.

As April slept, her thoughts and dreams took her back to the hospital in Puerto Rico.

▲

"April, these gentlemen have some questions for you," the doctor said. "How are you feeling?"

April nodded, as if to say that she was alright. She did not say a word. April just stared at the men in distrust.

"April," The older man said with a strong accent. "My name is Agent Garcia."

The man extended his hand. April stared at the older officer and hesitated. She then slowly extended her hand and shook his.

Agent Garcia continued, "This is Agent Martinez."

When April looked towards the other gentleman, she noticed something familiar about him. April did not know why; but she felt an energy from Agent Martinez that she could not explain. He was a very young, tall man with light brown skin and big brown eyes. The comfort she felt towards Agent Martinez was similar to the comfort she felt when she was near Balhib.

As April extended her hand, her eyes widened. She shook the agent's hand.

Agent Garcia looked at Martinez with a look that questioned her reaction. Agent Martinez shrugged his shoulders, not knowing what April's reaction was about.

"We wanted to ask you some questions," Agent Martinez said speaking much clearer than Agent Garcia.

April just stared with a concerned but tired look.

"Are you feeling well enough to answer some questions?" Martinez asked.

April nodded.

"April, do you remember what happened?" Garcia abruptly asked.

April wondered what they were speaking about. She shook her head with a look of confusion.

"April," Martinez continued. "Do you have any idea what happened?"

April stared silently.

Martinez explained, "There was an airplane crash. Eighty eight people were on board that plane. Eighty seven died."

April stared with fear and confusion.

"April," Agent Garcia said. "There were 87 people registered on that flight; not 88. What puzzles us is that, one, you were found on the plane; two, your name was not found on the list of passengers; three, all passengers were accounted for and pronounced dead and four, you were unharmed. Now, that raises a lot of questions April. Eighty seven people are dead. The one person who did not belong on that flight is not. What can you tell us? What…"

"Where was the plane coming from?" April interrupted.

"You do not know?" Garcia asked.

"No! I don't," April exclaimed. "Now, tell me where the plane was coming from."

Suddenly, the nurse dropped her tray of food behind the two agents.

Doctor Dupri interrupted, "Gentlemen, regardless of whatever you are alleging, April is still a patient… a child who has been through a very traumatic experience. You should give her more time to rest."

Agent Garcia then began to argue with the doctor in Spanish.

As the two men were conversing, Agent Martinez looked at April with a smile that told her that everything was going to be alright then he said, "Caballeros! We will return tomorrow. There is no need for us to stress the child anymore if it is only going to create more confusion. April, forgive us for the confusion."

As Martinez looked at Dr. Dupri, he said, "We did not come here to make accusations…"

"Still," Agent Garcia interrupted, "There are 87 people dead…"

"We will return tomorrow." Martinez said. "April… Get some rest princess."

The men then left the room.

The very next day, April was awakened very early.

"April?" the nurse said with strong accent as she placed a tray with juice and fruit next to April's bed.

As she was about to speak to April, Agent Garcia entered the room. The nurse immediately left the room.

As April sipped her juice, Agent Garcia began to speak. "April, I think Martinez and Dr. Dupri misinterpreted what I was saying yesterday. When we left the hospital, Agent Martinez was very quiet. I felt that he was upset with me. He was acting very strange. This whole situation is strange."

April, a bit scared said, "where is Agent Martinez?"

"I came here without him because… April, I'm not sure what's going on but…" Garcia continues as he stares out the window. "I have never witnessed a case like this…."

"Why are you here?" April asked

"Why are *you* here?" Garcia asked in return as he quickly turned to her. "

When Agent Garcia turned to April, he looked different. He did not look like the same person. His eyes looked different. It was almost like Garcia was possessed by the spirit of another person.

"I don't understand." April said.

"Why did you not stay?"

April gasped silently.

Suddenly, Agent Garcia's face changed completely. His face became that of another person; someone April has never seen before.

Garcia then whispered, "You must go back!"

April got scared, "Where? How did I get here? How do I go back? Why am I here?"

Then, Agent Garcia's face changed back. "What?" He asked. "Did you hear me, April? How did you get on that airplane?"

"What? What happened? Wait, come back. Please…" April cried.

"April," Garcia exclaimed. "What are you talking about? This is… I don't understand what is going on?" He continued in Spanish, "Esta nena está loca!"

"She is not crazy," Dr. Dupri interrupted as he entered the room. "She's a young child that has had a near death experience. She's been under a lot of stress. I understand that you have to do your job, Agent Garcia. However, I must insist you inform me when you need to speak to my patient."

"This is a very serious investigation Doctor…" Garcia replied.

"I understand that Agent Garcia. But, she was a victim in your investigation. And, unless you can provide proof that she is under investigation for any wrong doing, again, I must insist that you leave her be."

As the two men spoke, the young nurse entered the room to bring April medicine and juice.

"Dr. Dupri, this girl is not under your custody. She is under surv…"

"She is under my care in my hospital. I will not continue this discussion any further," Dr. Dupri exclaimed. "It is my professional opinion that you continuing to have conversations of this sort in front of this child will create more stress for her. I insist that you leave immediately."

Without uttering another word and appearing angry, Agent Garcia left.

"April, I'm sorry for this," Dr. Dupri said.

April just stared confused.

"How are you feeling today?" the doctor asked.

April continued to stare. Typically, this type of situation would make April angry. Before, she would have argued and asked a lot of questions and even cried. This time, feeling more mature and calm, April contemplated. She stared, trying to piece everything together. She was silent.

April trusted Doctor Dupri and the nurse. She felt like she knew them. She thought of Agent Martinez and the energy she felt from him. Although she only met him once, April felt that she was going to see him again. She felt that she could trust Martinez as well. April realized that the only way she was going to get answers was to be patient and learn how and who to trust. Once she learned that, the answers would come without questions.

"April, you must take your medicine," Dr. Dupri said.

Without any questions or argument, April put a pill in her mouth and drank the juice. She then fell asleep.

The next morning, April was awakened by loud thunder and wind. The rain outside crashed against April's window like stones.

It was morning. However, it still was dark outside. Because it was dark, April did not know what time of the day it was. She did not realize that she had slept for many hours. April wondered about the storm outside and stared out the window as she walked towards the restroom. While in the restroom, April heard banging. She began to feel a little frightened.

"What's going on out there?" April asked herself.

When she came out of the restroom, April found Dr. Dupri in the room.

"April..." Dr. Dupri said.

"What's going on outside?" April asked.

"There is a tropical storm, April. It is just east of the island; headed north. We are catching some of its winds and rains," Dr. Dupri explained.

April gasped.

"Don't worry April. You are safe in the hospital."

April stared out the window as police cars' lights flashed by.

"How bad will it get?" April asked.

"Oh, it won't get any worse than this April. Don't worry," the doctor replied nonchalantly while looking at the chart. "Did you rest well?"

Suddenly, the nurse entered the room.

"Doctór?" the nurse called.

She gestured for him to come out the room for a word. As they spoke outside the door, April noticed tension.

Behind the nurse and Dr. Dupri, April noticed nurses packing things and moving patients on their beds and wheelchairs. Still, she waited patiently.

When the doctor came back in the room, he approached April with a serious expression on his face.

"April," Dr. Dupri began to explain, "I was just informed that the status of the storm has changed. I have to speak with some people and I will return. You may have to be moved."

"Why are you always here?" April asked as she stared out the window appearing to be in deep thought.

"Excuse me?" the doctor asked with a surprised tone.

"I noticed that you and that nurse are always here. Don't you have families? Don't you go home?" April asked.

Dr. Dupri chuckled. "I don't understand. I…"

"I've been in hospitals before. I've never had just one doctor or just one nurse. Aren't there shifts?" April interrogated.

"Well, you are in Puerto Rico, April. I'm sure things are different here…"

"No." she replied. "I don't believe that. I want to know what is going on."

April then turned to Dr. Dupri and demanded as the doctor stared and the nurse witnessed, "When you return, you will explain everything to me. Everything!"

Dr. Dupri looked at the nurse silently and they both left the room.

April sat on the bed, laid back, turned towards the window and stared.

No more than an hour had passed before Agent Martinez came into April's room. April turned to Martinez with a concerned look.

"Why are you here?" April asked.

Without uttering a word, Agent Martinez extended his hand towards April and gestured for her to take his hand.
April looked at him curiously. She extended her hand and placed it in Martinez's.

Martinez slowly pulled April out of the bed and began to walk her out of the room.

April stopped, turned around, walked to her bedside, placed her robe and slippers on and took a sip of juice. They then left the room. As they walked through the hospital halls, no one noticed them because of the disorganization due to the storm.

While walking towards the door, April noticed a very familiar taste in her mouth.

"The juice," she thought. "Oh, my God! The juice! It's the juice!"

She stopped. Agent Martinez's hand slipped away from April's and he stopped.

"April!" he exclaimed.

"The juice! It's the juice," April said as she remembered that the juice that the nurse was bringing her was the same juice that was in her room in the golden world. Suddenly, she began to think back and remember. In her thoughts, she was taken back to the festival where she had passed out. Although her memory was blurry, she remembered looking at the people surrounding her.

"Those eyes…" April said silently.

April then suddenly remembered the nurse being one of the people around her when she was laying on the ground at the festival.

"The nurse… She was there!" April said.

Then, hastily, Agent Martinez grabbed April's hand and said, "April, we must go."

April asked, "Where are you taking me?"

Suddenly, everything around April went silent. Agent Martinez's eyes became very bright as he stared into April's eyes. April became very calm.

When Agent Martinez spoke, he spoke with the voice of Balhib.

"Answers will come, April," he said.

The noise around April then rapidly returned. April, calm and a bit startled by the noise, began to walk with Agent Martinez towards the door without saying anything else.

When they went outside, the wind was blowing hard and giant drops of rain were flying sideways.

There was a gold colored van with police lights parked in front of the hospital. The engine, lights and windshield wipers were on. There was someone in the driver's seat and some people in the back. Agent Martinez opened the front passenger side door and had April sit in front. Agent Martinez sat in the seat behind her.

As they drove away from the hospital, a red car with police lights and two regular police cars began following the van. The driver, who April did not recognize, drove faster and April realized that the driver was trying to flee from the cars behind them.

April became frightened.

"Relax, April. You will be alright," Agent Martinez said.

"What's going on? Where are you taking me? Who are those people following us?" April asked.

Suddenly, the driver of the van made an immediate turn, causing April to scream. The van began to move faster and faster. April could barely see out the window because of the torrential rain. There was debris on the road which made the ride more frightening. April screamed each time the van made a sudden move.

The other cars were still behind the van as the driver of the van made every attempt to lose them.

"Somebody tell me what is going on?" April demanded as tears fell from her eyes.

"Make a left here," a young woman's voice called from the rear of the van.

April turned around and looked towards the rear of the van but could not see the faces of those seated there.

"Who are you?" April asked.

The van suddenly stopped. They were on a small street where a police car had blocked them off in front. The other cars behind were stopped behind them. They were trapped.

"¡Sálganse del vehículo!" a man's voice said. He demanded for them to step out of the vehicle.

One of the people seated behind April, a man, stepped out of the van from the side door. April did not see his face. He was wearing a blue outfit with a hood. The man walked towards the cars in front of the van. As he passed April's window, April heard the man's voice.

"Tengo un paciente. Ella está muy enferma," the voice said.

April recognized the voice.

Suddenly, there were gun shots. The man from the van stumbled backwards as blood sprayed from his body. By the time he hit the floor, there were six gun shots.

There was a stunned silence. April was petrified.

All of the sudden, the van began to speed towards the car in front of them. The van crashed passed the police car, and drove away from the scene.

April began to cry hysterically. She could not believe what was going on. Since the day in the desert when she first saw the city and met Balhib, April had not been this stunned.

April turned to Agent Martinez crying uncontrollably.

"That was Dr. Dupri," she cried. "That was Doctor Dupri. You did nothing. Why did we leave him? April could barely get her words out.

Agent Martinez began to speak, "April…"

"No!" April interrupted. "You tell me what is going on."

As debris and wind hit the van, Agent Martinez looked at April remorsefully.

"TELL ME!" April yelled.

Agent Martinez slowly lifted his head to look at April. He then looked out the window and said, "We are here."
April turned around and looked out the window. They pulled up to an airport runway where a small jet plane was parked. The driver quickly got out of the van.

The young woman in the back of the van said with a strange accent, "We must move quickly."

Before April had the chance to look at her, the young woman left the van and made her way to the stairs of the airplane.

Still in the van, Agent Martinez said to April, "Please, April, understand. Things may appear a certain way to you. But you must trust that…" Martinez looked down. "… Answers will come. I will try my best to explain once we are in the air. We must hurry April. Please."

Martinez got out of the van, opened April's door and reached his hand out.

"Please come April. Your answers will come soon. I promise," He said.

April took his hand and stepped out of the van. She looked disappointed; almost disgusted.

They walked up the steps and boarded the plane.

As April looked for a seat, the airplane shook from the winds outside.

"Are we going to be safe in this storm?" April asked.

April heard a voice from the back of the airplane answer, "we will be absolutely fine, April."

It was the young nurse from the hospital.

"That was you in the van?" April cried with anger. "I thought you didn't speak English!"

"April…" The young girl attempted to speak.

"No!" April said silently with anger. "No more explaining! I'm done with this! Take me home! I don't want to listen anymore. I don't want to be around you people anymore. Just leave me alone!"

"No April!" The young nurse exclaimed with assertiveness and authority. She startled April. "You *are* going to listen! You are going to sit down; you are going to be quiet; you are going to behave and you are going to stop your childishness."

April attempted to speak.

"Sit down!" the young woman interrupted with a stern tone of voice.

April sat as she stared at everyone with a look of a humiliated child. Everything became silent as everyone sat down and the door closed.

April looked out the window and saw the police cars approaching the runway. As she was about to inform Martinez that the police were coming, the airplane began to drive up the runway. It began to go faster and faster and April looked scared.

The young lady looked over to April and said, "No worries child. You will be safe."

Suddenly, the airplane left the ground and they were on their way. In Spanish, the pilot of the airplane announced that they are going to feel a lot of turbulence but they will fly above the clouds. He asked that everyone remain seated with their seatbelts on until he announced otherwise. The pilot also announced that the flight to Philadelphia would take approximately 3 hours and 55 minutes.

Martinez translated. While Martinez was translating, April heard the pilot say Philadelphia. She became excited.

"We are going to Philly?" She interrupted.

"Yes April," Martinez answered. "We are taking you home."

"Why…?"

As April began to ask questions, she looked at the young woman and cut herself off as if she was afraid to ask.

The young woman sighed and moved to the seat next to April.

"My name is Mayet. I have been sent with you to keep you safe. You were not in the airplane that crashed in Puerto Rico. The crash was an accident but you were not on that plane." April stared and gave Mayet her undivided attention.

Suddenly, the airplane began to shake violently. April got scared and grabbed Martinez, who was sitting next to her, by the hand.

The lights on the airplane began to flicker as the airplane continued to shake uncontrollably. April wanted to scream but was too terrified. The fear was overwhelming. April held Martinez tightly and closed her eyes. The strong turbulence continued. Tears began to fall from April's eyes as her surroundings began to fade.

Martinez's voice faintly echoed, "No te preocupes, April. Everything will be alright."

▲

As the airplane landed in a small airport in Philadelphia, three police cars awaited them at the end of the runway.

"April, we are here." Martinez said as he stroked April's cheek.

Martinez, Mayet, April and two other people made their way out of the airplane and down the steps.

April looked afraid. Surprised that they survived the flight through the storm, April became concerned with the police officers that waited for them at the terminal entrance.

Showing no concern, Martinez grabbed April's hand and continued to walk toward the officers. Martinez reached into his pocket, pulled out his badge and showed it to the officers at the door without stopping. The officers simply looked at Martinez and nodded, allowing the group to pass. The officers stared at April as she walked past.

April felt very tired. She knew that there was a lot going on and she still had a lot of questions. But she remained quiet. She was happy to be home. Outside, there was a blue van waiting for them with a driver. They got into the van and drove off.

The radio played as they drove. The radio played commercials. April was just happy to hear something familiar. A radio commercial was just enough to put her at ease. As they drove along the highway, April stared quietly out the window and gazed at the houses, then the skyline. Then, she heard the radio station's DJ speak. It was a familiar voice, April felt chills. Hearing something as simple as the radio made April feel at ease.

She felt at home and, for the first time in a while, she was content.

On the radio, April heard a familiar song.

"I haven't heard this song in a minute!" April exclaimed.

The others showed no concern.

April felt very relaxed. Not really remembering the words to the song, April hummed along with the melody.

Then, as the song finished, the DJ stated that the song he had just played was brand new and that it was the first time he had played it.

Quickly, Mayet, who was seated in front, turned the radio off.

Confused and a bit amused, April laughed.

"No it's not. I heard this song a lot of times," April chuckled. "What is he talkin' about?'

Martinez, then says "We are almost there, April. Do you recognize this area?"

Distracted, April looked out the window and saw her old neighborhood. Dazed with a feeling of relief and joy, April let out a silent, "yeah!"

April stared quietly as the van drove around.

Almost immediately, the van pulled into a driveway of a single house in a quiet block in North Philadelphia. It was not April's home. It was a house prepared for them to stay. When April entered the house, it appeared that it was planned for them to stay there for a while. April had her own room. April found the house very appealing.

After looking around the house and changing into some new clothes that were left in her room, April began to feel restless and wanted to go outside.

"Would it be alright if I went outside?" She asked as she came down the stairs.

Martinez looked at Mayet with a smile and said, "I told you."

"Told her what?" April asked.

"I knew that you would want to go out, April. But I'm afraid that we cannot allow you." Martinez explained.

"See..." April began, appearing upset. "I knew this was going to happen and I wasn't even going to ask. I was just going to go 'cause I know that you were gonna hold me like a prisoner."

April was very upset.

"April, you are not a prisoner. We are just looking out for your safety. You saw what happened in Puerto Rico," Martinez explained.

"But I know this neighborhood. I'll be alright." April said.

Martinez looked at Mayet and sighed.

"Look April. I have to go do something very important. When I return, we will go for a drive. Is that ok?" Martinez said.

April looked at Martinez with a disappointed look and nodded. Martinez then left.

As the door closed, April looked at Mayet silently then walked away. She walked up the stairs, into her room and closed the door.

The day passed and April did not get to go out.

The next morning, April opened her door and went downstairs. She did not see anyone.

"Hello?" April called.

No one answered. April then looked at the door. Cautiously, April walked towards the door, opened it and looked outside. She looked around and saw no one. Scared, April quickly closed the door. On the table in the other room, April saw an envelope with her name on it. In the envelope, April found twenty dollars.

April again looked around and said, "Hello?"

No one answered.

With the envelope in her hand, April quickly walked out the door.

Outside, April felt different. She took a deep breath and relaxed herself. She was content.

April walked to the bus stop to go to the foster care home where she once stayed. She realized that she did not have change for the bus so she walked to a nearby corner store to buy some snacks and get some change. As she walked towards the store, April looked around and observed the neighborhood. She could not believe that after being in such a marvelous place like the city in the desert, she felt so content being in an old Philadelphia neighborhood.

"You are still my home Philly. And I love you," April said.

April walked into the corner store. As she pushed the door open, a bell jingled above. April took a deep breath and smelled the familiar scent of what she called "the Papi store-" a bodega.

Salsa music played in the back of the store as April browsed about. She grabbed a bag of ranch flavored corn nuts, a chocolate bar, some chewing gum and a large can of flavored iced tea. For some reason, April felt compelled to buy a bottle of water as well. April felt so at home, she could not wait to pay for the items and eat them all.

April walked to the front of the store to pay for her items.

"Four, fifty," said the cashier with a thick accent.

April handed the woman a twenty dollar bill.

The cashier handed April her change. "Gracias mami," she said.

"Thank you," April replied.

April then walked towards the bus stop and waited. She opened her bag of corn nuts. After eating one, April felt disgusted. She did not know why but, for some reason, April did not like nor did she want the corn nuts.

Then, April opened her chocolate bar. After one bite, April felt nauseous. April spat the chocolate out and put the rest back in the package. April wanted to go back to the store to complain, because she thought that maybe her snacks were bad. But, as she turned to go back to the store, she saw the bus coming and decided to stay for the bus.

What April did not realize was the there was nothing wrong with her snacks. April simply did not have the taste for them anymore.

When April got on the bus, she did not remember how much the fare was. When she was about to ask the bus driver how much the fare was, she notice the sign at the front of the bus. The sign stated that the fare was two dollars. As April looked through her money, she noticed that she only had one ten dollar bill, a five dollar bill, and some change.

April felt embarrassed. Still, without hesitating, April turned to the bus riders who were seated and asked, "Anybody got change for a five?"

No one answered.

The bus driver turned to April and said, "Look sweetie, you should've…"

"I got you," a girl appearing to be the same age as April said as she walked towards the front.

"Thank you," April said.

"You're welcome, sis," the girl said as she gave her the five bills.

When April got off of the bus, she looked back and saw the girl who gave her the change on the bus. The girl waved; April waved back.

April looked around and was at her old neighborhood. Everything was just as she remembered. She was standing right at the corner where she watched a girl she knew get mugged. As a child, April witnessed a lot of bad things. Once, as she was on her way home (April lived around the corner from the shelter) from school, she watched a man get hit by a car. As the man laid on the ground, the man who was driving the car stepped out, pulled a gun out and shot the injured man as he begged for his life. The thought of that moment angered April.

April looked around. Some things looked different from what she remembered. For some strange reason, April did not feel comfortable. She wanted to walk towards the shelter but something inside her did not allow her to make her way over. Instead, April decided to walk towards her old home, where she and her mother lived. As she walked, she did not see many people around. Cars were driving by, but not many people were walking around. As April looked at the broken down houses and the cracked cement on the ground, she visualized the beautiful city in the middle of the desert. She visualized the beautiful golden pyramids and crystal domes as she imagined children laughing, and the gentle breeze hitting her in the face. April stopped walking. She stood at the corner of the street, staring. She began to look around. April saw leaning houses with chipped paint. As a tear slid down her cheek, April turned in circles looking at her broken down neighborhood in disbelief. Seeing such a beautiful paradise in the middle of a desert made her wonder why could it not be the case for the community where she was born. April no longer wanted to see her old home. She remembers it as clearly as the present day. April made her way back to the bus stop.

At the bus stop, April noticed a sign on the light pole. It was an advertisement for an exhibit at the University's Museum of Anthropology. On the poster, there was a picture of a sphinx with pyramid behind it. April stared at the poster and visualized Balhib. Immediately, she wanted to go see the exhibit. Although April did not know how to get to this museum, she waited at the bus stop determined to find it.

When the bus came, April stepped on and quickly asked the bus driver how to get to get to the museum at the University. The bus driver told her that she would have to get off at Market Street walk to the El train and take the train to 34th street and walk towards 32nd and South Street.

April was pretty confident that she could make it to the museum safely without getting lost. It was still early and she was not concerned with running into any trouble or being missed at the house.

As April traveled, she stared. She did not pay much attention to conversations or any other sounds for that matter. April looked at people, the city and everything around her. Once she reached 32nd street, April asked a university security guard for directions to the museum. April walked. She was not even sure if she was going to have enough money to make it back to the house. Still, April did not care. She had her mind set on going to the museum. April still had her bottle of water. She pulled it out of her bag and drank. Even the water had a funny taste to it for her. But she drank it. April did not eat anything else because she did not want to waste anymore of her money. Besides, she was not even sure if she would like anything because of how her taste buds have been acting. April was not hungry anyway.

When April reached the museum, she went to the door where a group of what appeared to be college students waited. April decided to blend in with the crowd. Apparently, the museum was not open yet. April waited with the group who paid her no mind. Finally, the museum opened and April walked into the museum with the group.

As April attempted to walk past the front desk, a woman's voice called for her.

"Miss!" the woman called.

April turned to the woman.

"Are you with that group?" the woman asked.

April was honest and told the woman that she was not.

"Do you have ID miss?" the woman asked.

April shook her head no.

"Well, miss. You look a little young and these are school hours. I cannot let you in without an adult."

April looked disappointed and began to walk out.

The woman sighed and called for April.

"Wait!" the woman called. "I suppose it's better for you to be in here where it's educational than out there getting yourself into trouble. Why are you here any..? I guess I should be happy that a child would rather be in a museum than in the streets if they're not in school... Seven dollars sweetie."

April paid the woman and the cashier gave her a map of the museum.

"Thank you." April said quietly.

At the Egypt exhibit, April stared quietly. She looked at the giant sphinx that stood in the hall and thought of the great, magnificent beast that she met in the beautiful desert city. Looking around, she thought of Amisi and Khai and Balhib. She actually missed them.

As she stared, she wondered to herself, "Why couldn't we be like this? Why do we do the things we do?"

"They were so magnificent," a voice spoke behind April. It was Mayet. "Kemet, Nubia... You know, they were on the verge of creating so many great things before things made an unfortunate turn... Cures, flight... So much power... That's why we went back."

"Went back?" April asked with confusion turning towards Mayet. "What do you mean?"

"Time or dimension travel is not as difficult as you think, April. I mean, well, it *is* very difficult. There are a lot of rules, a

lot of conditions, and a lot of dangers. But it is very possible."
Mayet explained calmly as if it was a normal conversation. "For
instance, one cannot go to the same time and place; one cannot
communicate with others or interfere with the time or
dimension in which he or she had traveled. We just studied," she
explained. "There were, though, two occasions."

"What do you mean?" April asked.

Mayet turned to April with a big smile and said, "The answer
to that, April, is a big one. So…"

"…Answers will come, huh?" April interrupted with a smile.

"I knew you would understand." Mayet replied smiling back.

"Tell me about them." April said to Mayet as she looked at
the statues.

Mayet looked around at the exhibit. "Well, like all societies of
this world, April, they weren't perfect. They were not the most
righteous of societies," she sighed. "But they were closer to
magnificence than any society of this world. Their inventions,
views, sciences… They were superb. But, there was more to
them than anyone knows."

April turned to Mayet and asked, "Like what?"

Mayet looked at April and smiled. April smiled back knowing
what Mayet's response would be. They laugh.

Later that day, April, Mayet, Martinez were at the house. They
were seated and about to eat dinner. They had a guest as well.

Mayet introduced the young man. "April, this is Noel. He will
be staying here for a while."

He was a very young and good looking man. April was
somewhat captivated by his looks. Still, as they sat and got ready
to eat, all April could think of were questions she had had for
Martinez and Mayet since they returned to Philadelphia.

"So," April began as she looked at her plate. "Should I call you Martinez or Agent or what?" she said looking up at Agent Martinez.

Martinez chuckled and while chewing his food he said in fluent Spanish, "Me llamo Eugenio Martinez."

"Really?" April asked with a surprised tone.

Martinez laughed, "Did you think it would be different?"

"April, some of our names do have meanings or some sort of representation. But... many of us were named as people here are." Mayet explained with a chuckle.

"I was born and raised in Puerto Rico, April," Martinez explained with a smile. "My family is from the Caribbean. Two of my ancestors came to this," he paused, "...This world in the late 1700's. They were two of the very firsts to come here. They managed to stay away from enslavement by staying in mountainous areas. They took the name Martinez from a widowed Mestizo freed farmer who took them in, thinking that they were runaway slaves. The story was that, the newcomers- the man and the woman were unable to have children in their new world. The farmer got old and noticed that his new friends were not of this world when he saw that they were not aging like him. But, they became family to him and, when he passed away, he left them his land. As they adjusted to their new environment, they were always ill. Still, before passing away, they managed to have and raise a girl. She lived to be 120 years old. She had a girl at an old age. My mother told me this story and, as a child, I thought it was just a tale until I got older."

"What happened next?" April asked.

"...I noticed that I was not aging like the rest of my peers. But I was always getting sick. My mother still looked young. Yet, she was always in pain. She was not able to have me until an old age but she still appeared somewhat young. Eventually, she had me. When she turned 80 years old, she couldn't take being ill anymore and killed herself. I never knew my father. I understand that he was a local of African, European, and Taino decent. I never bothered looking for him."

April stared and gave Martinez her undivided attention.

"I then moved to the States; lived in Philadelphia…"

"Which is why you speak English pretty well," April said.

"Thank you," Martinez replied.

"Wait," April interrupted. "There's one thing I don't understand. Your world is so beautiful. Why would anyone leave it to come to this world…? Especially if they get sick and die younger than they would if they had stayed?" She asked.

Martinez looked at Mayet; Mayet sighed.

"April," Mayet, began to explain. "Although our world seemed perfect to you, things went wrong as they do in all worlds,"

"What happened?" April asked.

Mayet paused and took a moment to gather her thoughts. It looked like she did not know what to say. Suddenly, Mayet told April something very important. Something that April was not ready to hear. Still, it was time.

"April," Mayet began. "Sometime, in the near future, *your* world is going to come to a near end. The world you have known all of your life is going to be destroyed. Billions will die; a little over a million will struggle to keep humanity alive. There will be great devastation. Then there will be a great war, the likes of which no one has ever seen. When that war is over, many more will die."

April stared in disbelief as Mayet continued.

"Finally, when it comes to an end, people will recover. Generations will pass and humans will enter a utopian state… Do you understand that term, April?" Mayet asked.

April nodded.

Mayet continued, "People will be led into societies of greatness; few, but great societies. One society in particular will be the greatest of all and lead the world into a state of peace. There will be no wars. Humans will flourish more than ever. However, peace will be threatened again." Mayet paused and stared. "That threat returned... *Will* return to our world, April."

April listened.

"That threat *came* to our world. And technologies that were kept secret for our safety were put to use. Time and dimension travel. Dimension travel was halted and never used again after we realized that going to other dimensions only brought danger to those dimensions without helping ours. But time travel was put to use and many of our people were scattered throughout time for either safety or to find ways to help."

April quietly listened as answers to all of her questions just came.

"Other technologies were put to use. Our medicine, herbal and health technologies were always strong which is why we live for so long. But our leaders found other ways to help us. Some of our ancestors; very few were given natural gifts... Powers. Powers that were given to our ancestors that needed to evolve within our blood through years of adaptation... or 'fast' evolution, as we call it... "

"I don't understand," April interrupted.

"Well, how can I explain it? Some of our people were given a natural substance that potentially amplified a natural strength or sense. For example, let's say for our minds... Psychokinesis- the ability to move things with the mind. The person who was given the substance would not become psychokinetic; his or her child would be but only slightly. And that person's child would be more psychokinetic than the parent and so on. Through each generation that strength would evolve. That is why some people were sent to the past; so their decedents would…"

"So, you're telling me that there are people out there with super strength?" April asked with disbelief.

"Well, not strength in the sense of muscles," Mayet answered with a smile. "I am familiar with the super heroes in your movies and books. First, our bodies do have more potential than many are aware of. But, they are not without limits. To answer your question April, there are people with massive strength, yes. But, like I said, our bodies; the strength of our muscles and bones do have limits. We learned that when people began to die from the attempt to surpass the limits of our anatomy. Plus, when the bodies became stronger, stronger weapons were created. Still, there are so much that we are capable of…"

Mayet paused again.

"But, it did not succeed in many ways," Mayet said

"What?" April asked. "What did not succeed?"

Mayet accounted, "Many of those who were sent back were unable to survive. The environment was too different for them. Very few lived to have children. Those who did live were unable to have children. Our failure to make this plan work made us realize one very important thing that made us bring our project to a close.

"What?" April asked.

Mayet looked at April and said, "We cannot play God."

"There are very few who possess gifts, but…" Mayet stopped and stared away. "The second and final war will… has come," Mayet continued. "I will not see the end of this war, but it is said that this war will end all wars. After this war, peace and prosperity will reign forever.

"I don't know if I believe any of this," April said.

Mayet dramatically turned to April and said, "April, I cannot tell you everything. But, I must tell you this- believe your heart. You are going to witness things that you never thought possible and the only way you will be who you were meant to be is by believing the unbelievable and trusting your spirit, energy and heart. You and your people will be protected by the unexpected. You will…" Mayet stopped.

"What?" April asked anxiously. "And what will I become. Why are you protecting me? Do I become someone important? *Am* I someone important? Please… Tell me."

Suddenly, April awoke in her bed. It was morning. She felt as if she was dreaming. As she got out of the bed, she heard the front door open and close. April looked out the window and saw Mayet, Martinez and Noel, the young man, enter a blue car and drive off. April quickly put on her clothes and ran down the stairs. As she ran down the stairs, she noticed an envelope on the living room table. April quickly grabbed it and looked through it hoping that there was money. There was no money; only a letter. April disregarded the letter, threw the envelope back on the table and left the house.

April had some money left over from the previous day. She decided to catch the bus to the shelter where she lived. She did not know why she wanted to go there. She just went.

When April got off the bus, she saw the car that Martinez and Mayet were in parked near the children's home where she lived. April was confused. She did not understand what was going on. April stood at the corner where she could not be seen and waited. She looked around. April had a feeling that they were inside the home so she waited patiently. She was a bit afraid for she could not piece together what was going on.

After a few minutes of waiting, April notice a car slow down and stop next to the car that Mayet and Martinez rode in. The men in the car looked suspicious. They were at the blue car and looked around.

One of the suspicious-looking men got out of the car and walked to the corner. The other man in the car drove off. The man at the corner waited.

April became more suspicious. She was becoming more afraid. As she continued to watch discreetly, she noticed the car drive by several times. April suspected that the men were waiting for Mayet and Martinez. But, she did not know why.

After an hour of waiting, April noticed Noel come out the front door of the building. April then looked at the man at the corner. The man then turned around to look for the car with the other man and gestured for him to wait. April was getting scared. She knew something bad was about to happen, but she did not know what to do.

Noel walked over to their blue vehicle. He got in the car, turned it on and pulled up in front of the home, closer to the front door. The other man watched and took a few steps closer to the blue car.

Just then, April looked up the steps of the home and noticed Mayet and Martinez walk out the door with someone. April stared and tried to identify the person that was with them. As April was able to see clearly who was with Mayet and Martinez, she noticed that it was a child- a young girl. The girl looked to be a few years younger than April.

Suddenly, a rush of fear and confusion ran through April's body as she was able to see clearly who the child was- It was April. April gasped. She saw her younger self walking with Mayet and Martinez.

At that moment, trying to remember this moment in her life, April instead remembers the men who shot Dr. Dupri and she realized that the men waiting for Mayet and Martinez were two of the men who shot Dupri. Then, without any time for warning, the one man who was at the corner ran to the front of the building. At the same time, the car with the other suspicious men rapidly drove up and the men began to shoot.

April screamed.

As the men fired their guns, Noel ran out of the car to help. He was quickly shot in the head. Martinez was hit in the face. Young April was hit on her left hand and in her chest. Mayet was hit in the chest as well.

Suddenly, it all hit her. As immediately as the memory of it all hit April as she stood in front of her former home in Philadelphia; April woke up simultaneously from her sleep on Balhib's back. April gasped with overwhelming anxiety.

Noticing what had happened, Balhib stopped walking and said, "Welcome back April."

▲ Chapter 2
April

April was born April Nebettawy Lewis on April 13. She was born in Philadelphia, Pennsylvania and raised by her mother. April did have a father, but she never knew him.

April's mother always kept her really close. While all of the children in April's neighborhood played outside, April's mother would always keep her indoors. The child was very much sheltered. To avoid questions, April's mother did place her in school although it was not what she really wanted to do. In school, April was very quiet. She was not a very social child. Although no one ever picked on April, she did not have any friends either. It seemed as though April was alone. Nevertheless, April was loved. She was always happy to go home. Her mother showed her all of the attention she needed. April's mother would play with her. She would teach April new things every day; she would read her stories, play dress up with her, sing to her and treat April like a princess.

April was happy. She knew how much she was loved. In school, April would do well, but she did not socialize. Not because of conceit, but because of contentment. April, at a very young age, was content with her life.

In their surroundings there was crime, abandonment, resentment and negativity. But, in their home, there was love and happiness. As a very young child, April was oblivious to her unforgiving surroundings. In the classroom, she would do her work knowing that, once the day was over, she would see her best friend- her mother. During recess at school, April would sit

on a swing thinking of different games that she could ask her
mother to play when she would get home.

April did not know what her mother did during the day.
Sometimes she would wonder or imagine that her mother did
fun things. Her mother told her that she would be at work while
April was in school. But at a young age, April did not really
know what that meant. As she would sit on the swing in the
school yard, April would imagine that her mother's work place
involved fun things such as zoos or circuses. Why else would her
mother want to go to work every day, April would wonder.
Thinking of these things made April happy.

April was always thinking about her mother. When her
mother would pick her up from school, April would run to her
with open arms and a big smile. As they would walk home, April
would ask her mother about her day.

April remembered her mother sometimes being visited on the
weekends by people April did not know. April did not like those
days. Not because the people who visited were bad people. In
fact, the people who visited were very nice to April and her
mother. They always came with gifts. The reason she was not
really fond of those days was because her mother could not
really give her the attention April was accustomed to. As her
mother and her visitors spoke in one room, April would usually
sit in the other room and play with one of her new gifts; which
was fine with April. Still, she would have rather had been playing
with her mother.

As April grew older, she was able to be outside more. April's
mother allowed April to play outside every once in a while.
However, although April would speak to the other children in
the neighborhood, she would still play alone. Most of the time,
April would sit on the steps in front of her house and watch the

other children play, learn some of the games and later try to play the games with her mother.

The children in the neighborhood would refer to April as "the shy girl." Every once in a while, the girls who played jump rope in front of April's home would ask April if she wanted to play. April would simply smile and shyly say, "No thank you."

A day that would always stay with April was the day her and her mother witnessed a horrible tragedy. When April was 8 years old, as she and her mother were on their way home from the market, a man was hit by a car and shot in front of them.

The man was walking next to April and her mother. April vividly remembered the man saying hello to April's mother. After April's mother said hello in return, the man walked to the corner to cross the street. When the man stepped into the street, a car sped towards the man and violently hit him. April remembered her mother screaming.

When the man fell to the ground, the man who was driving the car quickly exited the car, ran to the man on the ground and shot him. Immediately, April's mother took hold of April and began running towards their home.

April's mother was a very quiet person. But that evening, the home was quieter than ever. April could not remember any other day when she received more hugs from her mother than that evening. April's mother quietly made dinner, bathed April and tucked her in. Once April was tucked in, April's mother lay down next to April, wrapped her arms around her and sang April to sleep.

The day after the incident, two police officers came to April's home. April was scared. She thought that she and her mother were in trouble. She asked her mother if they were in trouble. April's mother assured her that they were not. April did not know what the police and her mother were talking about.

Usually, as a child, the most that April remembered was what she would see at her eye level. As shy as she was, April rarely looked up unless she was looking at her mother.

After the police left April's home, her mother quietly picked April up, gave her a hug and a kiss; she sat on their rocking chair and just sang to April. April never felt too old to be rocked and sang to. It made April feel calm.

Since the day that April watched a man get killed, things became very different. April would remember seeing her mother just stare. When April would say something to her mother, her mother would become startled. There were also days when April remembered her mother being very sick. It seemed that the event really affected April's mother.

Weeks passed after the incident and it seemed that April's mother was more frequently sick. Also, the visitors who would come to April's house were visiting more often. That was a sad time for April. After witnessing a horrible event, she then had to endure watching her mother being sick. She did not get a lot of the attention as she normally got either. April felt more alone than ever. Still, her mother never failed to make April feel better in the evenings when she would go to April's room, sit at her bed, rub April's head and sing her to sleep. Many times, April did not understand what her mother was saying but just the melody and the sound of her mother's voice were enough to soothe April.

The saddest day in April's life was the day she was awakened by a stranger. She was a police officer. April was terrified being woken up by a police officer- a stranger in her own room. The officer rubbed April's face to wake her up.

When April opened her eyes and saw that it was not her mother, April jumped back and screamed. The officer pleaded with April to calm down. April asked for her mother.

With sadness in her eyes, the officer said to April, "Your neighbors heard noises coming from your home and called us. Are you alright?"

"Where is my mommy?" April cried.

▲

After witnessing the shooting of Mayet, Noel, her young self and Martinez; April was terrified. Standing unnoticed across the street from the building that was once her home, April watched as the police came. She could not understand. April looked at her hand and did not see a scar. She pulled the collar of her shirt down and searched her chest for a scar, but she did not find one. April did not get it. If that was her she saw get shot, she did not remember it.

"This didn't happen," April said. "This didn't happen. What is this? What's going on?"

Suddenly, the blue car that Noel, Mayet and Martinez drove in sped towards April.

"Get in April," A voice said from the car. It was Martinez.

As blood slid down the right side of his face, Martinez called for April again, "Please April, we have to go," he said.

Confused and afraid, April hesitantly opened the car door and got in…

When they got to the house, April saw the envelope on the floor. Quietly, she walked to the envelope. April picked the envelope up, took the letter out and began to read it.

The letter was written by Mayet. It said,

"Dear April,

Before you read the following, please understand that you need to keep an open mind. Please remember that there are many perspectives of life. As one may say, 'things are not always what they seem…'"

"April," Martinez interrupted. "Are you ok?"

April nodded.

"I need to clean up," He said as his face bled.

April nodded again. "… Are *you* ok?" She asked.

Martinez sighed and stared with watery eyes and said, "I should be."

Martinez walked up the stairs and April continued reading.

"First, I understand that the things that you are experiencing are not typical for anyone let alone a girl your age. The things that you are witnessing are enough for you already, which is why we try not to give you too much information when you want it. It is for your own benefit. I do not have much time to get into details, April. I am writing you to explain what is going to happen next.

When you wake up in the morning, April, we will not be home. Now, knowing you, I feel that you are going to attempt to follow us. Please do not. Although I know that you might, it is important that you do not.

Eugenio and I will be gone for a while. However, you will not be alone. Noel will be taking care of you while we are gone. Please forgive us for leaving you without explaining. You will come to understand all of this very soon. Also, forgive us for leaving you with someone you do not know. Noel is a very good person. We are confident that you will grow to trust and care for him as he will care for you."

April stopped reading as she remembered watching Noel get shot in the head. April began to cry. She then continued to read.

"The two of you will continue to live in the house. Noel will be making sure that you are taken care of. You will not have to worry about anything, April.

April, you will continue to learn and grow. You need to go to school and grow into a strong woman. You are to learn what you need so that you can become what we all expect you to become- A great leader.

I must go, April. Please remember a saying we always say where I am from, 'Everyone loves sunny days, but we will always need the rain.' I know it is a silly saying. But it will make sense one day.

Goodbye April.
Love,
Mayet"

When April finished the letter, she held it to her chest and took a deep breath. Afterwards, she wiped the tears from her face, folded the letter and sat at the table to gather herself. By this point, after all that had happened, April was becoming immune to the trauma of the harrowing events that continued to take place.

After a few moments, Martinez came into the room and saw April sitting. Saddened by seeing her so distressed, he slowly walked to the table and sat at the chair across the table from April.

"April…" Martinez said silently.

April sat quietly as Martinez reached across the table for her hand.

"What now?" April asked.

"I don't know," he answered. "…I mean, I do know. But I don't know how. The things that happened… This wasn't supposed to happen. This was not my mission."

"Your mission?" April asked.

Martinez looked down, sighed and said, "Mayet knew more than I did. I mean, there were things that she knew that she couldn't tell me…. What I do know is that I was to protect you but not here; not now. Well, now but not *you*," Martinez explained. "I was to… You know who that was with us right?" He asked.

"It was me. Right?" April asked.

Martinez paused, staring at April's hand as he held it. "Well… yes. But…"

"The younger me," April added.

Martinez stared silently and said, "Yes. But…"

"How come I don't remember any of this…? The shooting; you and Mayet getting me at the home?" April asked.

"Because it didn't happen to you," Martinez answered. "I mean…" Martinez stumbled on his words as he tried to explain something *he* didn't even understand. "April, I believe, history just changed."

▲

Khai called for Amisi. By this point, all that Amisi knew was that April was a stranger- a strange child who came from another world; a child who she simply watched over during her stay. Khai was about to explain some very important and overwhelming information to Amisi.

As Amisi walked into the room where Khai and Balhib were, she felt something was terribly wrong. They were in a brightly lit room. Still, the mood was dark. Balhib appeared very serious as he did most of the time. Khai also appeared serious. Yet, to Amisi, he gave off a sad energy.

"Yes?" Amisi said.

"Amisi," Khai began. He reached for Amisi's hand and guided her to the seat next to him. Khai then told Amisi the story of April. From the moment she first came to the city, to the event of her young body being shot; Khai explained to Amisi in the best, most understandable way possible. Although he did not tell her all he really knew, he did tell Amisi all she needed to know. There were some things about April's past that he knew but did not tell Amisi. He told Amisi about the time traveling and April's importance to their world. He told Amisi about the wars from the past and the war that is to come.

As Amisi tried to understand it all, Khai stressed the significance Amisi had in not only their city but in their entire world as well. Amisi knew she was somebody of importance, but she did not know the magnitude of her importance. And, although Khai expressed to her that she was more important than she knew, he could not explain to her why.

"Now I know how she felt," she said softly.

"Amisi," Balhib calmly said in his deep and noble voice. "You know the result of opportune, timely knowledge. You have taught others the very theory of it. The power of knowing one's destiny at the right time is exactly that- powerful. When one realizes his or her destiny at the perfect time... The power is inexplicable."

"I understand," she said as she respectfully looked at Balhib.

"It has begun," Khai stated.

Amisi looked at Khai not knowing what he meant.

Khai reached for both of Amisi's hands and, with a sad look upon his face, he said, "You are not safe here."

A scared expression quickly came over Amisi's face. "What do you mean?" She asked.

"They came after April. They will come after us and they will come after you Amisi," Khai explained. "You must not stay here."

Afraid, Amisi asked, "Where can I go? This is my home."

"Amisi, we are sending you to the past," Khai stated.

Amisi began to cry, "I cannot. I *will* not…"

"But you must, Amisi!" Khai insisted. "You are not safe here. You must be kept safe."

"Where?" Amisi argued. "In the past? Was April not supposed to be safe…?"

"You will go further back. Before this event took place. No one will know you. We will make sure that you are safe." Khai said."

Amisi cried. But after some thought, she finally said, "I will go." Convinced that she will be safe, she agreed.

"You will be sent to the city where April lived; just a few years before the incident."

Amisi thought for a moment then said, "I can save her. Send me to when and where I can save her."

"That is very valiant of you, my child. But you must save yourself before thinking about saving anyone else. You must keep yourself safe, therefore you must live quietly," Khai explained. "There will be people there watching you and giving you what you need…"

Khai sighed. "Just keep yourself safe…"

"I will find her…" Amisi said.

Khai sighed. "Look for her then, Amisi," he said. "But do only that. It is obvious to me that I cannot tell you what to do. When the time is right, you will know what to do."

The following morning, Khai and Amisi met with Saini at the medical dome. With Balhib staying behind, they then made their way to another dome located outside of the city- in the desert.

When they reached the dome, Saini explained, "Amisi, this is a very delicate procedure. You will be put to sleep. When you reawake, you will be there. You will be awakened by doctors of that time in an island called Bermuda. You will then be transported to the city where April came from."

"How does this work?" Amisi asked. "Please explain to me how it works," she pleaded as if she needed to know for her own comfort.

"Well, many years ago, we found that there is an area in the region where we are sending you that has storms created by a unique circulation of high winds. These storms at times interfere with the planet's magnetic field bridging a gap between time and space. We are now able to weather these phenomena with a chemical that will be shot out as you fly over the region…"

"Fly?" Amisi asked with fear as she is walked to a bed. "You mean…"

"You will be sent in that vehicle," Saini stated pointing to a spherical contraption just outside of the dome. "It is an antigravity apparatus that will float you into orbit. When you are over the region of which I spoke, you will reenter the atmosphere. Once in the atmosphere, the heat that will be generated from the reentry will cause the release of the "antiparticles" stored in the melt-away canisters surrounding the capsule where you will lay. These antiparticles will then combine with the super-heated particles in the atmosphere that will surround you as you are reentering. They will also combine with the highly magnetized particles in the region causing a series of quantum explosion, sending you to another time."

"How can you make sure I will be sent to the right time?" Amisi asked.

"We set the amount of antiparticles…" Saini attempted to explain. "It is very difficult sending one so far back. The time is determined by the amount of explosions. If there are two quantum explosions, it equals close to two years… Now, that does not mean that there will be hundreds of explosions, Amisi. We cannot even send you to an exact time. We were able to create a way to have microscopic explosions within an explosion significant enough to make a full leap."

Amisi, becoming tired as she lay down on the table said, "I don't…"

"Amisi," Khai interrupts. "I know that you want to understand what you are getting yourself into. However… It is time."

Amisi stared at Khai with watery eyes. Her fear was evident as she attempted to stall with questions. Saini sprayed Amisi with a mist. As Amisi began to fall asleep, Saini injected a fluid into her stomach.

"Startled by the needle, Amisi asked, "What was that?"

As tears slid down Khai's face, he said, "You will know when the time is right, my child."

Shivering, Amisi cried softly, "I'm scared."

As he grazed his hand across Amisi's forehead Khia softly said, "It will be alright, Amisi."

With tears sliding down her cheeks as she fell to sleep, Amisi looks up at Khai and said, "I love you, father."

Crying, Khai softly replies, "I love *you,* my daughter."

▲ Chapter 3
Amisi

She was in a city that she had never known, hundreds of years before her time. The lost young woman knew nothing of this time or place. All she knew was the information that was in the envelope left with her clothes by her bed in the hospital where she came to. Instructions on where to go and how to get there were written in a detailed letter inside the envelope.

In the envelope, there was a stack of green paper that Amisi had never seen before. The letter explained how to use this green paper. There was a card with Amisi's picture and name on it, a certificate with her name and another card with a lot of numbers on it. Her name had an added name to it. It read *Amisi Samuel*. The last name was added, for Amisi did not have one in the time from which she came time due to her status. The letter told her about the importance of getting used to her new full name and all of the numbers on the card and forms.

There was also a booklet with common terms and phrases used in that time for her to study, and a set of keys. The letter explained how to use these keys, as Amisi never used keys before. The letter also explained the importance of being calm and behaving "normal." For her safety, the letter expressed that no one would be helping her get adjusted. She was to be alone. She would be contacted. However, she would not hear from anyone for some time.

Amisi was instructed to dress in the clothes that were left at the bedside, leave the hospital, and board a yellow vehicle with the name Taxi written atop of it. Once in this strange vehicle, she was to ask its conductor to take her the address written in the letter. The long letter in the envelope explained as much about this world as possible. The letter explained to her what the vehicles were; what addresses were, the way of life of the people of that time. Of course, not everything about this world was written. Much of this strange world at this time would have to be learned by Amisi alone.

When the taxi stopped at the house, the driver made Amisi aware that they were at the destination she asked for. As instructed, she gave the driver of the taxi the amount of green paper stated in the letter. The letter even specified for Amisi to say, "Keep the change."

As she exited the yellow vehicle, she stared at a white door in the middle of a red two-story building stretched both ways down the street. It was a small street with red brick row houses on each side. Amisi walked up the three white steps in front of her and reached for the keys inside the envelope. She then unlocked and opened the door and walked in the house. When she entered the house, the lights inside automatically turned on. In the first room she entered, there was furniture, lamps, a table and two large shelves with books. Amisi was expecting to find a letter or something with information on what to do next. After looking around her new home, she found nothing but more clothes, a large bed with comfortable sheets, and more books about history and popular culture. She also found a safe that could be opened with one of the keys left in the envelope. Inside the safe were stacks of more of the green paper that she learned were called money. There were over a hundred stacks of bills of 100 in the safe. The letter did specify the importance of this money. Amisi was instructed to read about how money works and how to use and save it.

In the house, Amisi also found the bathroom and the kitchen, both of which she would have to learn how to use on her own. In the kitchen, there was food and fruit in the tall white box that she learned was called a refrigerator. The letter explained that she would need to replenish her food by seeking out the market place in the area each week and "purchasing" more food.

After spending time looking around her new home and taking it all in, Amisi sat on her bed exhausted, lay down, curled her body and cried herself to sleep.

For the next several days, Amisi stayed indoors. She was afraid for the first time that she could remember. For the first time in her life, she did not know what to do next. She was hesitant and insecure about all of her decisions and moves. Amisi simply sat at her window and observed. She did not know what else to do. She would watch the children play in the street. She would also watch how people interacted, especially the adults. Amisi knew about how people aged in this new home of hers. She knew that she appeared much younger than the typical adult in the city where she now lived. Amisi looked very young. She realized that her appearance might come into question. She thought of ways to make herself look older. At times, Amisi listened to the ways the adults spoke and practiced her speech and mannerisms to make herself seem older.

After a few days, Amisi gained the courage to sit on the front step of her house. It was very early in the morning. There were not many people outside. Amisi sat and smelled the air and watched cars drive past her home.

"I was wondering when you were gon' come out," a voice said a few steps away from Amisi.

When Amisi turned to the much older dark-skinned, heavy set woman with grey hair speaking to her, the woman became surprised.

"Whew, child! Where is your mother?" The older woman asked with a laugh. "You are kind of young to be here all by yourself?"

With her accent being evident, Amisi answered, "Well, actually, Ma'am, I'm…" Amisi stuttered.

"Look, child," the woman interrupted. "One thing you don't have to worry about around here is people being in your business. It's a small block. Although it's not the nicest neighborhood, we do look out for one another on this block. But, like I said, don't worry about anyone prying into your business. What's that accent from, anyway? You African or somethin'? Jamaican, right?" She asked.

Before Amisi had the chance to answer, the old woman said, "Forget it, it ain't my business. But if you need anything, don't you hesitate to knock on my door. Ya'll kids are all tryin' to be independent too darn soon. But don't you be stubborn if you need anything. Just knock. You hear me?"

A bit amused by the conversation, Amisi nodded with a smile and simply said, "Yes, Ma'am."

"And don't be havin' your friends over at all hours of the night, throwing those college parties, you hear me?" The woman said with a smile. "We got little babies on this block; school kids."

Not quite understanding the old woman's 21st century urban accent, Amisi just smiled at the woman as she gestured for Amisi to knock on her door if she needed to. The woman then went inside her home.

As days followed, things became more comfortable for Amisi. One day, Amisi decided to go for a walk around the neighborhood. As she was about to leave the house she heard the old neighbor say, "You not gon' lock your door?"

Amisi turned around and, realizing what the woman was trying to tell her, she took the keys out of her pocket and locked the door.

As days passed, Amisi walked further and further away from her new home to familiarize herself with the neighborhood. Once comfortable with the area, Amisi finally decided to go to the market to buy food. She was finally learning how to survive on her own.

After several weeks of being on her own, April would walk around the neighborhood still trying to get to know her new surroundings. Amisi also continued to observe and study how people behaved.

Suddenly, one day as Amisi was walking from the market, Amisi heard, "April, come April." A mother called her child.

Amisi gasped and turned. Behind her, Amisi saw a toddler run towards her mother reaching for her hand.
"April?" Amisi said to herself wondering if that was the strange child with whom she became friends in the future. 'It can't be," she thought.

Curious, Amisi slowed down and allowed the mother and child to pass her so that she could follow.

Not knowing as much of April's history as she had liked, Amisi wished that she had asked Khai, Balhib and even April more questions.

"It cannot be a coincidence," Amisi said to herself as she observed the mother and child.

As she followed the two, she began to notice that they were walking closer to her new home. Amisi's eyes lit up. They walked closer and closer to her house. Then, a few doors down and across the street from Amisi's new house, the child named April and her mother walked up the stairs and went inside.

"It cannot be a coincidence," Amisi again thought.

That evening, Amisi could not sleep. Aside from feeling a bit ill, she lay awake thinking. She wondered if she was sent back for more than just her safety. She knew in her heart that she was there for something greater than her own life; and she knew that April had something to do with it.

As days passed, Amisi's health felt different. She continued to try to adjust to the new environment. As she adjusted, she would sit outside her door at the top step of her row house in the city she did not know and watch the children play. She especially kept an eye on the little girl named April. She did not want to try to make contact with the child or her mother. She just watched from a distance. Amisi knew that she could not interfere with anything or anyone from that time for the sake of the future… Not yet anyway.

Amisi would not speak to anyone except the older woman. Most of the time she would just observe; watch others' behaviors learning the lingo and ways of the residence of her new environment. In the evening, alone, she would write in a journal. In one entry, she wrote,

> *"If this truly is our past, I wonder how we made it. Such resentment they have.*
> *I learned that they endured 500 years of enslavement, colonization, murder, rape and thievery- words I did not know much of until I came to this place. It is no wonder…*
> *Without any reparations, they were expected to assimilate and 'catch up' to the world after being taken away from it. Even today, one cannot live without judgment and lack of understanding of their*

continuous struggle. Even as elected leaders, they still have much to make up for.

…Still, I live among them and I cannot help the feeling of slight bitterness towards them for their unwillingness to amalgamate for strength and growth. They have such potential; such power… Yet, in many vital cases, they do not treat each other as brothers therefore it is difficult for them to grow.

…So many shades and languages but all the same. I, a woman of them, dare not speak a word for I may be judged and asked, 'Where are you from?' with a look as to say, 'She does not belong.' They are my people. Yet, I call them 'them.' Still, I love them so… It hurts me to see them hurt themselves for 500 years' worth of reasons beyond their control.

…A new nation is what they need. They were never given a new beginning. In my opinion, that is what they need. …"

The following morning, Amisi sat at her usual spot at the top step in front of her house. She sat with her knees against her chest and her forearms rested on top of them. She would just stare as the children on her street played. As she watched, she would look over to the house where the young child named April lived. The child would never come out to play with the other children. If she did come out, she would be with her young mother to walk to the market. It seemed as the mother was very protective of the little girl who could not be much older than a toddler.

"So innocent when they're young, ain't they?" The older woman asked Amisi as they sat outside. "It's like I'm they're babysitter though."

Not knowing what that meant, Amisi just listened.

"They're parents either go to work or just go… Somewhere. And these kids just hang around. See, now, they stay on the block; play nearby. But eventually, they're gon' get bored with all that and find something else to do. Chances are it'll be something they're not supposed to be doin'…" the woman lectured. "Then, well… I won't be their babysitter then… I mean, it ain't always like that. Take that nice young lady down the block. I don't know her name… She's new around here too. Her little girl is the sweetest little thing. April. That's the little girl's name. I heard her call her a couple of times. See, that's how it should be. Parents should always be with their babies. Some people say that's being overprotective. I say that's being a parent."

Amisi just stared and pondered over the older woman's words.

"When's the last time you had your hair done?" The older woman asked bluntly.

Amisi simply reached for her braids and smiled with a slightly embarrassed look.

"Now don't be all embarrassed, child," the woman said, reminding Amisi of how April responded to being referred to as 'child.' "Look, I'm not only askin' because your hair looks a mess. I'm asking because I'm going to the hairdresser tomorrow and I'ma need some company. Did you wanna come with me?"

Amisi smiled and nodded.

"Good," the woman said. "Now you're gonna have to bring some money 'cause it ain't free."

Understanding the woman's frankness, Amisi smiled. She appreciated and found humor in the old woman's frankness. That evening, Amisi did not sleep much. But, she did dream. As she dreamt, there were explosions. The first explosion took her to a helicopter.

Amisi faintly remembered the sound of the helicopter rotor barely waking her from a semi-comatose state.

"King Edward Memorial is nearby," a strange voice said as they are flying over the ocean.

"No. We have to get to the airport," another voice argues.

"But she's…"

"Listen," the second voice interrupts. "You got your money and orders. Do as you are instructed… The airport, please!"

"Yes, sir."

Another loud explosion startled Amisi. This explosion took her to a room where she was barely awakened again by loud beeping noises and men in white coats speaking frantically. She then faded to sleep in her dream and was reawakened by more beeping and a man in a white coat speaking softly to her.

"Where did you come from?" The man asked as he stared at a chart.

"Doctor?" A woman said. "You are needed in…"

As the doctor left the room, Amisi vaguely remembered footsteps make their way to her bedside. She dreamt seeing a hand place an envelope on the table next to her bed.

"Welcome to your new home, girl," a woman's voice whispered.

Suddenly, there was another explosion. The explosion awoke Amisi. As she breathed heavily in fear, she looked towards her window and saw heavy rain pour against her window. She knew what rain was. It was seldom seen where she was from. Although it did rain in her world, it did not rain much where she lived.

The loud thunder made Amisi jump. She then stepped back, sat on her bed and watched the rain pound her window for the rest of the night.

The following morning, Amisi and the old woman walked to the hair salon and waited for their turn.

That day, Amisi made an important decision. She knew that assimilation was very important. That day, she decided to take out her natural braids and press her hair straight. It was a day that marked major change in Amisi's new life.

After a few months of learning how to live in her new world, Amisi, still reserved and to herself for the most part, made progress in assimilating to the surroundings. She was used to her new hair style. Her hair began to grow back after breaking off from the heat put to her hair months before. Amisi had a television and a radio in her home. She wore clothes that made her look older and more part of society. Although she felt sick at times, she was content with how her new life was going so far.

Amisi still sat in front of her home and watched the children play. She would still discreetly watch the child named April as she and her mother would walk pass daily. Amisi would still sit and have short conversations and go on her occasional hair salon visits with the older woman.

Although the older woman did not really pry into Amisi's business, they always found something to talk about. Sometimes they would walk together to the market. Amisi thought the older woman to be like a distant relative.

In the evening, Amisi would write in her journal and then think. She thought that, eventually, she would have to introduce herself to the woman whose child was named April. She felt that she needed to get close to them. But, she did not know how. Also, after learning about society's norms through her readings and television, Amisi realized that she needed to go to 'school' or obtain a 'job' or at least appear that she was doing those things. She did not need to work for money; she had plenty of money for years to come.

"If people are not asking questions already, they soon will be," she thought to herself.

So, Amisi decided; three days per week, she would leave her home in the morning and not come back until the afternoon. On those days she would either go to museums, parks or the movies. April became fascinated with movies when she learned about them. When she would get home, she would sit and speak with her friend.

The old woman would never ask her about what she did. She would just speak to Amisi about the latest neighborhood gossip or a story about the neighborhood's past. Amisi sat and listened until the sun went down.

During her first winter, Amisi became very sick. She was not used to this weather and she did not like the cold. She did not understand this weather. Still, Amisi did like watching it snow when it did.

For two weeks, Amisi was cared for by the older woman. The woman helped Amisi get used to the climate. Eventually, April got better and became more adjusted to the environment.

Months passed and Amisi continued to do what she had been doing since she arrived at the city. But now, she added new activities to her day. Along with traveling around the city visiting museums, parks and keeping busy, she would sit in a busy park and read for one hour.

One day as she made her way home from the Center City Park, Amisi noticed a young man appearing everywhere she was. He was slightly taller than Amisi and slightly darker. He wore denim jeans, a black winter cap, a slim fitted jacket and black boots. He carried a black side bag. She saw the young man on the public bus and remembered that he was at the park as well. She thought he looked suspicious.

When she got off the bus, April noticed that the young man got off from the back doors of the bus. As she walked towards her street, she noticed him follow behind her. Amisi, not being afraid, quickly turned around and confronted the man.

"Why are you following me?" Amisi asked sternly, catching the young man off guard.

"Whoa! Chill girl!" the young man exclaimed with the local lingo. He laughed with slight arrogance as he was taken aback by Amisi's confrontation.

"What does that mean? Who are you?" She interrogated. "Why are you following me?"

"I'm not following you. What are you talking about?" He said with laughter. "I live down this block."

"Why are you laughing?" Who are you?" Amisi asked again. "You *are* following me!"

"Look, shorty, I'ma just go home." The man said as he pointed to a house just a few steps ahead.

"Shorty? I'm not short." Amisi said.

The man simply looked at Amisi with a smile and a slight confused look, said, "Excuse me," and walked past Amisi. He walked to the house as Amisi watched him carefully. He opened the door and went into the house.

Amisi remained where she was for a moment and thought. She watched the house, thinking that maybe he was lying. She watched the house to see if he was going to come out and run or do something out of the ordinary. She waited but he did not come back out.

Dumbfounded, Amisi began to walk home. She walked slowly, thinking. She did not understand the situation. When she walked past the house that the young man entered, the door opened. She then saw the young man walk out. He had his jacket off and had a cup of juice in his hand. Amisi just looked at him with a suspicious look.

As he sat down on the step in front of the house he said to Amisi, "I have a confession. I was following you."

Amisi turned to him with a wary look.

"I followed you yesterday too," he said.

Amisi walked towards the young man with an upset look and asked assertively "Why are you following me? Who are you?"

The young man laughed and said, "Chill! I'm not trying to hurt you or nothing, *shorty*."

Amisi looked at him with an angry look when he called said 'shorty.'

He laughed. "Where are you from anyway?"

"Why are you following me?" She asked.

"What's your name?" He asked.

"Why are you following me?" Amisi asked again.

"What's your name?" he asked again with a slight laugh.

"Why are you following me?" Amisi asked sounding frustrated.

"Look, I wasn't tryin' to stalk you or nothin'," He replied. "I just think your cool and all."

"What does that mean? I do not understand you," Amisi said, even more frustrated.

Amused by Amisi's behavior, he said, "Will you calm down?"

"Why are you laughing at me?" She asked.

"I'm not laughing at you," He replied.

"You are!" She said.

"Nah, sis," he laughed. "I just think you're cute. That's all."

"Cute??" Amisi responded.

"Cute," the young man stressed. "I think you're cute. Don't you understand the word *cute*? You know, cute; pretty? Do you understand? Habla Ingles? Pale' vu?" The young man teased.

Amisi looked at him confused. She then blushed. Calmly she then said, "I don't know what you just said but I *do* understand what you are saying." Suddenly her mood changed and she became suspicious and a bit defensive again.

"Ah. You are just a boy," She said. She then began to walk away.

"Boy?" the young man asked, sounding insulted. "I'm a grown man. I'm a college man. I'm older than *you*!" He exclaimed.

Amisi continued to walk away without turning around.

"I'll see you tomorrow, alright?" the young man yelled.

Amisi, without turning around, smiled slightly.

The next day, Amisi sat at the park on the bench where she usually sat. As she read, someone sat next to her on the bench. Not paying attention to the person sitting on the bench next to her, she continued reading.

"So, you're just gonna act like you don't see me, huh?" the person asked.

Amisi looked up and saw that it was the young man from the previous day. She barely recognized him. This time he wore dress pants, a thin, long jacket, a tie and shiny shoes. He did not wear a hat. He had short trimmed dark hair.

Appearing frustrated, Amisi asked, "Why are you following me? Who are you?"

"Heh, is that all you know how to say?" he asked. "Where are you from?"

Amisi stared at the young man for a moment with her eyes squinted. She then returned to reading her book.

"It's like that, huh?" the young guy said under his breath. "Look, I saw you a few times in the park. I walk through here on my way home from school. I recognized you from around our neighborhood. So, yesterday, I waited around here at the park until you left. I followed you 'cause I was hoping you'd notice me. I… I think you are very pretty and you are truly interesting." The young man explained in a mature manner.

Amisi sat quietly for a moment.

Thinking that he may have made a mistake, the young man grabbed his black bag stood up and said, "Well, I'll see you around."

As he began to walk away, Amisi said, "You look different today."

He stopped, turned around and said, "You mean, I don't look like a boy…?"

"I apologize for that," Amisi said with her thick accent. "I have a habit of… Well, like I said, you look nice." Amisi then turned to her book and continued reading.

The young man sat back down and said, "Well, I'm going to work. I don't always dress like a 'boy.'"

"It is not the way you dress. I just…Never mind," Amisi said. What is your name?"

The young man smiled, extended his hand and said, "Bamidele. You can call me Dell. My parents were like African American hippies."

"Hippies?" Amisi asked as she shook Dell's hand.

"Never mind. It's Yoruba… My name. It means…"

"Yoruba. African? I know of Yoruba," Amisi interrupted.

Dell smiled. "You do, huh? Well, now we're getting somewhere. Well, what's your name?" He asked.

"Amisi," she answered.

"Amisi? That's a nice name. So, where are you…?"

"So, you go to work?" Amisi interrupted.

"Why…? Umm… Yeah," Bamidele answered. "So you don't have to worry about me following you home today." He then chuckled. "I go to school in the morning. I'm in *college*," he stressed with a smile. "And, I work at a firm three days a week.

Well, sometimes four. You know, sometimes, I work on Saturdays for extra hours.

Amisi smiled. She did not really understand what Bamidele was speaking about.

"A firm?" She asked.

"Yeah, a firm. You know... Lawyers and stuff? I do filing and copying... Umm... Just a little something until I graduate. I gotta make money."

Not really knowing what Dell was talking about, Amisi just nodded. She found Dell interesting.

"Well, look. I gotta go," Dell said. "Can I see you tomorrow? I don't have to work."

Amisi nodded. "I will be here," She said.

That afternoon, Amisi went home to find sadness on her street. As she walked towards her home, she looked at a group of people standing in front of the house where the toddler named April lived. Some people were crying. Amisi stood in front of her house and saw the older woman next door.

"What happened?" Amisi asked.

The old woman, with a sad look on her face, quietly said, "Poor baby. It turns out; she had some sort of a disease."

"Who? A disease?" Amisi asked as the anxiety built in her.

"Little April. Little April was sick. She died," the older woman said as a tear came from her eye.

Distraught and in disbelief, Amisi said, "No. It can't be. How?" She asked.

"Baby," the woman said. "Sometimes things just happen."

Not knowing how to react, Amisi said, "Not this. This can't..." Amisi then stopped speaking and stared at the house. She then saw two men roll out a small bed on wheels with a small body out of the house. The body was covered.

In disbelief, a woman reached for the cover and pulled it from the child's face. The woman then yelled out a cry. And as Amisi saw the face of the young child, she realized that it was true. The little girl was dead. Amisi quickly felt a pain in her stomach and began to cry. She then went inside her house.

Inside, Amisi began to pace back and forth. "It can't be. It can't be," she kept saying to herself. She then sat down. "I don't understand."

Amisi stayed inside for the rest of the evening. She could not figure out what was going on. She wondered if the little was really April. She did not want to believe that it was April and that she had passed away. The troubled young woman did not want to leave the house. She stayed in for a couple of days. For the next two days, Amisi attempted to convince herself that it was not the April she knew that passed away. Amisi stayed home.

Finally, after two days, Amisi came out of the house. It was late in the afternoon.

As she came out of the house, the older woman saw Amisi and said, "I was about to come knockin' today. You had me worried. You alright?"

Amisi nodded.

"Child, sometimes these things happen… It's hard when it's a baby. I know…" The older woman said. She then sat silently.

Amisi just sat and stared. After a few moments, she stood up and said, "I am going to walk to the market. Do you need anything from the market?"

The older woman shook her head and said, "No thank you, child. Be careful."

Amisi turned around locked her door and walked down her steps and began to walk to walk to the market. As she walked around the corner, she saw Dell walking towards her. It appeared that he was coming home from work. As they passed each other, Dell did not look at Amisi and walked past her without saying a word.

Not understanding why he did not speak, after a few steps she remembered what Dell said to her in the park. "So, you're just gonna act like you don't see me, huh?" She said sarcastically.

Dell kept walking and did not turn around.

Feeling a bit embarrassed and confusedly sad, Amisi turned back around and began to walk away.

"You playing games with me or what?" Amisi heard Dell say as she walked away.

Amisi turned around and looked at Dell. He looked upset.

"Games?" She asked.

"Yes. Games. You playin' me?" Dell asked as he walked towards Amisi. "Because I remember you calling me a boy but..."

Suddenly, remembering that she said that she would meet him in the park two days prior, she interrupted Dell and said, "Oh, my. I am terribly sorry. Games... No," she said. "A child on my street passed away and it affected me more than I expected."

"I'm sorry...," Dell said. "You okay?"

"I am," Amisi replied. "I did not know her very well. But she was just a child. She reminded me of a friend I lost..." Amisi then grabbed Dells hands. "I am sorry."

Caught off guard by Amisi's affection, Dell then said, "Umm... Listen... Where are you going? May I walk with you?"

Amisi nodded and said, "Yes, please."

▲

Months passed and Amisi and Dell became closer. Amisi met Dell's mother. He took of care of his mother, because she was sick and unable to work. He would tell Amisi stories about his past, which helped Amisi understand his respectful and hard-working personality.

And although Amisi was still very private and did not share much with Dell, Dell was very understanding. He liked her very much and did not want to ruin what they had by asking a lot of questions. But, every once in a while it would frustrate him that he knew little about her past.   Amisi would tell him stories. She would take stories about her life and change them around to make them fit into the new world in which she lived. However, she did not share much.

One day, while at the park, Dell asked Amisi, "When am I going to meet *your* parents?"

Amisi did not answer. She could have simply said that they were dead or something without going any further with it. This would have satisfied Bamidele. But she could not. She simply did not answer.

Upset, Dell stood up, grabbed his bag and said, "I'll see you later."

"Wait," Amisi said.

"I'm not gonna do this anymore, Amisi," Dell said. "I don't try to pry in your business but, if you want this to go any further, you gotta let me in.

"Bamidele, please sit." Amisi grabbed him by the hand and pulled him to the bench. "You have to understand, I want to tell you. I really do. But…"

As Amisi looked at Dell, she realized that if she is going to make it in this world, she needed to trust someone. She felt that he was the one to trust.

"I am not from here," Amisi said.

"Really?" Dell said sarcastically. "I got that."

"You do not understand." Amisi said in a sad tone. "I had to leave my home because I was in danger."

"Danger? What kind of danger?" Dell asked. "Is someone after you? Tell me."

"I cannot..."

"Why not?" Dell interrupted.

"Because I don't even know everything," She said in a frustrated tone. "I was sent here by my father..." Amisi stopped, not knowing what else to say.

"Go on." Dell said.

"It's getting dark, we should go. I promise, Bamidele. I will find a way to tell you in a way you can understand and I will tell you all.

Dell looked over to Amisi with a disappointed look and said, "Yeah."

As they made their way home, they did not speak. They held hands as they walked. Amisi felt awkward. She did not know what to say.

Dell walked Amisi to her house. Seated outside was Amisi's older friend, her neighbor. Still appearing disappointed, Dell kissed Amisi on the cheek said, "Goodnight," and walked away.

Amisi watched Dell as he walked away. She then sat on the top step of her front door.

Night had fallen, but some of the children were still playing outside. Amisi enjoyed watching the children play. It made her feel at ease.

"How are you feeling this evening, Ma'am?" Amisi asked. Amisi has grown used to calling the older woman *Ma'am*. She never bothered learning the woman's name. Being used to being called Ma'am, the older woman never bothered telling Amisi her name.

"Oh I'm fine, child," the woman answered. "Just getting old. Getting old."

Amisi just looked at her friend and smiled.

"You do know that, right?" The woman strangely asked.

"Know what, Ma'am?" Amisi asked.

"That I'm getting old." She answered.

"Well, Ma'am. I suppose so." Amisi said.

"The reason I say that is…" the woman took a deep breath and smiled. "Well, child. I ain't gon' be around forever,"

Amisi looked at her friend, wondering where she was going with the conversation.

"There's gon' be a time when you're gonna have to befriend someone new… Trust another person; other *people*."

Amisi just looked at the older person.

"I've seen that boy every day since he was little child. And, I tell you, he's a good boy. He really likes you. He don't play around. He takes good care of his Momma and I think he wants to take care of you, too. Now, like I said, I ain't gon' be around for you too much longer. I'm not young like you," she said with a slight laugh. "So, if you wanna start trusting other people, he'd be the one."

Amisi, staring at the older woman, did not know what to say.

The older woman laughed as she began to stand up. "You don't gotta say nothing," she said. "I'm just a wise old woman who's seen it all." She taps her finger on her temple and repeated, "…seen it *all*. Goodnight child."

"Goodnight," Amisi replied. She then looked over to the house where the little girl died, and sighed. Thinking about April and her old home, Amisi felt overwhelmed. She then went inside and went to bed.

The next day, Amisi waited for Dell in the park. She read a newspaper as she sat. While reading, she heard a young woman playing with her young child. The woman sat on a blanket as her child crawled around her. Amisi stared. She enjoyed observing the calm, peaceful bond between the woman and her child.

The mother sang to the baby an old American nursery rhyme. She sang, "This old man, he plays one. He plays nick-nack on my thumb. With a nick-nack, patty whack; give a dog a bone. This old man came rolling home."

Amisi stared in admiration.

Then, she saw Dell walking to her. She quickly became nervous. Amisi was not familiar with this feeling. She was unfamiliar with many of the feelings she had been feeling lately. She knew that she liked Bamidele. She knew she could trust him with basic information for now. It was too soon to tell him everything. He would not understand nor believe her. She tried to remember what she planned on telling him but her mind went blank as he came closer. Dell then sat down.

"Hey," he said.

"Hello, Bamidele," she said. "How was school?"

He exhaled and said, "Well, school is school. You know."

"No. I don't. Tell me," Amisi replied.

"Ok. Well, in my class, we are going over current events," Dell explained. "It's a Sociology class. We are focusing on urban culture. We got into this huge discussion about the violence in the Black community. Some people say it's about economy, a sense of modern colonization and abandonment; others say it's about Blacks just being 'savages' and uneducated criminals who look for any reason to commit a crime..."

"What do you think?" Amisi asked.

"Heh," Dell exhales. "I mean, come on... I think there are a lot of factors... Is this our first conscious, political conversation?" He laughed.

"What do you mean, *Black*?" Amisi asked.

"What do you mean, what do I mean? I mean... Black people; people of color. Anyone who is of African descent... I mean, that could be anyone nowadays to some people..." He stated. He seemed passionate about the subject. "Our people are so separated; you can't even say who's what anymore. Languages and shades and mixes separate us today. I mean, Black can mean anything to a lot of people nowadays. To me, it means... Anyone who has the slightest bit of African in them and has experienced enslavement, struggle, colonization and is willing to accept their African heritage and use it as empowerment. They don't necessarily have to have experienced those things," he amended. "But, at least accept that it happened, and... And, as a person of color, help those who are suffering from what I call 'post traumatic slave disorder.'

"Which goes into what you think..." Amisi said, pushing Dell to get to his point.

"I think we, as a community, suffer from fear. We don't trust anyone. I mean, who can blame us? Anyway, we fear change, things that are different. We fear failure but, when we become successful, we're skeptical and even vulnerable... I mean, we are unconvinced that it's gonna last. We think it's a set up. We develop this 'you only live once' attitude. We don't trust the people we once did trust, and we act irresponsibly..." Dell continued. "I guess, in the end, we have become so accustomed to struggling in many cases that we are content with it; and, therefore, we continue the cycle ourselves. I mean we don't even need racist people anymore... I think the violence and the drugs and weapons were planted in our community and, through media and other discreet means, we were taught how to keep the cycle going. Plus, we are too dependent on the government. And every time we come close to learning how to break away from this cycle, we are stripped away from resources that we need the government to provide or we are set back somehow. I mean, take the last election…" He paused, thinking that he may have talked too much. "There are so many things that I think about it. I mean, I have complaints about us, the government, the crime… I can go on for hours. I apologize." He then laughed.

"Why do you laugh?" Amisi asked.

"Heh." He chuckled. "Because, I just rambled on and you just sat there and…"

"I admire your passion," Amisi said.

"What do you think?" Dell asked.

"About what?" she asked.

"About what we're talking about," he replied. "Our community issues…"

Amisi chuckled slightly and said, "Well, it's really not my place to say. I'm not from…"

"Now, how could you say that?" Dell asked slightly upset but with a smile. "Just 'cause you're from another country and you speak another language…? See, that's another thing. Our own people…" Dell said as he stroked Amisi's skin. "It's like no one wants to be associated with us. It's 'their' problem. Not 'ours…'"

"No, Bamidele. That is not what I am saying." Amisi interrupted. "It is a long story…" To avoid argument about what she truly meant, Amisi spoke on her opinions. "What I meant was that I have strong opinions about it. But, I hesitated to speak on it, *because* I am not from here."

"I think you have just as much right as I do. You live here now, right?" Dell said.

"I suppose so," Amisi responded. "Where I am from," Amisi went on, trying not to give too much information about her world, "The people are happy. We know our history- thousands of years of it. We learned about the struggles of our ancestors and about their antagonists. But…" Amisi stopped, not knowing what else to say. "I suppose… Regarding here, now… There must be a point when one cannot be afraid anymore."

- "There was one who was not afraid; actually two or three… And thousands who followed them." Dell replied. "But they were killed…"

"Then there must be another one… And another if need be." Amisi stated.

"… And then there are those older people who speak up against drug dealers and criminals in their neighborhoods, and their houses get burned down; their families get threatened," Dell continued. "I mean, we do have politicians now. We had a president. It's not like we are not succeeding. But those who succeed have responsibilities. They are responsible for 'more important issues,'" he said with a tone. "When they obtain those positions, they are no longer responsible for just *our* community. We become a small portion of their responsibilities… And then, the true goal gets lost. Our community then, once again, gets left in the hands of the criminals and corrupt so-called leaders… The goal gets lost," he repeats

"What is the true goal?" Amisi asked.

"Equilibrium, I guess," he answered. "Our own greatness; not modeled after anyone else's. But our own free greatness. The continuation of our interrupted legacy," Dell said with passion, raising his hand.

Amisi smiled.

He then continued with a quieter and serious tone. "… And to be able to obtain all of that without having to justify or explain to anyone *why* we deserve it."

Amisi stared. She admired Dell's passion.

"So, you gonna tell me where you're from?" Dell asked with a smile on his face.

Amisi smiled and asked, "What if I told you that I was from the future and that, where I come from, greatness is the norm?"

Dell laughed, "I'd believe you. As great as you are, it would be hard not to believe."

Amisi smiled and blushed.

That evening, Dell walked Amisi home. She held his hand as they walked. Amisi was happy. Not just because she was with a man that she really liked. She was really happy because she finally felt like she was living an actual life.

As they approached her house, they saw bright flashing lights. Red flashing lights shined from Amisi's house. As they got closer to her house, she realized that the flashing lights were coming from an ambulance parked out front of the house next door to Amisi's house. It was her friend's house.

"Oh, man. What happened?" Dell asked.

Amisi could not speak. She knew something was terribly wrong. She walked quicker to the older woman's home. She then began to run. When she got to the house, the ambulance drove away.

"No!" Amisi said. "What happened?"

The last time Amisi saw an ambulance, it drove away with the little girl's dead body inside. She feared that her old friend was dead.

Then, the door to the old woman's house opened. A woman walked out. The woman looked a bit older than Amisi.

"Are you Amisi?" the young woman said.

Amisi looked puzzled. "How did you know my name?" she asked.

"This letter is for you," the woman said as she handed Amisi an envelope with her name on it. "She asked me to give this to you."

"I did not know she knew my name," Amisi stated. "What happened?"

The young woman sighed. "She'd been sick for some time now," she said as she locked the door. "It finally took its toll on her. She lived a full life, though," the woman said with a slight smile as a tear came from her eye."

"How did *you* know her?" Amisi asked quietly.

The woman smiled as she walked to her car and said, "She was a good friend. She took care of me when I moved to the city years ago," she paused to think. She sighed, then said, "I will really miss her."

The woman got in her car and drove away.

Amisi was sad. She did not know what to do.

Dell took hold of Amisi's hands and asked, "Are you alright? Do you want me to stay?"

Amisi thought for a moment. Feeling that she may need to be alone as she read the letter, she said, "No, thank you, Bamidele. I think I should be alone. I hope you understand."

"I do," Dell said. "I'm sorry." He then kissed Amisi on her forehead and went home.

When Amisi went inside, she sat on her sofa and took a deep breath. She then opened the envelope and unfolded the letter.

The letter said,

"Dear Amisi,

I got your name from an envelope in your room when you were really sick a while back. I hope you don't mind. You never told me your name. And I thought there was a good reason for that, so I never called you by your name.

I am writing you this letter because I have been really sick. I'm not sure how much longer I have so I wanted to write something before… Well, you know.

I really don't know what to write. But I felt like I just had to.

I've lived in this house for a very long time. My mother lived in this house for many years before me. Throughout those years, many girls just like you have come to the house that you live in now. They were all quiet; they all kept to themselves; they were all always sick. None of them ever worked.

The difference between all of those girls and you, child, is that they were all afraid. Now, I know you were a bit scared but, you weren't afraid. You weren't afraid to come out. Now, those girls came out to get their food and stuff. But, that was all. When I would speak to them, they wouldn't say a word. Some girls would come and live in the house for years without coming out. And I'll be honest with you, girl. A couple of them even took their own lives in that very house (I hope it's not a bad thing for me to tell you that). You are different. You became my friend. You became part of this community. I just wanted to thank you for that.

I never knew where you girls came from or why they sent you here. But after meeting you, I now know that it's for a reason greater than anything I will ever know. I appreciate being a part of whatever it is you are a part of. You brought me hope for my children and I don't really know why.

Before I go, I just want to tell you some things; some advice. One, don't let this world scare you, no matter what. Two, although you have changed in your physical appearance in some ways, never change who you are inside for no one. You are special. Three, always remember where you come from, but don't forget to keep your eyes on what's ahead of you. You don't wanna trip. And lastly, remember that sometimes we search the world and try our hardest to find great things only to find that they've been with us all along.

Thank you.
Love,

Ms. April
(Yes. Same as that poor little girl)."

Amisi gasped as her eyes widened.

Amisi then began to cry. She then gathered herself and stood up, went outside and walked to Dell's house. Still crying, she knocked on Dell's door. When Dell answered the door, Amisi, with tears coming from her eyes, hugged Dell. Dell held her for a long time.

▲ Chapter 4
New Life

That evening, Amisi told Dell everything. It took Dell a moment to gather himself and actually believe Amisi. He did not want to believe Amisi. However, she was so compelling. With so much emotion, she told her story as Dell sat in front of her and took it all in.

He believed her. Question after question, Dell inquired on every possible thing. The conversation lasted for days. Amisi felt relieved. She felt closer to being home more than ever.

Years passed and Amisi and Dell remained together. Amisi remembered the words from the letter she received from her old friend. She often thought of Ms. April.

Dell graduated from college. And, although he did not need to work because Amisi still had a lot of money, he chose to work. Dell wanted to be a teacher. But, he continued to work at a law firm until he became certified to teach. His mother passed away from her illness just a year before his graduation.

Amisi attempted to get used to death, for it continued to rear its head. Still, it was a concept she had difficulty accepting. She supported Dell through the grief of losing his mother and in his decision to work. Amisi loved Bamidele.

Amisi first learned about death at a young age. It was one of the very few times she witnessed death. When she was very young, her mother was killed in an accident. It was never clearly explained how her mother passed away. All Amisi knew was that it was an accident. She told Dell about it and it made their connection stronger.

By this time, Dell was not officially living with Amisi; but he stayed over her house most of the time. Dell even spoke to Amisi about marriage. Where Amisi came from, marriage was the grandest thing in one's life. It was a spiritual bond. And Amisi felt somewhat impassive about it. She had no family and no friends. When Dell would speak to her about marriage, she would draw away from the subject. This would upset Dell. After knowing everything about Amisi; after everything they had been through together, he felt that it should be the next step. After all, he loved her.

Eventually, without marrying, Amisi became pregnant. It was unexpected. Since she continued to feel ill, she did not think she could become pregnant. And when she did, she became fearful. She thought that she would either lose her life or the child. However, months past and she had a healthy pregnancy. Amisi was comfortable with the world enough to see a midwife but not until later in the pregnancy. Dell was afraid as well. Still, he was supportive and caring. He took good care of Amisi.

Months passed and although she became physically ill at times, Amisi maintained a healthy spirit. She and Dell lived in her house. After Amisi told Dell that she did not want to wed, Dell felt resentment. But, he carried on as he loved her. Although Amisi had no family or friends other than Dell, she became accustomed to her new way of life. She was content. However, her contentment was going to be challenged again and again.

One evening, in the later stages of Amisi's pregnancy, she and Dell were walking in a usually quiet part of Center City Philadelphia. As they talked and held hands, they were confronted by a group of boys. Young, and not quite adults, they were big, well numbered and ready to start trouble.

Not afraid of confrontation yet taking Amisi's health and safety into consideration, Dell tightened his hold on Amisi's hand and continued to walk through the group.

Immediately, the group of boys began to taunt the couple by making passes at Amisi and attempting to intimidate Dell. Dell was an educated good man. Still, growing up where he did, he was never the one to intimidate easily. Seeing that the group was going to continue harassing them and knowing that there was no one to help, Dell pushed Amisi behind him and began to challenge the boys. They began to hit Dell. Fists were flying everywhere. Amisi began to scream for help to no avail.

With several guys surrounding him, Dell continued fighting and holding his own. Amisi was pulled away from Dell by several others. Dell pulled Amisi away from the group and yelled for her to run. As they were running, Dell was struck in the head and knocked down. Amisi, not seeing Dell fall, continued to run but then turned around and saw him on the ground. She was then surrounded by the group while two of the boys began to kick Dell.

Suddenly Amisi's adrenaline rose to its limit. She then heard her mother's voice. In her thoughts, Amisi was taken back to when she was a child.

"Amisi," she heard her mother call.

She then heard Dell call, "Amisi!" as he was continuously being struck.

Again she heard her mother call as she remembered being in her room at home. She then saw the group of boys surrounding. Back and forth, she heard her mother and heard Dell calling her. Back and forth, she was taken from her childhood memory to the violent altercation. Suddenly, in her thoughts, she remembered her mother screaming. Amisi then screamed and blacked out.

Moments later, she was awakened.

"Oh God!" she heard Dell exclaim silently, with surprise. "Amisi," he said as he stood up and walked towards her. He took Amisi by her arm and helped her to her feet and asked, "Are you alright?"

As Amisi stood up, she looked around her and found the boys who surrounded her lying on the ground around her in a circle. They were dead.

Shaken, Dell took Amisi by the hand and silently said, "We have to go."

Amisi, scared and shaken as well, then fell to her knees and began to cry uncontrollably.

Dell grabbed her by the arm and tried to pull her to her feet and said again, "Amisi, we have to go."

Crying, Amisi then said, "I killed my mother."

That evening, Amisi could not stop shaking. As she sat in the living room of her house, Dell was in their room packing their clothes. During this time, he had the television on to see if what had happened would be on the news. It let him know how much time they had to leave. It was reported on the news that 7 bodies were found dead in the street from an apparent electrocution.

"*...the bodies were found after police were responding to an emergency call when neighbors heard screaming,*" the reporter on the television said. "*Police did not have any comments although it was said that there were no down power lines in the vicinity and the skies were clear. So far, police have no witnesses.*

Returning to our top story, it is now being reported that the death toll has risen to 4,130 from what is being called the worst earthquake in recorded history. And officials tell us that that number is expected to increase dramatically. It is being predicted that it may rise to the hundreds of thousands. The earthquake in Sumatra, Indonesia reached magnitude 9.7 in the Richter scale, crumbling buildings, opening the ground and creating tsunamis that traveled as far west as the eastern coast of Africa and as far east as the west coast of North and South America. Thanks to the Tsunami alert systems we have in place, many lives were spared. Unfortunately, we can't say the same for many other countries. We are now getting a report from our sister station in Los Angeles, that there was indeed much damage and even deaths…"

As Dell packed, he did not listen to the television. All he thought of was the need to leave the city. He knew that there were at least two survivors from the incident with him and Amisi. He also knew that the police were going to be investigating. He felt the need to leave immediately. After packing all that he could, he went downstairs to get Amisi.

"Amisi, I know this is difficult for you but we must leave," He said.

Amisi just stared.

"Amisi," Dell repeated. "We have to leave."

In a slight daze, Amisi looked at Dell and said, "Leave? Leave where? Where are we going?" She asked.

"What do you mean?" Dell asked. "We can't stay in Philly. We have to go."

"Go?" Amisi asked. "No. I cannot go?"

"Amisi," Dell argued. "Seven boys are dead. How…?" He paused trying to piece it together. "And the others…? There were at least two…"

"I cannot leave," Amisi interrupted.

They began to argue back and forth.

Dell could not understand why Amisi did not want to leave.

Amisi understood why Dell wanted to leave but she knew that she could not leave the city.

Suddenly, she yelled, "I cannot leave."

Dell stood quietly. He was speechless for a moment. After a moment of silence, Dell struggled to get his words out.

"It's this whole April thing, isn't it?" He asked.

Amisi looked at Dell in silence.

Upset, Dell continued. "You found April… Two of them in fact; and they are both dead, Amisi. Dead!" He yelled. "There is no…" He stopped and, disgruntled, he walked away.

The next few days were silent. Amisi and Dell were distant from one another. Although they lived in the same home, they were worlds apart. Needing food, Dell quietly mentioned to Amisi that he was going to the market to get food.

Amisi simply nodded.

The afternoon passed and Amisi was at home not feeling well. In fact, Amisi felt worse than she'd ever felt. She began to feel terrible pains. Dell was not yet home and she began to become very scared. She felt that maybe she was in labor. Suddenly, she felt warm fluid running down her leg, which assured her that she was definitely in labor. She became more afraid and looked at the door, hoping Dell would walk in. In excruciating pain, Amisi called for Dell in hopes that he would somehow respond. She looked at the telephone. In the time that she had lived in the city, she had never used the telephone. However, she did know how to make an emergency call. But, she did not want to. She wanted Bamidele. But the longer she waited, the worse the pain became; the worse the fear became. She could not wait any longer. Amisi picked up the telephone and called for an ambulance.

Meanwhile, Dell was out taking a walk around getting his thoughts together. He had not yet gone to the market because he needed to think. Dell knew that he was in a unique situation. Life had not prepared him for what he was currently experiencing. He did not know if he was ready to be a part of this lifestyle. Still, he had a child on the way. He was in this now whether he wanted to be or not. After some thought, Dell realized that his love for Amisi was greater than he could imagine. Dell realized that he would do what Amisi needed him to do. He then turned around and without going to the market, he began to walk home. Little did he know; Dell was being followed.

As he walked home, a young man followed behind waiting for the right moment. During this time, Amisi was in the ambulance, on her way to the hospital. She was in labor and scared. In pain though, all she could think about was Dell.

As Dell walked, all he could think about was his future with Amisi and their child. Unfortunately, deep in his thoughts, Dell could not see what was in his immediate future, for he had a predator on his trail.

Amisi finally made it to the hospital. She was in terrible pain. The moment to have her baby came quickly. The midwife present was in disbelief in how quickly her labor was progressing. The midwife spoke to Amisi to keep her calm.

"Is the father in the picture?" the woman asked bluntly.

"Yes," Amisi said. "But he does not know I am here. He went to the market and…" She breathed.

"Now take it easy, we'll have someone find him. Let's just get this baby because it looks like it doesn't want to be in there anymore," the midwife joked.

The birth of the child was near. Amisi then screamed in agony.

All of a sudden, as he walked, Dell felt a sudden feeling of danger. He knew that something was wrong. Just as he was about to start running home, he was confronted by a young man- a boy in fact. The boy looked familiar.

"I know you," Dell said.

"Where's your girl at?" The boy said. Just then, he pulled out a gun and shot Dell in the chest.

In the hospital, at the moment Dell was shot, Amisi felt the worst pain she had felt yet. Although it was a contraction, Amisi felt something more. She knew something went wrong. Amisi screamed again and cried. Just then her child was born.

As the baby cried, so did Amisi. So many emotions went through her that she was distraught. She was still in pain, she was terribly scared, she did not know where Bamidele was; and she knew something was terribly wrong. All the while, Dell lay dying in the street not too far from their home.

"We had a police car go to your house to find your husband," the midwife said.

When Amisi heard the woman refer to Dell as her husband, it gave her a soothing sensation. She then knew that that was what she wanted- for Dell to be her husband. It was in fact what she needed to make her transition complete. She cried.

"Would you like to hold your daughter?" The midwife asked.

Amisi nodded and smiled.

"While we are waiting for the father to get here, we should get the paperwork started," the nurse said. "Did you have a name picked out for your daughter?" she asked

Amisi thought for a moment. She thought of the name of three people who brought her to this point in her life emotionally- the young stranger who became her friend and changed her world, the old stranger who became her friend in her new world, and the toddler who although she mistook her for someone else, she grew very fond of, if only for just a brief moment in her life.

As Amisi was giving her response to the nurse, the man who she wanted to finally marry lay dead from an assailant's gunshot.

"April," Amisi said.

"And will she be given her father's last name," the nurse asked.

"Yes," Amisi answered. "Lewis. His name is Bamidele Lewis."

▲

Part TWO

▲ Chapter 5

Time passed and Martinez and April continued to live in the house. Not knowing what to expect, Martinez was always alert waiting to be contacted by someone. As time passed, he became less and less anticipative. Martinez began to simply live as a guardian and nothing else. They had plenty of money so he did not have to work. His life became routine. He would jog every morning and work out for an hour; he would then make sure April made it to school safely. Then, he would read several global as well as local newspapers in a coffee shop in the neighborhood; then watch more news at home. He would document any abnormality that he would see in the news.

At times, he would feel sick, so he would take a nap during the day. Still, he always made sure that April made it to school and then home safely.

"Why can't I sometimes walk home or take the bus?" April asked with a slight laugh one day when Martinez picked her up from school.

Martinez responded, "I have to protect you April."

April stared at Martinez.

"What?" Martinez asked wondering what she was thinking.

"Genio," April called; short for Eugenio, Martinez's first name. "It's been a while now. I don't even think people know about me…"

"Right," Martinez interrupted. "And the moment I let my guard down, something will happen."

"Like what?" April asked. "Besides, don't you think they would have done it by now? Plus, I mean, no offense, but what are you gonna do? You are one person."

Martinez did not respond. He sat and drove quietly.

April thought of what she had said, "Look," she sighed. "I didn't mean it like that…"

"They *don't* know about you," Martinez said.

"What? What do you mean?" April asked.

"I mean, they killed who they were supposed to kill," Martinez answered. "Right? I mean, from what they saw- the people who wanted to kill that little girl; they saw her die. So to them, it is probably over. They don't know about you," Martinez tried to rationalize.

April didn't know what to say. She really did not know what Martinez meant.

Before April could respond Martinez explained, "But, just as we don't know why you don't remember that incident or why you are here, we don't know if it's over. Plus, there is…" Martinez looked at April.

"The 'Great War?' Ooh, can't wait for that!" April said sarcastically.

"When will you be convin…?"

"I am convinced!" April exclaimed. "It's just not often one is told that their life is based on a war and time that hasn't even happened yet. I don't know how to react."

That evening, Martinez watched the news:

> *"Our top news story tonight is the devastation in Colorado where an earthquake hit 8.1 on the Richter scale killing several hundred people with possibly hundreds more missing or buried. This only one day after the 18th anniversary of the record breaking earthquake in Indonesia that killed hundreds of thousands. Now,*

18 years ago, experts linked the record breaker to the Super Volcano which lies under Lake Toba in Sumatra. Now, experts are linking this earthquake to the Super Volcano which lies under Yellow Stone Park. What does this mean? Stay tuned. We'll have more information- things you should be concerned about and more, later in the newscast."

Martinez stared at the television.

▲

Two years passed and April attended college. She was very much interested in history and the sciences. One of her classes was Environmental Science. It really intrigued her. "Now, although I'm going to somewhat drift into another topic today, I hope that you all read the article on alternative fuels and atmospheric regeneration over the weekend," April's young class professor stated as he entered the lecture hall.

The professor– a young, tall, skinny, well dressed, light brown-skinned gentleman with glasses, looked around the room, looking for a response. No one responded as the students pulled out writing instruments and their books.

"I take that as a… Yes," he said. "Alright… So, Global Warming… It's a term we've all heard for years, especially in the beginning of this millennium. We've seen it on TV and the movies; we've had political figures talk about it, and now… Well, we are living it." The young professor continued. "What about its affects? Anyone?" He looked around.

April stared at him as she listened carefully. At the same time, she thought about what just occurred over the weekend wondering if the professor is going to bring it up and get into a deep debate or conversation about it.

"Anyone?" The professor asked again. "Well, over the weekend…" April's eyes lit up, hoping that he was going to say what she was waiting for.

"Over the weekend, and old movie came on about the near extinction of humans due to climate change. Anyone see it?" He asked.

April became disappointed.

Students called the title of the movie out.

"Right." The instructor responded. "And what was the main cause of this event? See… unlike the movies, it's not an event that's going to happen overnight. We are not going to freeze to death or burn to death. Not tomorrow or the day after tomorrow. But let's talk about the facts and that will lead us a little into the article we read." April stared losing interest.

"Let's talk about three things- North Atlantic Oscillation, the Atlantic Heat Conveyor, and Desalinization." The professor continued.

April's attention began to drift away.

After class, April began to walk towards the corner where Martinez picked her up every night. She had gotten used to being picked up by Martinez.

What was unfortunate was the fact that the only time she saw Martinez anymore was when he picked her up from the university. He would then drop her off at home, sometimes eat and then leave for one reason or another for the rest of the evening. Often, Martinez would tell April that he was out monitoring the neighborhood or meeting with people from the local community to hear about changes in the community. April joked that he had a girlfriend that he did not want her to know about. Martinez would insist that it was not true and stressed that there was no time for that type of recreation, especially with what was coming in their near future.

As April walked, she heard someone call her. It was her young professor, Mr. Coffey. April turned around. She smiled but kept walking. Although April enjoyed listening to debates in the class and sometimes even made small comments, she was not much of a conversationalist outside the class. April walked.

"Ms. Lewis," Mr. Coffey called as he jogged towards her.

April stopped and turned around. She was a bit agitated but did not show it.

"I'm sorry to bother you," the young instructor said. "But I just was wondering…"

"Yes, Mr. Coffey," April said sounding a bit uptight.

"Please, call me Anthony," he said politely. "I just had a concern. Now, some of my students are sometimes weirded out by my… Well, friendliness and show of concern but, look… You put a lot of time and money into these classes and I'm all about helping people…"

"What's your concern, Mr. Coffey," April interrupted.

They young professor chuckled and said, "Well, on your first two exams, I was blown away… I mean, top grades in the class. Plus, although you did not say much, you did seem pretty interested in the class…"

"Are you offended that I'm not showing you attention anymore, Mr. Coffey?" April mocked, clearly joking.

Caught off guard with April's teasing, Mr. Coffey did not know what to say. He stood silently.

"I'm sorry, Mr. Coffey. That was inappropriate of me," April stated. She was still trying to get the hang of being mature and social.

"That's quite alright. Again, call me Anthony," the professor said. "I'm really not that much older than you; although, you do look pretty young to be in college," he laughed.

As April was about to respond, Mr. Coffey interrupted, "See? Now, I am being inappropriate. I apologize."

April smiled.

"Anyway, you seem to be losing interest in the class and you've been doing so well," Anthony said.

"Why didn't you talk about what happened this weekend?" April asked.

"What….the earthquakes?" Anthony asked. "Well, April, I mean… It was pretty… devastating, to say the least. But, I have a job to do."

"It is Environmental Science. And…"

"Yes, April but we have to follow the syllabus… We can't always cover what the student wants, when they want it. But that isn't the reason you've lost interest," Anthony explains." I mean, that just happened. You've been…"

"Two years ago there was the Colorado disaster. Eighteen years before that there was the one they called the big one in Asia that killed a lot of people," April argued. "Not to mention the great tsunamis several years before that…"

"I think we are getting off topic here," Mr. Coffey said. "Besides, those types of things happen all the time. They have been happening for thousands of years."

"But don't you see a pattern? And I don't think we are off topic, these are environmental issues we need to discuss. The other things you teach, I already know." April argued.

Stumped, Mr. Coffey smiled silently. "April," he began. "There are a lot of things that we need to cover in this class. We are not scientists hired by the government and… Look, if you would like to have discussions of the environment having to do with what is on the syllabus, by all means, bring it up in the lectures. If it is not on the syllabus, please, set up a time… I'd be more than happy to have a discussion with you about it. I am fine with that. But, please, if you are going to fail my class, please don't let it be over your lack of interest in what I am paid to teach you. Bottom line… you have to learn and pass exams on what is taught in the class. I am impressed with your knowledge, and I just wanted to make sure you were… I just wanted to make sure you were okay."

As April thought about what Mr. Coffey said, she saw Martinez drive up.

"I have to go," she said.

Mr. Coffey nodded.

As she walked towards the car, April turned around and called to Mr. Coffey.

"When can we meet to finish our discussion about these earthquakes?" April asked.

Mr. Coffey smiled with a slightly confused look not expecting her to have asked what she did.

"See me after class…" He replied.

April smiled and entered Martinez's car.

As they drove away, Martinez asked, "New friend?"

April reacted with a slight attitude. "He's my professor."

"Professor?" Martinez asked surprised. "Aren't they usually older?

April did not respond.

"What were you talking about?" He asked.

April became agitated. "Why?" She asked.

"I was just asking… Having conversation..." Martinez said. "I mean, what professor socializes with students?"

"What, are you jealous or something?" April asked with a troubled tone. Not wanting to give Martinez any more reason to ask questions about Mr. Coffey, she said, "I needed to ask him about his opinions on the earthquakes and stuff. Just to get a professional opinion. I just wonder if it has anything to do with… Anything."

Martinez sat silently. "Jealous…" he scoffed. "Jealous of what? Why…?" Martinez became speechless.

"You are ridiculous," April stated.

"What?" he asked.

"For months, you have been leaving me alone and…" April stuttered. "Socializing… What if I *was 'socializing'* with him? I need to be socializing with someone," she argued. "I mean, you tell me that I should be living a normal life… Well, as close to normal as possible. But you leave me alone every night to do who knows what."

"I…"

"I know what you say you do," she interrupts. "But, I don't know that. You could be out with women and stuff."

"Women?" Martinez asked sounding insulted. "April, I told you…"

"I know. I know…" April interrupts again.

"Fine," Martinez interrupted. "I will take you with me to see…"

"I don't want you to take me anywhere to prove anything to me," she exclaimed. "I just want you to spend time with…" She stopped.

There was an awkward silence in the car.

Then, not used to having these types of discussions, Martinez said the first thing that came to mind. He was a bit irritated about April not understanding what he does, although he did realize that he really should spend some more time with her.

"You still have some maturing to do, April," he blurted out. "These past months, I have been trying my best to…"

Insulted, April widened her eyes and looked at Martinez upset. She then interrupted him.

"How can you say that to me?" She asked. "Do you have any idea how much I've had to endure? How much I was forced to change about myself? Do you know anything about what has changed about me? Do you know anything about me? The difference between the 'me' 3 years ago and the 'me' now. Mature?? What…?" April was disgusted. She had no more words to say.

The rest of the evening was silent. Martinez stayed home. He did not know that April felt the way she did. Although she joked about him leaving her in the evenings, he did not know that she thought about it that much. He felt bad. Still, he was a bit bitter about April saying that he was jealous. He thought to himself that it was absurd for April to think that way. Martinez was up all night thinking about it.

Days passed and the relationship between April and Martinez grew tense. April was becoming resentful towards Martinez. She felt that too much time had passed and she began to feel skeptical about what Mayet and Martinez told her would happen. April was convinced that something *was* going on- she did travel in time; she did witness the lives and the deaths. Still, as time passed, she could not help but become frustrated because it was not happening quickly enough. Of course, she did not want the world to end or for war to break out. She was just feeling tired of doing nothing but waiting. She was getting older and becoming bored with her life.

One day, as Martinez was taking April to school, April asked Martinez to not pick her up after class.

Confused, Martinez said, "I have too. What do you mean? Why not?"

"I'm not coming straight home after class," April replied.

"I don't understand. You know that you can't just…"

"I was told to live a close to normal life. Right?" April interrupted. "Well, I'm going out."

"Out?" Martinez asked, sounding irritated by April's attitude. "Yes we told you to live a normal life but not without caution. I…"

"I'm not really going out. I am meeting with someone. Mr. Coffey." April said.

"Mr. Coffey? Your Teacher?" Martinez asked

"Yes…"

"I can't allow that," Martinez quickly responded. "You don't know him. He…"

"'He,' what?" April interrupted again. "He doesn't meet your approval? He's a college professor. We are just going to talk, which is more than what I can say for what we have been doing. Eugenio, I have stayed in that house for too long. I have to get out and socialize. I am going crazy."

"You do not know him!" Martinez stressed. "For all you know, he could be someone out to kill you."

"Why would he…?" April said with a high pitched tone. "Did you even hear what I said? *We*…," she pointed to herself and Martinez, "do not talk! We do not socialize. You say 'Good morning' to me, take me to school, pick me up then say 'Good night' to me. That's it. Now, I appreciate everything you do for me. But, I am a human being, not a…" She stopped not knowing what to call herself.

Martinez stopped the car in front of April's school. He sat silently.

As April opened the door to get out, Martinez said, "I didn't know. If you could just tell me what you need; what you want… I can do better. I don't know how… This wasn't supposed to be my job."

April turned around. She looked at Martinez and said, "That's the problem Eugenio. You keep seeing this as a job. If you could just see it as our lives…" She paused and appearing highly upset, she asked quietly, "Do I have your *permission* to go out after class? I will not be late and I promise I will be safe."

Martinez thought for a moment then said, "Fine."

April, looking a bit sad then said, 'Thank you," and closed the door.

As Martinez drove away, he thought about what April said. He began to understand what she spoke about. He understood that she was bored. Martinez appreciated April's honesty but wished that he knew what to do. He knew he needed to keep her safe. However, he understood that her happiness and emotional welfare were important as well.

Martinez viewed April as a child. However, he realized how mature she really had become. Technically, April was a woman now. Still very young, she had grown a lot since she'd been back to her world. She was not like Martinez, Mayet and the rest. She did not stay young like them. But, it was noticeable that she did not age like her present day peers either. Although she grew, there was something different about her. She was unique.

When Martinez arrived at the house, he thought about April. He wanted to leave again to find April and follow her; to protect her. But, then, he decided not to. He thought that she should not be sheltered any longer. April needed to grow more. And, for her to do that, she needed to know how to be on her own. All evening, Martinez paced back and forth thinking about her. He was nervous; paranoid. But, he stayed home.

Meanwhile, April met up with Mr. Coffey, her professor. At first, the conversations with Anthony were simply about class topics. Eventually, April began to express her opinions about society, politics and the topic that she'd wanted to talk to her teacher about, the earthquakes. However, April found that it was very difficult holding a conversation with someone who knew nothing about her; nothing about what she truly knew. She needed to be very cautious.

April and Anthony spent the whole afternoon at the college campus. They were outside on a bench. As it became later and darker, it also became cooler. Anthony asked April if she wanted to go somewhere warm. April did not know how to respond. She was very cautious.

"I mean, well, do you want to go get something to eat?" Anthony asked.

"I am pretty hungry," April answered.

"What do you like?" he asked.

"Well, I don't eat a lot of meat," she answered.

"Ok," he responded. "I know a great place downtown. Do you mind getting in a car with a stranger?" Anthony asked.

April smiled and said, "No."

They walked to his car and left.

As they walked towards the restaurant from the parking lot, they walked past an area that was eerily familiar to Anthony. He shivered.

April asked him what was wrong.

"I guess you are too young to know about this. I don't even think you were born. But, when I was a little kid…" Anthony paused.

"What happened?" April asked.

"Heh," Anthony chuckled. "That's funny. It was the same night of the Great Earthquake you were asking about. Weird. Anyway, it was only in the news a couple of times even though it was one of the craziest, most tragic, unsolved mysteries in this city's history."

April listened quietly.

"My uncle was one of them," he continued. "Seven teenagers, killed; right down this block," he sighed. "Kids. They were found lying in a circle, practically burnt to a crisp."

April didn't know what to say. Still, she felt strange walking down this street. For some strange reason unbeknownst to her, she played the image in her head as if she were there. April was frightened.

The mood was eerie as Anthony continued his story.

"With the terrible tragedy that happened in Indonesia... I mean the people thought the world was going to end. So, I guess they didn't put as much effort in this case as they should have. No one ever found out what really happed. There was one guy who said he survived it. My mom knew him. She was going crazy about it. Anyway, the guy said he witnessed it. He told this crazy story about magic and stuff. No one believed him. A year later he was arrested for murder. Last I heard, he killed himself," Anthony walked silently for a moment. He then shook his head and said, "Crazy."

April again did not know what to say. She just looked down the street and continued walking.

When they got to the restaurant, they ate and sat quietly. April could not think of anything to say.

"So..." Anthony began. "You had questions about the earthquakes?"

April smiled. "Yes," she said.

"Why are you so interested in that?" He asked. "I mean, it is interesting and scary if you think about it. But you seem especially interested in what happened so many years ago. I've never met anyone your age so caught up in that. Now, older folks... They still talk about it. It was very scary."

"I don't understand why it's not a fear among everyone," April stated. "Shouldn't everyone be scared? I mean, hasn't anyone noticed that it seems like the earthquakes are getting stronger and more frequent."

"Yeah," he responded. "But what should we do, sit in our homes waiting for the world to end. As scientists point out, these are things that have happened for thousands and thousands of years. And we've survived," Anthony explained.

April, knowing more than the typical person of that time, really wanted to get further into the reasons of her intense interest. However, she needed to be careful with what she said.

"But what if we don't," April asked. "Didn't something happen a few thousand years ago that almost wiped out all humans? It took our population from millions to the lower thousands, right?"

Anthony laughed. "Now what would a person your age know about that?" Anthony continued to chuckle. "You really are into this… Why *would* you wanna know…?" Anthony rubbed his head not knowing how to react to April's interest in the subject.

Not knowing how to explain, and understanding Anthony's reaction, April said, "Let's just say that it's a field that I know I am going to be working with in the future."

Anthony smiled. "Interesting," he said. "Well, yes. You're right April. History does tell us of such an occasion. There was a Super Volcano eruption that almost wiped us out. But they're saying that nothing like that will happen again for thousands of years." Anthony became more interested and asked, "Is that really the field you wanna get into? And do you really think something is going to happen?"

"Well, not really," April stuttered. "I know that the world isn't going to explode," she laughed. "What really interests me is, how would the people react if something were to happen? How would we survive? Would there be wars? Would there be hostility for power over what's left?"

Anthony looked at April curiously, took a deep breath and simply said, "You are…"

"What?" April asked. Wondering what Anthony was going to say about her.

Anthony did not answer.

"I am what?" April asked again

"You are something." He answered.

April smiled. "Something?" She asked.

With a very serious look; a look of fondness, Anthony said, "Something special."

April smiled.

After they ate, Anthony drove April home. While driving, it was quite silent for a few moments. Anthony appeared as if he wanted to say something but he struggled to get the words out.

Suddenly, he said, "Is that your boyfriend who picks you up from school?"

April laughed and said, "My boyfriend." She blushed slightly. "No!" She exclaimed.

"Oh," Anthony said. "You're brother; cousin or something?"

"No," April answered. "I guess you can say he's my guardian."

"Oh," he said again. "Guardian? He looks kind of young to be your guardian. And aren't you kind of old to… I'm sorry. It's none of my business. Forgive me for asking."

April sat and thought for a moment. She did not want Anthony to wonder what was really going on. She needed to think of something.

"Umm… My mother passed away a few years ago," April told him, saying whatever came to mind. "She raised him. We were raised sort of like cousins. He took me in 'cause I had nowhere else to go. But I'm moving out soon. He's got a girlfriend."

Anthony really did not believe April's story. But, he did not want to ask questions, fearing that he may push her away.

"I'm asking," he said cautiously, "because… Well, I think you're a cool person and, I know I'm probably a lot older than you but, you are very interesting and pretty and…"

April began to blush.

"I was just hoping we could go out again," Anthony said shyly.

April pointed out her house without responding to her professor's gesture. He parked in front of her house.

"Well, it was just a thought. I just…"

"I'd really like that," April answered maturely. "That is, if you don't mind hanging out with a student. Or is that something you do on a regular basis?"

Anthony smiled then laughed. "No. I mean, I don't mind 'hanging out' with one of my students. And no, it is not something I've done before. Besides, I'm not asking as a professor. I'm asking as a man who is very interested in a woman," he replied.

April smiled and said, "Ok. How about this weekend?" She asked.

Anthony responded, "Yes. Can I still talk to you after class before the weekend?" He joked.

April said, "of course." She then opened the door and said, "Thank you for dinner. Goodnight."

When April opened the door to the house, she found Martinez sleeping on the sofa in the living room. He had a thick blanket on top of him and there was a bucket on the floor next to him. It appeared that he was sick again. Knowing that Martinez slept in his room with the door closed whenever he was sick, she realized that he was up waiting for her. April felt bad. With a small space for her to sit on the sofa, April slowly and quietly squeezed herself by where Martinez had his head. She felt his head and noticed that he was very warm. She gently rubbed his head. He was in a deep sleep. April looked at Martinez as he slept.

"Goodnight Eugenio," she said. She then kissed him on the forehead, got up, locked the door and went upstairs to her room.

As she walked up the stairs, April did not notice the strange phenomenon occurring in the living room. Just above Martinez, there were objects floating in the air. Up towards the ceiling floated books, and other objects from the living room. But, as Martinez awoke from hearing April close her door, the objects fell to the ground. Martinez quickly gathered his things, shut off the light and went to his room at the very top of the stairs. April, hearing Martinez's door close, came downstairs and saw that Martinez was no longer on the sofa. She sighed and went back to her room.

The following morning, April woke up earlier than usual. She got dressed, cooked breakfast and set a plate for Martinez. She covered the plate, quickly grabbed her bag and made her way towards the door.

"You go out one night, and suddenly, you don't need me to take you to school anymore," Martinez said as he came down the steps.

He surprised April. She gasped.

"You were sick last night. I didn't want to bother you," April said with slight attitude. "I cooked you breakfast," she said as she pointed to the covered plate on the table.

"Thank you," Martinez said quietly.

"I wasn't trying to…," April started. "I just wanted to let you sleep late."

Martinez sat down at the table and looked at the plate pondering.

"If you...If you want to go. You can," he said without looking at April. "I mean, you should be able to come and go as you please without me monitoring your every move. You should have freedom."

April stood silently for a moment.

"It's not freedom that I want," she said silently.

"Tell me April. What is it that you want?" Martinez asked.

April thought for a moment. She then said with a sad tone, "I don't know." She then left.

As Martinez sat staring at his plate, a tear came from his eye.

Later that day, April was on her way to the corner where she usually waited for Martinez. As she walked to the corner, she saw Mr. Coffey. He was coming out of the bookstore across the street. She did not know if she should call for his attention so she just stared. Then, Mr. Coffey turned and saw her. He smiled.

April smiled back.

He began to walk towards her.

"Hey!" he said.

April smiled.

"Waiting for your friend?" he asked.

"I don't know," April answered. I don't think so."

"Well are you or aren't you?" Anthony asked.

"I guess not," April said.

"You alright?" he asked. "You two fighting?"

"Why do I feel like you think he's my boyfriend?" April asked.

"You said it, I didn't," he responded. "Are you ok though?"

"Yes, I'm fine," April stated with a big smile. "And no I am not waiting for anybody."

"Good," Anthony responded with a smile. "...Because, I have to be honest. I'm glad I saw you today."

"Why is that?" April asked still smiling.

"Well, because, I don't think I can wait until the weekend to hang out with you again," Anthony replied.

April laughed. "Really?" she asked as she blushed.

"You wanna go somewhere?" Anthony asked.

"Sure!" She answered.

"Good! Let's go." Anthony extended his hand out.

Hesitant, April took Anthony's hand and began walking with him.

As April walked across the street with Anthony, Martinez pulled up in his car unnoticed. He was there to pick April up. Instead, he sat as he watched April walk away with Anthony. Martinez did not know what to think. However, he did feel something. He felt a feeling he had never experienced before. It was a sadness that he had never felt. He felt a strange feeling of helplessness. He sat in his parked car for a moment trying to decipher his feelings. Then, he drove away.

That afternoon, April and Anthony went to a restaurant to eat.

Anthony began to speak to April about their last conversation.

"I was thinking about what you were saying about these earthquakes and stuff," Anthony said. "In what is now Colorado, La Garita erupted 27 million years ago and…"

Thinking about how much she had missed out by thinking about disasters and the past and the future, April did not want to speak about it anymore. She cut Anthony off.

"Honestly, Anthony, can we talk about something else tonight? I just want to talk about something more positive." April said with slight smile.

A bit surprised, Anthony replied, "Ok."

"So," April began. "Tell me about yourself."

Anthony smiled. "I'm not sure if I should. Would that be appropriate?"

They laughed.

"I think after two dates, we are pass the line of appropriateness," April said.

"I guess so," Anthony replied. "About myself… Let's see. I don't know where to start."

"How about you tell me how someone so young is a professor," April said.

"Well, I'm really not *that* young," Anthony responded. "But, I… Well, to answer your question. I was one of those child genius kids in school. When I graduated high school, I went straight to college; got my degree quicker than most people. Technically, I'm not a professor yet. I won't get my PhD for another 6 months. Shh! Don't tell anyone," he whispered with a smile.

"So, how old *are* you?" April asked.

Anthony laughed. "Now, you know it's not polite to ask a man his age."

"Tell me." April said.

"Seriously, though. I want to hold off on telling you. I mean, it's really not a big deal, but I don't want to risk it becoming an issue between us," Anthony said.

"Is there something going on between us?" April asked.

Anthony sat silently.

"Is there?" April asked again.

Anthony smiled. "I really don't know. I really can't say."

"Is it because you are my *'professor'*?" April asked with a smile.

"Well, I have to be cautious. You know?" Anthony responded. "I just can't be hanging out with my students unless it's related to class. Unless," he paused, "unless it's something that's going to be taken seriously, I really shouldn't risk… Well, I shouldn't put effort into it. If it is something that's going to be taken seriously, I will 'risk,'" he quoted, "going through the complications. Do you understand what I mean?"

April stared at Anthony and said, "Yeah. I understand."

He then smiled and reached for April's hand and held it.

That evening, Anthony and April stayed out later than the last time they were out. They talked all night about themselves. April told Anthony about her mother and her childhood. Of course, she left out the part about going to a distant time where she met Balhib, Amisi, Khai and the others.

She spoke about wanting to be a leader and the reasons why she was so curious about the environment.

Anthony spoke about his mother and how the incident with his uncle tore his family apart. He told April about how his mother became obsessed with the incident to the point where she began to use drugs. By that time he was old enough to make his own decisions and he decided to use his intelligence as a tool to get out of the bad situation that he was in. He spoke about being home alone and staying up all night and sometimes waiting for his mother to get home. He spoke about being really afraid at nights and making it through the nights by reading library books and newspapers until he fell asleep.

April felt that she could relate with Anthony because she was alone with her mother as Anthony was alone with his. And although April's mother did not use drugs, the way Anthony felt when his mother was not home was similar to when she lived in the foster homes. April grew fonder of Anthony as she learned more about him. He was intelligent, handsome and she liked the way he thought.

Anthony took April home very late that evening. Before exiting the car, April leaned over to Anthony and kissed him on the cheek. When she entered the house, she found Martinez lying on the sofa once again. She stared at him for a moment. He stayed up waiting for her again. April felt bad, because she knew that Martinez meant well. But she felt that she needed to move on with her life. She had to live.

Before their relationship became strained, April really, secretively, had hopes for something bigger with Martinez. Maybe it was a young girl's crush on a man who cared for her. Maybe, since April never really had a man in her life, she had hoped that she could have had something special with the first one who came around to care for her. Yet, at the same time, she felt that those feelings were hopeless feelings of need- the need to be loved the way her mother once loved her.

"But you don't know how to do that, do you?" April said softly, staring at Martinez. "Why would you want to anyway? I'm just a child. A child that you think is going to lead this world…," She scoffed as her eyes watered, staring at him as he slept. She then walked up the stairs.

As April walked away, Martinez opened his eyes. He heard every word April whispered. As he was alone with his thoughts, his eyes grew tearful. Martinez was used to being serious and tough. He was not used to the emotions he had recently been feeling.

The following morning, April awoke early and made breakfast for herself and Martinez. She ate and waited for Martinez to come downstairs dressed and ready to take her to school, as he always did. April sat and stared at Martinez's untouched plate as she waited. She continued to wait but he did not come. She knew he was home because his car was outside and his jacket hung on the hook where he would always put it. As time passed, she couldn't wait any longer. It was getting late and she needed to leave for class. April walked to the steps and looked up to Martinez's door. She paced back and forth in front of the steps wondering if she should go knock on his door. April walked up one step and came back down. Finally, feeling anxious, she walked up the stairs and went to knock on Martinez's bedroom door. But, she stopped. Suddenly, a rush of sadness ran through her body. Sad, April went downstairs, put her jacket on took one more glance at Martinez's door and walked out of the house.

Later on that afternoon, April sat in her Environmental Science class. Usually, April would sit in the front of the class. However, this day, she sat all the way in the back.

As he lectured, Mr. Coffey glanced continuously towards April's direction. She did not appear to be paying attention. Mr. Coffey thought about calling on April to get her attention. But he did not want to anger her or embarrass her. She might have been in a bad mood. Not knowing what was wrong with April and concerned, Anthony continued with his lecture anyway.

After class was over, another student approached Mr. Coffey not allowing for him to follow after April. The student needed to speak to Mr. Coffey about something important. So, unfortunately for Anthony, he had to watch April leave. After meeting with the student for about a half hour, Anthony quickly packed his things and began to hastily walk out the building. As he exited the building, Anthony looked around and did not see April. He then walked to the corner where she usually waited and she was not there. Anthony then walked to the bus stop in hopes to find April there. She was not there. Disappointed, Anthony walked to his car. On his way towards his car Anthony saw April standing by his car.
Anthony smiled.

April still appeared disconnected; as if she had a lot on her mind and was thinking of it all at once. She stood at Anthony's car not even realizing that he was approaching.

"Hey, are you alright?" Anthony asked.

April looked up and saw Anthony. "Hey!" She said in a dejected tone.

"Are you alright," he asked again.

"Huh? Yeah. I'm fine." April answered. I was gonna go home but... I don't know."

"What's wrong?" Anthony asked. "You look like you have a lot on your mind. Did something happen?"

"Can we hang out?" April asked.

Apprehensive, Anthony looked at April like he was unsure if he could be with April that evening. "I don't know," he said. "I have to go see my advisor. You know? I have to discuss my dissertation."

April became more disappointed looking. "I understand," she said.

"I can drive you home though," Anthony said.

"I don't feel like going home," April responded.

Anthony laughed. "Wow. You sound like a child who doesn't want to go home to their parents."

April became angry by Anthony's comment. She grunted with anger and began to walk away.

"Wait a minute, April. I was just joking. Where are you going?"

April did not answer and continued walking.

Anthony called for April but she kept walking. Feeling that April needed to calm down, he let her walk away.

It was late in the afternoon and it began to get dark out. April did not know where to go. She just walked. She was headed in the direction of her home but she was still very far from there. As she walked, she thought of her mother. It was the first time she thought about her mother in a while. April was so caught up with what was currently going on with her life; she really did not have much time to think about anything but the present issues. As if she was not sad enough, she became even sadder when she realized that she had not thought about her mother in a while.

"What would you do Mommy?" She thought. "Yeah right," she cried. "You wouldn't even be in this situation. You were too strong and independent to be thinking about men," she thought. "…You didn't need anyone."

Suddenly, she stopped. With tears coming from her eyes, April came a realization.

"I'm not ready for this," April thought. "I *am* just a child. Look at yourself April," she said to herself.

At that moment, across the busy street, April saw a group of teenaged school students appearing to be following two young girls. One of the girls wore the same uniform as the teenagers in the group. The younger one apparently went to another school because she wore a different uniform. The two girls who were being followed looked terrified. Then, April saw the group of kids throwing things at the two girls who looked related to one another. Without a thought, April crossed the street.

When the two girls saw April walking towards them, the youngest, about to cry, asked, "Excuse me, can you help us?"

Speaking in a calm tone, April asked, "What's wrong?"

"They're messing with us," the little girl said. My sister picked me up from school and they've been following us…"

"One of the girls keeps bothering me in school and I finally said something to her and now they want to fight me," the older girl said as the group kept taunting them.

The group got louder, now taunting April.

April continued to walk with them.

"I don't want to fight," the girl said.

Understanding that the child may feel that fighting is wrong, yet feeling that sometimes fighting is unavoidable April asked, "Why don't you want to fight her?"

The girl became agitated and rolled her eyes. "*Because*, if I fight her, I know I'm going to beat her. But then, I'll get in trouble in school," The girl explained. "Then, I'll get jumped by her friends and, if I'm with my sister… I don't want her to get hurt."

Just then, one of the girls from the group began to run towards the girls and April. April quickly turned around. The girl stopped. Something about April's presence made the girl stop immediately.

"What?" April said assertively. "Were you about to hit me?"

"Not you!" the tough girl exclaimed.

Then, the other teenagers began to instigate. One of the boys in the groups said, "I'll hit her."

The group laughed.

April sternly walked to the boy without saying a word. The group then began to surround the two girls. April stared at the boy and he did nothing.

While all of this was going on, Martinez saw it as he drove up the street. He saw April and he stopped. He parked across the street. About to get out of his car, he stopped and thought to himself that he should not get involved. He knew that this was something that April needed to deal with; something she needed to experience. She was getting to the point in her life where she needed to strengthen herself and this was a good moment for her to experience. Martinez knew that stepping in would only weaken April. He knew that April was going to encounter situations much worse than this, and so he sat in his car and watched. If the situation became extremely violent, he would get involved. But, for the moment, he needed to allow April to gain confidence in herself by dealing with this on her own; even if it was a minor incident in comparison to what was to come in April's future.

The youngest girl screamed in fear. April then quickly stood between them and the group. Although this was a group that one would assume would not be intimidated by anyone, especially a young woman, they did appear to be affected by April's presence.

Seeing this made Martinez smile. Though he already knew that April was special, seeing her effect on the group without even saying a word convinced him for good that April was indeed special.

All of the sudden, a car drove up. It was Anthony.

"No!" Martinez said silently with agitation.

Anthony ran to the group and began to yell at the group. Some of the teenagers from the group ran away. Those who stayed tried to confront Anthony but he told them that he took pictures of them and that he was good friends of the principal of their school. One of the kids did not care and continued to threaten Anthony. The other students walked away when they heard what Anthony said.

"Don't let me find out you're bothering these girls again," he yelled as the young people fled. He then pushed the boy and the boy walked away.

Speechless, April just looked at Anthony.

"You girls okay?" He asked them.

Across the street, Martinez watched in frustration. He then drove away.

April looked at the girls and asked, "Are you going to be alright?"

"Yeah," the young girls answered. "We live right around the corner."

"What about in school," April asked. "Are they going to keep bothering you?"

"I'll be alright in school," the girl answered. "My mom is thinking about transferring me to a private school anyway. I'll have my cousins walk with us until then."

April began to walk the girls towards the corner.

"Maybe I should walk you home and tell your mother what happened," April said to the girls.

"I don't know, April," Anthony intervened. "Maybe you should just let them tell her. You are a stranger. Plus, they're alright. Right girls?"

"Yeah," the girls answered.

"No," April responded. "I think…"

"April, come on," Anthony said. "They've been through enough. The last thing they need is interrogation from their mom."

After thinking about it, April decided to not speak with the girls' mother. She felt that Anthony *was* smart enough to know what was best. He *was* the teacher. April then walked the girls to the corner.

Anthony then grabbed her hand and pulled her towards him. Before April could express her opinion about the situation, Anthony expressed his.

"You are truly amazing, April," he said. "I mean, stepping in between those girls and that mob. That was real cool. Not the smartest thing to do, but cool."

April looked at Anthony. "I could have handled it. I was getting through…"

Anthony laughed. "Getting through? To who? Those kids?" He asked. "April, they were going to attack you. There was no getting through to them."

Before April could respond, Anthony continued.

"I really like and appreciate your passion. I get it. You want to be a leader. But, April, you can't just put yourself in danger like that."

"I honestly don't think I was in any danger, Anthony," April responded. "I..."

"April," Anthony interrupted. "You should leave the tough stuff for the guys. I mean, you really could've gotten hurt."

"What?" April said with disappointment. "That's very..."

"I didn't mean it to sound sexist, April," he interrupted again. "I'm sorry. It's just that, when I saw you surrounded by those kids... First, I couldn't believe it was you. Then, fear rushed through me. I got scared for you. What I'm saying is, I couldn't imagine or allow seeing you get hurt. I guess... What I'm really trying to say is that I really care about you. I got into protective mode. I don't want to see you hurt."

April fell silent. She didn't know what to say. Anthony's words made her forget her reasons for rebuttal. April was touched. This was the feeling that she felt she had been needing. She remained silent.

"I'm sorry," Anthony said. "I didn't mean to get deep. I hope I'm not scaring you with what I'm saying."

April then looked up and, with a smile, she softly said, "Not at all."

After thinking for a moment, April then asked, "What happened with your meeting?"

Anthony smiled and said, "When I saw how sad you looked earlier, I called my advisor and rescheduled. I thought maybe you needed someone."

"Really?" April asked surprised. "That meeting was very important, wasn't it?"

"Yeah," Anthony replied. "But you are more important."

April felt special. She actually felt human again for the first time in a long time. She then hugged Anthony tightly.

"I should take you home," Anthony said.

"Can't we spend some time together?" April asked as they entered the car.

"I think we've had enough excitement for one night." Anthony replied.

April, thinking about how mature Anthony sounded, respectfully complied. She understood that Anthony was wise. Therefore, she thought, she was going to listen to him at all times. This was April's next step to having deep feelings for him.

"Plus, I don't want your guardian to get worried." Anthony said.

"Oh, he's not thinking about me," April responded.

Not knowing how to respond to April's comment, Anthony realized that the reason April appeared upset earlier may have had to do with issues at home.

He then said, "Well, maybe he *should* be thinking about you. The one night he didn't pick you up... You almost got hurt."

April became silent once more.

Anthony then took April home.

When April returned home, she saw Martinez sitting in the living room.

"Oh," April said. "You're home."

"Yes," Martinez replied.

"I didn't think you'd be here," she said with a slightly malevolent attitude.

"Why wouldn't I be?" He asked.

"I just figured, you'd be out with your secret wife or doing whatever it is that you do," she responded while taking off her jacket.

Martinez sighed. "Just..."

"What Eugenio?" April said loudly. "Just what?" Just grow up?"

"That's not what I was going to say," he replied.

"Then what were you going to say?" She asked.

Martinez stood silently.

"I thought so!" April said.

"Just like you have been feeling discouraged and disheartened, April," Martinez explained, "I have been feeling the same."

"Yeah right…" April said.

"Listen!" he exclaimed.

"I am human just like you. The way that our relationship has fallen apart has had its effects on me. But, I have a responsibility….a responsibility that was bestowed upon me when Mayet passed. If you don't want to get it into your stubborn mind that I am doing my best to not only take care of you, but also prepare myself for the time that is destined to come… If you do not want to understand that I am trying to protect you…."

"Trying to protect me??" April asked with frustration. She then laughed. "Protect me? Where were you tonight, huh?" She was very upset. "I must admit; I've been feeling sad and alone these past few months. *And*, I was kind of hoping *you* would help me with that. But, I understood. I understood that you weren't able to do that. I understood that, on the emotional side of things, you may not have been the right candidate. But I knew that if I truly needed you for protection… I mean, if I was being attacked or something… I was satisfied in knowing that you would at least be there for me with that!" She laughed furiously. "But after tonight, I realized that you can't even do that…"

Before Martinez could get his words out, April began to walk angrily up the stairs.

"I think it's time for us start preparing to go our separate ways," April said.

Sad and disgruntled, Martinez responded, "You know we cannot do that."

"Why not?" April asked. "This isn't even *your mission*!" She said mockingly. She then went to her room and slammed the door.

Martinez became very frustrated. He did not know what to say or how to feel. He had never been in this type of situation before. The anger he felt was overwhelming. Everything that he had done was for April, he thought. Even that evening- he had stayed in his car *for* her benefit. He was not going to allow anything to happen to her. The things that she knew nothing about; the things that she took for granted were all for her. There were times when he risked his life for her. Not just because of the mission but also because he truly cared for her. Thinking about the situation made Martinez more and more furious. He stood in the living room trying to calm himself. Still, the stress of the mission combined with his feelings and the situation with April made it difficult for Martinez to control what he was feeling. As he tried to calm down, objects in the room began to shake. Suddenly, a glass that was placed on the coffee table floated in the air and violently flew against the wall shattering into pieces.

"Damn it!" Martinez said.

Suddenly, April opened her door thinking that Martinez threw the glass on purpose. She yelled, "And you say that I need to grow up!"

Frustrated, Martinez grabbed his jacket and walked out of the house.

The next day, April met with Anthony. They sat at a bench in an empty playground. She explained to him that she has been

living with Eugenio for some time and that the other people
who were supposed to take care of her were murdered. She
explained that they were like a foster family to April after her
mother passed away. April told Anthony that things were
becoming strained between her and Martinez, because he did not
allow her to do anything. She said that Eugenio treated her like a
child and she was becoming sick of it.

Anthony defended Martinez. He expressed his understanding
of Martinez's protective behavior.

"You are a beautiful young lady; you're fragile. I'd want to
keep you home all to myself too," Anthony joked. "But
seriously, when he was left alone to take care of you, he had to
devote a huge part of his life to you," he regressed. "You gotta
understand…"

"I know. I know," April interrupted. "I don't want to talk
about it anymore."

"Hey, maybe he has a thing for you," Anthony said. "Maybe
he doesn't see you as a little girl anymore. Maybe, he's acting this
way out of frustration from seeing the little girl growing up
before his eyes and liking what he sees." He said then laughed.

"What? Yeah right!" April exclaimed. That's just…" April
paused to find the word. "…Weird. Anyway, I said I don't want
to talk about it anymore.

April went on to think about the possibility of what Anthony
said being true.

"What if?" she thought, as she expressed an appalled look on
her face.

Still, deep inside, April felt a sense of hope that what
Anthony said was true. But as she thought, April became angry
because, if it were true, Eugenio would never show it. April
doubted it. Plus, it did not matter to her. She was beginning to
have feelings for Anthony.

"April, I need to talk to you," Anthony said. "I know that we are only at the beginning stages of…" he paused. "…Of whatever we have. But, before this goes further, there is something I need to tell you about me; a secret."

April gazed at Anthony with a look as if to say that she did not need any more issues.

"Anthony," April said. "I don't think I…"

"I think that I need to tell you this because," he interrupted, "well, I don't want to go further with you and suddenly catch you off guard with it. I don't want there to be any surprises."

"What is it, Anthony?" April asked.

Anthony looked at April trying to find the words and then said, "A long time ago, I killed someone."

April's eyes widened. She could not believe that such a kind and intelligent person could ever take another person's life.

"H… How?" April stuttered. "Who?"

Anthony began to explain. "A long time ago, when my uncle was killed, things became very…" He paused. "Things became very messed up. My mother went crazy, my family was torn apart. People I knew weren't the same. Even though I held it together, I still became very angry and resentful. I wanted to hurt the people who hurt me." Anthony's face began appearing sadder. "From what I understood, there were a couple of people involved. One of them was killed," he paused. "And, even though, I knew it was wrong, I was happy. But I know that there was another person who was responsible. And, April, I was young, I was really young and stupid."

As Anthony began to cry, April reached for his hand.

"It's okay," she said.

Sobbing, Anthony continued. "I actually went looking for the people involved. Anyway, I found out that there was a girl involved…a young woman. So, I went looking for her," he continued to sob. "You gotta understand April I would never hurt anyone, especially a girl, I swear!"

April tried to console Anthony. Anthony then wiped his eyes and tried to calm himself.

"Sometime later; years later, I found out where the girl lived and," he began to sob again. He cried so hard that he couldn't even speak. "I mean, I didn't kill her immediately. I poisoned her. She died about two months later from complications that looked like cancer. No one ever knew…"

April, not knowing how to respond, just held Anthony's hand.

"That's not the screwed up part," Anthony sobbed. "Later; years after my uncle's death, I found out that the girl or woman or people who were accused of killing him…? My uncle and his boys were actually plotting to kill them long before the night they were killed," Anthony stuttered for a moment. "He was following the girl. He was even responsible for the death of an old woman who was protecting the girl he was after," he cried. "He killed the old woman the same way I…" he couldn't speak. "The same way!" he cried. "Isn't that crazy?" he asked hysterically. "April I think I killed an innocent woman… I don't even know why… I…"

April, speechless, felt sorry for Anthony. She understood how a rough life could lead people down the wrong path. Although she could not understand how Anthony- an educated, kindhearted person, could do such a thing like taking another person's life; she believed that his sorrow was sincere. She believed that long ago, Anthony was in a place where he had no control of his life due to what his uncle and family handed to him. It was a very different place from where he was presently. April felt that Anthony was a changed man and that his past was just that. After some thought, she actually felt respect because

Anthony, through so much turmoil, had still managed to become the person that he presently was. She wanted to be there for Anthony more than ever.

Later that afternoon, Anthony and April were still together.

"I was thinking April," Anthony began. "I know it wouldn't be the right thing for us to live together but, I was wondering…"

Suddenly, as they walked from a small diner to Anthony's car, April saw Martinez. April gasped.

"April, what's the matter?" Anthony asked. He looked up and there was Martinez.

"What are you doing here?" April asked.

"I need to speak with you," Martinez said.

"Can't it wait? I'm busy," April said as she grabbed Anthony's hand.

"April," Martinez said. "It's very important."

"Leave me alone, Eugenio," April said with a mean tone. "I don't have anything to say to you."

"April, this has nothing to do with," Martinez stopped. "It's very important."

"Maybe you should go," Anthony said to April.

April then looked at Anthony with a disappointed look.

"I don't think it'd be right for me to get involved," Anthony said to April but then paused. "Look," Anthony said to Martinez, "Can I just speak to her for a second?"

Martinez just looked without answering.

Anthony then pulled April aside and said, "April, in my opinion, this guy is really protective of you. He looks like the jealous type. You gotta go and handle that. I don't want to get involved because it could get ugly and you don't want that. Just go ahead with him. I'll see you tomorrow."

Defiant yet understanding, April agreed and said goodbye to Anthony with a kiss. She then walked towards Martinez.

As she walked towards Eugenio, April said, "I can't believe you're doing this."

"I'll explain in the car," He said.

When they entered the car Martinez said to April, "April we have to leave the city…"

"What?" April asked loudly, "You are going too far with this…"

"April," Martinez interrupted, "It's beginning."

Not believing Martinez, April asked, "What are you talking about?"

"April, I don't have any proof to show you right now, but I think that guy is…"

"NO!" April exclaimed. "Don't start that, Eugenio. You are going too far!"

"What are you talking about?" Martinez asked.

"You are not going to use Anthony to get your way," April argued.

"Use…?" Martinez began, "No, April. You don't understand."

"No, Eugenio!" April continued. "Stop it! You are doing too much. You are jealous!"

"April!" Martinez yelled. "You are in danger! Now, do you want to get your head out of the clouds or do you want to die?!"

"I cannot believe you!" April exclaimed.

Suddenly, Martinez made an abrupt turn.

April yelled.

Martinez began to drive faster. As April became afraid, Martinez made sharp turns and ran stop lights.

"Fine April," he said. "You want to do it like this. We will do it your way."

April became more afraid. "Where are you taking me?" April asked in fear.

"I tried to protect you by telling you only what you needed to hear," Martinez mumbled in anger. "I tried to protect you by keeping you away from certain things. But you insist on making things difficult. Now I have to do what I did not want to do."

The car came to an abrupt stop. They were parked at a vacant warehouse in a deserted area of the city.

"Get out," He said.

April was scared. She began to speak. "I…"

"Out!" Martinez yelled.

April got out of the car and followed Martinez.

He unlocked a chain in the massive doors to a freight elevator outside of the building. In the elevator, he pressed the button for the basement.

"Where are you taking me?" April asked silently.

Martinez was silent.

When they got out of the elevator, Martinez demanded that April take off her jacket. They were in a very dusty, empty room. The room was large. It looked like an old court used for sports. Everything was grey and brown. There was old sports equipment lying on the ground. There were old weights, medicine balls, and other types of balls on the ground. There were ropes and chains as well.

April, afraid, took her jacket off and placed it on a lone table next to the elevator.

Martinez began to speak in a tone that scared April.

"I tried to be kind and gentle with you," he said. "I tried to keep things from you for your…"

April interrupted, "I never asked you to…"

"Be quiet!" Martinez yelled.

April jumped in fear.

"Eugenio!" She screamed. "You are scaring me. I don't feel good." April began to sweat and appeared dizzy."

"Shut up!" He yelled again.

As he continue to ramble on about the things he had done for her from the time they came to the city, things started to occur that scared April more.

First, dust from the ground began to float in the air. Then, as the dust began to form a sphere around Martinez, heavy objects on the ground began to shake. The equipment on the floor began to float all around.

April grew more afraid as she could not believe what was going on. Her body began to tremble in fear. She began to sweat and pant.

Martinez began to yell, "You need to understand, April! The time is near and you need to be prepared!"

"Eugenio," she gasped as she became breathless.

Suddenly, a weight flew into the wall crushing an old clock. April screamed.

"You couldn't just learn the way you were meant to learn," Martinez grunted.

April, as she became more afraid, suddenly began to itch. She was confused and more afraid.

"What's going on?" she asked.

"Now, I told you that you need to be mindful of your surroundings. You cannot trust everyone. This Anthony…"

"You leave Anthony out of this!" April said breathlessly.

"No April! You need to know!" Martinez said as he sent another heavy object crashing into the wall.

April screamed. She then asked, "How are you doing this?"

At that moment, as Martinez began to see April become more and more aware of the situation, he sent a large object in April's direction.

April screamed. All of the sudden, a bright blue light came from April's hands creating an electrical field around her and destroying the large object flying towards her. Then out of great fear, without any thought, April pushed the electrical field towards Martinez, setting the dust particles that floated around him on fire, creating a ball of flames around Martinez. The objects that floated in the air suddenly dropped to the floor.

April, drained from all of her newly discovered energy and fearfully confused, breathed heavily and became dizzy. Her eyes then rolled back. She fell to the ground and blacked out.

April was unconscious. As she slept, April saw her mother's face. There were no words; there was no sound. All she saw was her mother. April cried.

"April," a voice softly whispered.

Her eyes opened slowly.

"April," the voice said again as she slowly awoke to find herself lying on a bed in a dimly lit room.

Still afraid but weak, she sat up to find Martinez seated next to her.

"I'm sorry, April," Martinez said.

April did not speak.

Martinez smiled.

"What?" April whispered.

"You!" Martinez said. "I knew it was in you but… Wow!"

"How did…?" April said but became too dizzy to finish her words. She laid back down.

"Here," Martinez said as he handed April a cup. "Drink this tea. It should give you energy. I think I should get you some water. You might be dehydrated."

"What happened?" April whispered. "How?"

"I don't know how, April," Martinez answered. "I did know… But I don't know how."

"I thought I was going to die," April said. "I thought I killed *you*."

Martinez laughed. "You could have. That's why we need to start practicing; preparing you."

"Why...?" April stuttered. "You... How...?"

"April, just like you, I have a gift that was passed down to me. As Mayet explained, it has gotten stronger with each generation. I have the ability to use the energy around me to move things. I was able to create a field of energy around me to block your... Well, heh. If you wanted to, you *could* have killed me though," He paused. "Anyway, this is where I would come to strengthen my gift. I must admit and apologize. The desire to strengthen my powers got the best of me and I would spend all hours of the night here practicing."

"Leaving me alone...?" April said.

"No April! I knew you were safe." Martinez insisted. "Well, until Anthony came into the picture."

April became mad. "Don't start..."

"April, please," Martinez said as he placed his hand in April's arm. "Can we talk about it later? You have to regain your strength."

April shook her head. "No," she said. "You are jealous."

"April. I love you," Martinez said suddenly.

April became stunned.

"Is that what you want to hear?" he asked. "I do love you. And I want what is best for you. If Anthony is the person you want to be with; then, I care for you enough to allow that if it makes you happy. Whatever it is you want, April. But there are things about him that you should know..."

"Like what?" April asked.

"He's killed someone." Martinez answered.

April's eyes widened. She became angry. "I cannot believe you!" She exclaimed.

"April, it's true…"

"I know it's true. I just can't believe that you would check up on him like that," April argued.

"But, if you know it's true…" he responded. "April, it was for *your* protection!"

"Yeah, I knew it," April said. "He told me. And he has suffered and has been remorseful since the day it happened."

"What did he tell you?" Martinez asked.

"How did you know about this?" April asked. "He said that no one knew."

Martinez fell silent for a moment.

Feeling exhausted, April thought for a moment. She understood that it was indeed for her protection.

"Can you take me home?" April asked.

Martinez nodded. He gathered their things and helped April up.

As they drove home April began to think. "Back there," April said referring to the old building. "When you talked about your gift, you said 'just like me.' Does that mean that my mother…?"

"Yes April," Martinez answered. "But your gift is much more powerful than anything I have ever even heard of."

"Then, what does that mean?" April asked.

Martinez sat silently for a moment then said, "I don't know."

"Did you mean what you said or did you…?" April stopped what she was saying. "Never mind."

They both sat silently as Martinez drove home.

Two days later, April sat in Mr. Coffey's class. She sat back in the front of class again like she used to. When Anthony saw her, he smiled. After class, Anthony caught up to April.

"You didn't call me," he said. "I mean, I didn't call you either but, I figured you needed time, so…"

"It's ok," April answered. "Everything is alright now."

"Oh," Anthony responded. "That's good."

"Yeah, it is," April replied.

"So…" Anthony said. "Any thoughts on moving out? I was thinking…"

"Umm… I think I'm just going to stay where I am," April said. "For now. I mean, I don't even have a job."

"Oh," he responded. "Well, I can help you… If you'd like."

"I couldn't," April said.

"So, what happened?" Anthony asked. "You two patch things up? You look happier today."

"Well, I'm still a little mad at Eugenio. But I think it'd be better for me to stay where I am until I… Until I uh, graduate," April said.

Anthony did not know what to say. "Well, I…" he stuttered. He then smiled. It was not a sincere smile. Anthony seemed upset but did not want to show April.

"You ok?" April asked.

"I, umm… April," he said. "I think, maybe, it'd be best if we stop seeing each other."

"No… Why?" April asked.

"Come on, April," he responded. "You live with another guy. Now, I am not jealous. I just understand…"

"I…" April did not know how to react.

"Look! You two have something. There is something special," Anthony said with a sad fake smile. "I know you are not telling me everything, and I know it's really none of my business. But, I understand. The two of you have something bigger than what you and I will ever have; something bigger than anything I could understand. I can't get in the way of that."

April thought for a moment. She thought of her feelings for Eugenio. She thought of what he had said to her two nights before. But, she also thought about how good of a person Anthony was. What she had with Anthony, she built on her own. That was important to her. Plus, he was willing to give it all up for what he thought would make her happy. That made her appreciate him and trust him more. That made her care for him more.

As Anthony began to say his goodbye, April walked up to him and passionately kissed him on the lips.

"I will do whatever you want," April said with a smile. "I will tell you everything. I will make you understand. I will let you in."

Looking confused, Anthony smiled and said, "Okay."

That day, having gained April's trust, Anthony listened to everything she had to say. As he listened, he laughed and smiled in disbelief. Still, April tried her best to convince him that what she told Anthony was the truth.

April even felt comfortable enough to tell Anthony about the gifts she and Martinez had. At that point, Anthony began to appear disbelieving and even upset.

"April," he said. "If you don't want to be with me, you don't have to try to push me away with these crazy stories."

He began to walk away.

"No," April said. "Please believe me."

He appeared angry and asked, "Why would you go to these lengths to…"

"Wait" April said vigorously. "I think I can show you."

"I don't have time for this, April," Anthony said slightly angered.

April clenched her fists and closed her eyes trying to show Anthony something but nothing happened.

Anthony began to walk away.

"Please!" April cried out.

Suddenly, April gathered all of her emotions inside of her. She took her anger, love, hatred and whatever sort of emotion she had within her and focused as hard as she could. Suddenly a spark of energy shot from her finger to a light pole above Anthony. Sparks fell from the light onto Anthony's head as he stood in shock.

April jumped with excitement. She began to laugh happily. Just as Anthony could not believe what he had just witnessed, April could not either.

"What the...!" Anthony exclaimed. He was in shock.

April continued to jump with excitement. She hopped over to Anthony and hugged him.

"Now do you believe me?" she asked.

Not knowing how to react, Anthony took April by the arms and slowly pushed her away.

"What is this?" he asked in a shaken tone.

"What? I told you," April responded.

Anthony stared at April with a very serious look and said, "Yeah, but..."

It took a while for Anthony to gather his emotions. After an hour, Anthony was able to think clearly. He had a lot of questions. April was happy to answer him.

"No wonder you were brave enough to confront that mob," he said referring to the incident with the group of teenagers; insinuating that April would not have done what she did if she did not have her gift. "And... And your friend Eugenio?" Anthony asked. "Does he...?"

"Yeah." April responded. "He can move things with his mind. It's actually pretty cool."

"Is he stronger than you?" He asked.

"Well, it looks like he is. But he said that I'm actually much more powerful than he is. I don't know…" April responded.

"And all of this for the end of the world…?" he asked.

"Well," April seriously began to explain. "It's not really the end of the world. There will be a lot of turmoil, destruction and a great war. A war that I'm supposed to lead. Then another war- the final war they say…"

"What about Eugenio?" Anthony asked. "Is he a leader?"

"I don't know," April answered. "I don't think so. That's a good question. But, I don't think so."

"How could they put so much pressure on you?" Anthony asked. He then began to joke. "I know if I had power, I wouldn't let you be alone. You are too precious."

April smiled. She then hugged Anthony.

"Do you still want to leave me alone?" April asked. "I really wanted you to be a part of… this. We need all the help we can get. Plus, I really would like for you be a part of my life."

Anthony smiled and said, "How could I possibly walk away from this?"

April smiled.

"But what about Eugenio?" Anthony asked. "Didn't you say he was jealous of me?"

April thought for a moment.

"I have to tell you something," April said warily.

"What?" Anthony asked, seeming a bit worried.

"You said that no one knew about the woman you…" April said hesitantly. "But…" she paused. "You have to promise me you won't get mad."

Anthony looked upset. "April, did you tell him about…"

"He knew!" April exclaimed. "That's what I was saying…! How did he know?"

"I don't know, April," Anthony replied, sounding frustrated. "That was in the past and I told you with hopes that it would stay that way."

"I know. I know." April said. "But he knew."

Anthony sighed. "He checked into my past? He must have dug really deep. He must have really been trying to get you against me."

April stood speechless.

Anthony was silent for a moment as well.

"I can't do this April," Anthony said sadly. "I can't be with a person who is so connected with a person who wants to do this to me… Do this to me for what reason? I don't even know this guy. He doesn't even know me."

Anthony began to walk away.

"Wait," April called. "I can fix this. I can convince him…"

"April, he's already convinced" Anthony stated. "To go that far…"

April grabbed Anthony by the arm. "Please. Let me try,"

Anthony looked skeptical and pulled away.

"Please! You allowed me to show you what I showed you," April pleaded. "You allowed it to go this far. Please. Give me a chance."

Silently, Anthony nodded in compliance.

April smiled.

Later on that day, April went home to find Martinez in good spirits. He cooked for April.

"You ready to go practice some?" he asked

April looked at the food on the table and smiled. She was happy to see that Eugenio was in such a good mood. She was especially happy because this meant that it might be easier for her to speak to him about Anthony.

"This is nice," she said.

"I haven't cooked in a while. I figured…" he said as he set the plates on the table. "After what happened, we'd celebrate a new beginning. Is that ok?"

April smiled. She felt that it was the right time to speak to him about Anthony.

"I wanted to talk to you…" She said.

Martinez had a bad feeling about what April was about to speak to him about. He stopped what he was doing and sat down.

"It's about Anthony," April continued. "I spoke to him about what you accused him of."

"April…"

April put her hand up to stop Martinez. "I am not mad about it anymore. I'm not trying to start an argument. I'm actually in a good mood," April insisted. "Just let me finish. I spoke to him about it. And, like I said before, he was honest about it. And, Eugenio, he is so remorseful about it. He is such a nice guy. Since the incident, he has really changed. Actually, he was misled into doing what he did. He thought that the person was… What I'm trying to say is that he was set up. He really is a good person and has really made up for whatever he was a part of."

Martinez just sat silently. He listened.

"What are you telling me, April? What are you really trying to tell me?" Martinez asked. "Do you care about him, April?" he asked.

April felt uncomfortable having Martinez ask her that question although she knew, in order for them to move forward, he needed to ask and she needed to answer.

"Yes, I do," April answered.

As soon as April answered, a pain went through Eugenio's soul. April felt a pain as well. Still, April had already convinced herself that she needed to move forward with her social life and this was the first step in doing so. She knew it would hurt. However, April also knew that Martinez would always be a part of her life because of what had been happening. So, she needed to find a way to connect her new life with the life she had been living. She needed to have Martinez accept her new life and those she wanted in it.

Martinez sighed, "Ok, April," he said.

"Ok?" April asked. "That's it?"

Although Martinez still did not feel right about Anthony and felt suspicious, he felt that the right thing to do was to allow April to live her life and strengthen herself by experiencing life…without him holding her hand through every experience. Although it hurt, he knew what he needed to do. He realized that it was not about him. What was important was that April became stronger- physically, mentally *and* emotionally.

"I think he should know what's going on," April said.

Eugenio's face became very serious. "No April," he insisted. "We still don't really know him."

"I know him," April stated. "Besides, don't you think we need to start recruiting; getting more people on board."

"I agree, April. But there are ways we have to…"

"I already told him about us," April interrupted.

"No!" Martinez said in shock.

Immediately, April realized that she may have actually done something wrong.

"April… Do you realize what you might have done?" Martinez asked.

April did not respond.

Martinez shook his head. "You may have not only put our lives in danger; you may have just put the whole future at risk."

April sat silently.

"Why, April?" Martinez asked in anger. "Why? Because you wanted attention? Because you couldn't be patient? Because you wanted to be selfish? Don't you realize that…?"

Upset and feeling defensive April felt compelled to argue. "Isn't my responsibility to…? Weren't you the one who told me to live my life? I tried to do that. But, I also took into consideration the fact that I kept being told that I was going to be this leader. How can I be this leader by myself?" She asked remembering what Anthony told her. "I figured he'd be one more person with us and someone who was willing to keep me happy…"

"You! April," Martinez yelled. "You, You, You! Don't you realize that it's not all about you? Yes, you are to be our leader. But it is about the people; not you! And because you wanted to be selfish and childish, you put the people's future in jeopardy. That's not how one leads!"

April became extremely angry. Hearing Martinez call her selfish and childish upset her. Although, deep inside, she felt that he was right, she still felt upset. Maybe it was her childishness that Eugenio spoke about that kept her from admitting her faults. Still, April continued to be defiant.

"I am tired of you speaking to me like this. You are not my father. You are nothing to me. As a matter of fact, you are beneath me," April said. Then, a flash of energy shot from her hand to a vase inches away from Martinez.

Martinez' eyes widened in disbelief, as the vase shattered all over the table and floor. He could not believe what April had just done.

April walked out. Deep inside, April could not believe what she had done either. As she walked out, she felt ashamed. She held back tears as she left the house.

That evening, April contacted Anthony. She wanted to meet with him to discuss how the conversation between her and Eugenio had gone. Anthony quickly met her near her school and took her to his home.

A few days passed and Martinez, not seeing or hearing from April for so long worried him. He went to April's school and did not see her. He drove around the city and he could not find her. Finally, Martinez went to the home of one of his contacts who he only went to during times of desperation. The contact was a police officer.

"Why didn't you come to me sooner?" the police officer asked as he sat at his home desk.

"Well, I came to you about this Anthony guy just a couple of weeks ago," Martinez explained, "I didn't want to…"

"If she goes missing, I have to know immediately," the officer said.

"I thought I could find her myself," Martinez explained. "I didn't want to put our communication at risk over something I could have done on my own. I tried without risk first; now I am here. Can you tell me where he lives?"

"Ahh!" the officer grunts in frustration. "He might have moved but I got an address for you."

The officer prints out an address and handed it to Martinez.

"By the way," the officer stated. "It's actually a good thing you came by today. Something came to my attention and I think you should check it out."

Interested, Martinez sat at the desk. "Tell me."

"Well, you know we couldn't even ID a suspect because, if we did, it would raise too many questions about us, right?"

"Yeah?" Martinez responded.

"Well, how about this?" the officer called for Martinez's attention. "This was just brought to my attention; like it just came into existence. None of us understood what this meant. Nine years ago, a letter was sent to the police; my unit in fact. The letter said, 'Four months, she will perish. In four centuries, she will never have existed.' Weird, huh?"

Martinez thought for a moment. "Nine years ago?"

"And it was *just* brought to me," the officer said.

"'Nine years ago,'" Martinez thought out loud. "Four months." He continued to think. Suddenly it hit him. "April."

"No," the officer said. "I'm going with…"

"No!" Martinez interrupted. "You can't. You should stay here. I will find her. We wouldn't be having this conversation if something is going to happen to her. I will find her"

Martinez left the officer's home in search of Anthony's house. When he found the address, it was not a house at all. Martinez found that the address led him to a warehouse. Martinez looked for a front door.

When he found the front door, he saw a doorbell. He rang it. Anthony answered the door.

"Eugenio?" Anthony asked.

"Yes," Martinez answered.

"We weren't formally introduced," Anthony said as he reached his hand out to shake Martinez's hand.

Martinez did not shake Anthony's hand.

"Look," Anthony said as they stood at the door. "I know that there has been trouble between you and April. And I told her that I did not want to get in between the two of you. But she came to me. Apparently, she felt that you have been disrespecting her and I felt bad and took her in. You see I care about her."

"May I see her?" Martinez asked as he looked in the door.

"Please, come in," Anthony said.

Martinez walked in and saw a large space. It looked like the inside of a warehouse but with household furniture and appliances spread out. It looked like a giant house with miniature furniture.

"I actually bought this place with the intention of starting a business. But when the economy went bad, I lost my house so I had to move in here," Anthony explained in a friendly manner. "Crazy, huh?"

"Where is April?" Martinez asked.

"She had the sudden urge to get some take-out," Anthony answered. "So, I let her take the car to get some. She'll be back real soon."

Martinez looked perplexed. April didn't have her driver's license. Plus, he had expressed to April that she needed to be careful. He felt that she was at risk being out like that.

"I know what you are thinking," Anthony said. "I was surprised that she knew how to drive. I guess she learned by watching you for so long. And, don't worry. The store is literally around the corner. She'll be home soon."

"Home?" Martinez thought. *"This isn't her home."*

The door then opened. It was April. When she entered and saw Martinez, she was surprised.

"What are you doing?" April asked.

"I'm taking you home," Martinez said.

"What?" April said.

"Now, wait a minute." Anthony said.

"You stay out of this. This has nothing to do with you," Martinez said assertively.

"Of course it does!" Anthony responded. "I'd…"

"No, Anthony it does not," Martinez stated. "There is way too much here for you to understand. I appreciate what you are trying to do but I must insist…"

"April," Anthony called. "Say something."

April, knowing that she was wrong in the first place, thought for a moment.

"Stay out of this," Martinez said as he reached for April.

Anthony walked towards April as well.

Just as Martinez was about to take April by the hand, Anthony grabbed Martinez. Martinez then pushed Anthony.

Suddenly, April yelled at Martinez and pushed a flash of energy towards Martinez. Just as quick as April used her gift, Martinez put up a field of energy to block April's energy. The flash of energy ricocheted and hit Anthony in the leg. He then fell.

April screamed and ran to Anthony.

Martinez didn't know what to do.

"April," he said.

Crying, April yelled, "Leave, Eugenio! Leave us alone!"

Feeling bad about what had happened, Martinez wanted to help, but he knew that it was more important to get April to a safe place.

But, she was emotionally hurt.

"April, you have to…" he said.

April looked at Martinez crying and said, "Leave me alone. You've helped me enough."

Martinez left.

Martinez did not go home that night. He drove around thinking about what had happened. As he thought, he tried to piece the events together to try to understand where he went wrong. Until dawn, Martinez drove around thinking.

"We could have killed him," he thought.

Then, he stopped his car. Thinking about the strength of April's power, it was like a powerful lightning bolt. Could a normal human being have sustained such power? As he theorized conspiracies, Martinez also considered that he may just be trying to come up with excuses to go back for April.

Maybe he really did fail. Maybe he should just leave April with Anthony and just protect April from a distance.

Still, Martinez continued to think about the possibilities of April's powers and how no normal human being could have endured them. "Anthony should be dead", he thought. Martinez wanted to follow Anthony around. But he wondered if it were the safe thing to do. Or would it waste time? He then thought that he needed to take the chance in confronting Anthony immediately.

"If I confront him and I am wrong, I will just have to live with April hating me forever," he thought to himself. "If I am right and I don't confront him now… She may be in danger."

Martinez quickly returned to Anthony's home. He was polite enough to ring the doorbell again. There was no answer. He waited and rang again but no one came.

As Martinez was about to turn the doorknob on the large door, the door opened.

"It's crazy," Anthony said without being seen. "I was convinced that you were just gonna go ahead and leave us alone." He then came out from the shadow of his door. "I guess it was just wishful thinking, huh? You're not going to make it easy for me, are you?" He said with a smile on his face.

"I can't." Martinez responded. "She's my…"

"…Responsibility." Anthony interrupted. "I know. I heard," he said still smiling. "I suppose, you can't just let me take over, huh?" he asked.

"I can't do that," Martinez answered. "I don't know you."

"That's right we haven't been properly introduced. I'm Anthony. Anthony Coffey," Anthony said as he extended his hand once again to shake Eugenio's.

Martinez looked at Anthony's hand but did not shake it.

"Where is she?" Martinez asked.

"You know, that's the second time you did that," Anthony laughed. "I'm really beginning to feel disrespected. Well, I don't want to make you feel bad," Anthony said. "But, just as you left, April passed out. She's in bed now. Whatever it was that she did, it made her very weak and, well..." Anthony chuckled, "Heh, so much for your responsibility, huh?"

Martinez became upset. He then asked, "Your leg? Did you not get hurt?"

Anthony looked at his leg and thought for a moment. He then smiled.

"It was pretty scary," Anthony said. "I guess I fell from the fear of it. It didn't even hit me."

Martinez thought for a moment then said. "Still, it did hit the area where you were standing. It should have at the very least stunned you or something."

"Is that right?" Anthony asked.

Martinez nodded.

Anthony stood quietly for a moment.

"Would you like to come in?" Anthony asked. "You are more than welcome to stay until she wakes up."

Martinez walked into the home and looked around.

"Would you like something to drink?" Anthony asked.

"No, thank you," Martinez answered as he stood near the door.

Eugenio had a strange feeling at that moment. "What are your intentions with April?" he asked abruptly.

"My intentions?" Anthony asked. He then smiled. Knowing that April was just up the stairs in the loft, Anthony searched for the right words. He then laughed. "I like April…"

"What are your intentions?" Martinez asked again.

Martinez felt that he needed to take another risk. He was already there. Now, he needed answers; real answers. There was no turning back. He needed to provoke Anthony. Martinez felt that, if his feelings were right about Anthony, he needed to push him to the point of aggravation in order to get the truth.

Anthony stood down the steps in front of the door where Martinez stood. He looked at Martinez without knowing how to answer.

Calmly, Martinez said, "You seem much older than April…"

"So do you," Anthony interrupted. He then laughed. "I don't think you…"

"It's very different. And I was not finished,' Martinez said. "You've been around for a while, haven't you? …In Philadelphia?"

Anthony nodded as he stared seriously at Martinez.

"So, you were around when…"

"Maybe you should leave," Anthony interrupted.

"I know what your intentions are," Martinez said as he walked down the steps. Then, he took a chance. He took the greatest risk and said something that he knew would either bring out the truth or bring disastrous consequences.

"You want to kill her," he said.

If he was wrong with his accusation, it could possibly create more obstacles for the future; damaging the trust he had gained from April and losing a potential ally. Still, Martinez felt that the chances of Anthony being an ally were slim.

Anthony was silent for a moment. "Kill her…?" he asked

Martinez looked at Anthony silently.

"I do," Anthony answered.

Martinez knew that Anthony was being sarcastic.

"I *am* going to kill her," Anthony said. "You see, I've already tried but she's special. She's very strong."

Martinez followed Anthony with his eyes as Anthony spoke. Martinez felt strange. At first he thought that Anthony may have been joking. However, he started to feel different about how Anthony was answering him.

"Wait a minute," Martinez said realizing that Anthony may not have been joking at all. "You're telling the truth."

"I'm not playing this game with you anymore," Anthony said with an arrogant tone.

"You were one of the people who killed the little girl," Martinez said referring to the incident with the young April.

"No!" Anthony answered with a slightly different voice. "I would have done *that* differently."

Anthony was telling the truth.

"I came when her mother came back." Anthony chuckled. "When she came back, it was like we hit the lottery. We didn't understand why it was so... Anyway, we followed her around. Well, *they* did. I was still young and learning. She was well protected though. Some old lady and a few others..."

Martinez walked towards Anthony. Suddenly, Anthony picked up a desk as easily as he would pick up a pencil. He threatened to throw it at Martinez. He then stopped. He did not want to wake April.

"Tell me more." Martinez said.

"Sure. It's not going to matter in a few moments. You are just like the others," Anthony said as he arrogantly laughed. "When I got older, I became angrier. You see, this whole thing-April, her mother, her protectors and trying to kill her; the future, it destroyed my family. I didn't even know why our mission was to kill her but after what went on with my family, I didn't care. And on top of my anger, I became stronger; and on top of that, I became smarter. See, if we killed her it would continue, she would keep coming back. Even if we were to kill her mother…," he stopped. "I didn't really want to kill her anyway. But, like I said, she's too strong either way. So, the plan became to weaken her. Surround her with death. When I was younger, I realized that if she was surrounded with sorrow and negativity, it may make her afraid. You know, we easily killed one of her protectors right in front of her and her mother. That scared her mother and, then, we realized, maybe that was the key… Weaken her. Make her afraid; make her weak. Make her feel that she can't do it on her own. Discourage her." Anthony paused, "You were going to die anyway, Eugenio. You were just another pawn that enables us to take away April's strength."

Quickly, Anthony took hold of Martinez. Anthony held Eugenio tightly as his face and voice changed. His voice became deep. Martinez could not move. Then, in a flash, heat and a strange energy forced its way from Anthony's body to Martinez's.

Anthony let Martinez go. Martinez fell to the ground.

Anthony chuckled and then said, "Heh, you are strong. A regular human being would be a pile of dust right now." He then kicked Martinez and sent him flying towards the other end of the floor.

Martinez, appearing very weak, stood up and said, "Tell me more."

Not understanding Martinez's actions, Anthony walked towards Martinez appearing evil and angry.

"She is going to be torn from the inside out," Anthony said with a deep and evil voice. As he picked up heavy objects and threw them at Martinez he said, "There will be no April. Not because she will be killed physically; she will be destroyed emotionally. She will be too weak. That was the answer all along. Destroy not her but her spirit, her power, her name."

As Anthony threw objects at Martinez, Martinez pushed them away with his gift. Anthony displayed massive strength as he continued to pick up heavy objects. He also smashed things with his bare hands. His anger and arrogance made him completely forget that April was upstairs.

"This tore my family and world apart," he said. "It's ironic how I tore you two apart. I'm going to tear April apart in many ways. But first, I'm going to tear you apart."

Then, Anthony balled up his fists and began to run towards Martinez about to hit him with all of his might.

Suddenly, Anthony stopped. In midair, Anthony was still. He could not move.

Martinez began to laugh softly as he stood up. "Tear apart… That's funny," Martinez said with an angered yet slightly calm tone. Then, with his power, Martinez turned Anthony around, still in the same position he was in.

Anthony struggled to move but could not. He tried to move his fists but he could not. He was stuck; held by some powerful force. As Martinez turned him with his mind, Anthony saw April standing at the steps with tears in her eyes.

"Do you have anything else to say?" Martinez asked.

Anthony said nothing.

Suddenly, Anthony began to scream in agony as his limbs began to rip away from his body. As easily as a piece of paper, Martinez tore Anthony apart into pieces.

April was shocked by Martinez's power. She could not believe what she had just seen. And, after hearing what Anthony had just said, April began to sob.

"Did he kill my mother?" she cried as she ran towards Eugenio.

"No April," Martinez answered.

"I saw that face in Puerto Rico," April said. "The face on Anthony... When Garcia came to me... Was that...?" April asked.

"I don't know, April." Martinez said as he took April by the hand and walked her out the door.

"Wait!" April said. She then extended her hand towards the area where Anthony's blood was and ignited a spark of electricity causing a fire.

As they snuck away from the scene, Anthony's home burned down.

April became weak again. Martinez helped her to the car.

"What now?" April asked breathlessly.

"Make you stronger." Martinez answered. "The time is near." They drove away.

"You must continue to go to school," Martinez said as he drove. "You must go to your class and appear that you know nothing about Mr. Coffey."

April nodded.

Weeks passed and April successfully continued to live normally without any suspicion from others. She also learned how to use her gift better.

During these weeks, April was sad. However, the situation with Anthony was just another incident added to the many that made her stronger and more prepared for what was to come. But, after continuously thinking about what had happened, April became depressed. Her depression became obvious to Martinez. On some days, Martinez would have to make April wake up from bed. She lost the urge to go to school. April became quiet as well.

One day, Eugenio found April crying in her room. He approached her as he asked her what was wrong. April did not want to answer him. She sat quietly on her bed as tears came from her eyes.

Martinez just sat with her as she cried. He put his arm around her and waited.

April leaned into Martinez. "I don't know what's wrong," she said. "I just feel weak."

"April, it is ok to feel weak," Martinez said. "You've been through a lot."

"How can you say that?" April asked. "How…" she cried. "How can…?"

"April," Martinez said. "One cannot know how to be strong unless they know how it feels to be weak."

April sat quietly.

"I think this was something that needed to happen in order for you to become a stronger leader," Martinez said.

"Leader?" April asked "How the hell can I lead if I'm so naïve to be deceived like that?" April asked, letting out what she's been holding in for a while. "He played me! … So easily! Now, how…?"

"April!" Martinez interrupted. "Think for a moment. In the future, what if someone comes along and tries to deceive you again, would you know what to do?"
April was silent.

"Of course you would!" He exclaimed. "That's why it had to happen. Otherwise, who knows what would have happened in the future. Just be thankful it didn't happen when it was too late. Part of being a leader involves learning from your struggles. Like I said, you can't know how to be strong unless you know how it feels to be weak."

April nodded and smiled.

"You know, I read that…" she paused as she wiped her eyes. "It is the *great* leaders who actually create leaders."

Martinez smiled and asked, "So, what does that make me? Are you saying that I'm a great leader?"

April smiled, laughed and said, "Well, I'm not a leader yet."

Martinez hugged April, laughed and said, "Right. Not *yet*."

Just then, as April leaned into hug Martinez back, their lips met. They then kissed.

An awkward silence overcame the room. April and Eugenio looked at each other silently.

Martinez sighed. He then said, "I have a surprise for you."

April's face lit up with excitement. "What is it?" she asked.

"Well, it's outside," he answered. "I'm surprised you didn't hear him outside."

"Him?" April asked. "Him who?"

April followed Eugenio as he went down the stairs. She waited inside as he went outside to bring in her surprise.

When Eugenio walked in, he brought with him something that made April smile excitedly.

"I've always wanted one!" April exclaimed. "Aww!"

It was a small puppy; a baby Pharaoh hound. Martinez handed the scared puppy to April. April became very happy.

"I figured that you were lonely with just the two of us," Eugenio said. "What do you want to name him?"

"I don't know what to name him," April replied.

Martinez smiled and said, "You'll come up with something."

Martinez then stood and watched April as she played with the small puppy. He began to look sad. He then sat down, appearing weak.

"Eugenio, what's wrong?" April asked.

"Nothing," Eugenio answered. "I guess I am just tired. I'm going to go lay down."

Knowing that sometimes Eugenio felt ill, April did not think much of it and simply nodded. "Do you need anything?" She asked.

"No. I'll be fine," Eugenio answered. He then went up the stairs and lay down.

The next day was a Saturday. There was no school. April woke up early to take her new puppy for a walk and to make breakfast for her and Eugenio. April waited for Eugenio to come down the stairs but he did not. Thinking that he may still be feeling ill, April began to prepare Eugenio's breakfast on a tray to take it up to his room.

After fixing the tray, April made her way to Eugenio's room. April knocked on his door but he did not respond. She then opened the door. As she quietly peaked in, April saw Eugenio laying in his bed asleep. It was very warm in his room. After placing the tray on the table next to Martinez's bed, April quietly walked over to the bedroom window and opened it slightly. She then walked over to Eugenio's bedside. She noticed that Eugenio was completely under his blanket. She wondered why he was covered up so if the room was so warm. She pulled the blanket from over Eugenio's face and gasped from what she saw.

"Eugenio," she cried.

Not dead, but appearing nearly dead, Eugenio looked terribly ill. His hair appeared to be falling out. His skin was pale and covered with sweat.

April shook Eugenio for him to wake up.

Eugenio's eyes opened slightly. "April," he said breathlessly. "I wanted to tell you."

"What do you mean?" April cried. "What's going on?"

"April, you have to remember, this will make you stronger," Martinez said as a tear came from his eye.

"How?" April asked as she cried. "How will *this* make me stronger? What is this?"

Eugenio cried without saying a word.

"How did this happen?" April asked.

"Anthony," Eugenio said.

"No!" April cried.

"He poisoned me with some sort of energy," Martinez said. "I thought I fought it off but..."

"I saw him," April said. "It's all my fault. I could have stopped him. I brought you to him," she cried.

"April!" Eugenio said as loudly as he could. "What happened, happened for a reason. You need to look at it from the perspective of our future. All of this already occurred in the future. It's what created the cycle that led to your birth. It is what makes you the leader of our future. If it would not have happened, you probably would not be here today or tomorrow. You have to understand...Things happen in order for other things to fall into their place."

April cried as she held Eugenio's hand to her face. "You mean fate?" She asked.

"No April," he answered in a weaker tone. "I do believe in fate. However, I also believe that one has to have something much stronger."

"What?" April asked

"Faith," he answered. "I've realized that no matter what happens, April, there is so much faith in what you can do that those in the future will stop at nothing to make it happen; no matter how many attempts it takes. They will continue to send whoever necessary back to recreate April over and over again until she comes to do what she was meant to do."

"What?" she asked as she cried.

Eugenio looked at April with tears in his eyes and said, "Save them and reign over their world in peace."

April cried.

Eugenio then said, "In the drawer, you will find the contact information of a man who will know what to do," Martinez said as he struggled for air. "He will know what to do. He will take care of my body. But then you must live on your own."

April cried. "No! You will be ok!"

"April," Eugenio said. "In a moment, I will pass. Now it is time for you to grow on your own.

"I can't do it alone," she said. "What will I do without you?"

"You will not be alone," Eugenio said. "You have an army waiting for you."

"But I mean you," April said. "I don't want to be without you."

"They will come to you April" he answered appearing to drift away from consciousness.

"Please don't leave me," April cried.

"Your faith with guide you," he responded.

April sat silently for a moment and thought.

"April," Eugenio whispered. "I love you."

Realizing that she would have to endure yet another suffering blow; the hardest since her mother's death, April sobbed.

"I love *you*, Eugenio!" she cried.

Eugenio then breathed his last breath.

After spending the morning crying at Eugenio's side, April went downstairs. She was still very distraught as she would be for some time. At the bottom of the stairs, April's new puppy sat and waited. April sat at the bottom step and began to pet her new friend.

Crying, April said, "I know what to call you. I will call you Angel. You will be my angel; my protector."

▲ Chapter 6

"AAHH!!" yelled someone outside April's home.

It was the beginning of winter and April, now a year older, ran outside. She stared in disbelief and everyone stared in fear. No one knew what to do. One neighbor ran out of his house with a gun. As he was about to shoot, April yelled for him to stop.

Since Martinez's death, April had lived as an ordinary citizen in her neighborhood. She continued to go to school and interacted more with the people she was told that she was to save one day. Everyone knew her by seeing her. However, they did not know much at all *about* her. Everyone knew and respected her as the young single, college student who lived in one of the only single homes in the neighborhood.

"No!" April yelled as she ran in front of the man.

"What are you doing?" another neighbor yelled to April.

A pack of wolves walked slowly down the street.

The dogs in the neighborhood had been acting strange for the past few weeks. But, this moment topped the peculiarity. All of the domestic animals did something no one expected. Instead of attacking and appearing territorial; or instead of running away, the animals from the neighborhood walked slowly towards the wolves, turned and began to walk with them. The people stood dumbfounded.

A woman ran inside her house scared. She looked at her television and watched as the news interrupted the regular shows to talk about strange incidents occurring not only in the city, but also across the globe.

"Reports started coming in stating that regular house pets were becoming abnormally quiet and obedient; and when they would rest, they would only do so at the front doors of homes," A man reported.

He spoke about zoo animals behaving as if they had been trained for years by professionals. When zookeepers would speak to them, the animals would act like they understood humans. Soon after, he explained, the animals at zoos began to inexplicably escape the zoos and disappear. All over the world animals were being shot and killed because people were terrified by their behavior.

In Africa, elephants, lions, leopards, hyenas and other big animals were roaming into neighborhoods and towns in packs. People were horrified. Many animals were attacked by the masses.

The same happened in Asia. Tigers and bears were doing the same. In South America, snakes, cougars, alligators and other wild creatures were said to be invading villages and cities.

Animals were making their way into populated areas for reasons beyond human comprehension. However, after so many animals were slaughtered, people then began to realize that the animals were actually not attacking humans. Some children would run up to animals and pet them, terrifying their parents. But the animals would not harm them. As they were coming into neighborhoods, the creatures would set themselves up in specific orders. They would have several different wild animals spread out through blocks in these orders. House pets would stay in the homes at the doors.

Scientists were baffled. They could not explain this phenomenon. Eventually, humans began feeding the animals although scientists and other officials urged against it. This went on for some time. Schools were closed, economies were halted. People did not sleep for the first few days. But, gradually, humans became more comfortable and began to live as normal as possible.

Then, one early morning when it was still dark outside April's window, she heard a lot of noise. Wolves were howling; dogs were barking and howling. The noise gradually got louder. Other animals were calling and crying. April sat up quickly. She was terrified. A sense of panic stormed through the neighborhood. Everyone ran outside their houses. Then everything became quiet. The animals all looked towards the sky. Suddenly, a great light exploded in the sky. People fell to the ground and screamed. The lights and power from all of the houses and street lights went out. The animals flinched but stood their ground. Chaos hit the neighborhood like a bomb. The sky lit up as bright as noon. There was sudden warmth in the air.

April stood and stared. She looked at the animals and saw them looking as if they were on guard. One wolf that stood in front of April's home looked at April and made a gesture for her to get inside. April gasped as her eyes widened.

Then, as if she felt an overwhelming power, April ran down the steps in front of her house to the middle of the street and yelled, "Everyone, in your homes now!"

Suddenly, immediately after April yelled, all of the animals turned to the people and began barking, howling, and making whichever noise they made to make the people get inside their homes. House pets were pulling on their owners to get them into their homes. People began to run into their homes. As April ran into her house, she turned to look outside and saw a man fall to the ground shaking. Then, Angel, April's dog, slammed the door shut and sat in front of the door.

"You know what's going on don't you?" April asked the dog. Angel sat at the door without any sort of response.

Then, April felt the ground shake. From inside her home, she could hear her neighbors scream in terror. She heard a gunshot. April quickly stood up and ran towards the door. But Angel did not let her open it. She then ran to the window and saw a man lying in the street holding a gun with blood pouring from his head. It appeared that he had shot himself. Although trying to remain calm, April did not know what to do.

Suddenly the lights in her house turned back on. April ran to the television and turned it on. The television was blank. She turned the channel and found that all of the other channels were blank as well. Finally, she found a channel that had the message that said "Emergency Broadcast." April listened carefully as a man's voice spoke:

"… All citizens are to stay in their homes until further notice," the voice said.

"…The east coast is now feeling the effects of the blast. Officials in your area are preparing emergency procedures for these incidents. We are assessing this incident and taking all steps to make sure that you are safe. Again, the eruptions occurred in more than one area of the globe; the worst being in Indonesia, causing massive tsunamis and earthquakes. The air in many areas has become highly unhealthy as sulfur and ash are being pushed into the atmosphere. The Northeast region of our country will be experiencing dark skies, tremors and some ash flurries. Please remain indoors until further notice. Again, this is not a test."

April was terrified and needed to know more information. "'Eruptions,' he said eruptions," April said to herself. "There was more than one? Not only in Indonesia?"

April searched for a channel that was on the air. She then found a channel with someone speaking live. Then, April heard a knock on her door.

When April walked to the door Angel, her hound, moved out of the way letting April know that it was safe to answer. When April answered the door, she saw an older woman with two children- a boy who was a toddler and a girl who appeared to be about ten years old.

"You seem to know what you are doing. All I have are my grandkids and we're scared. Can we stay with you? I'll give you money," the woman said.

April shook her head informing the woman that she did not need to pay. She then gestured for the three to enter her home. The woman was very appreciative.

"My God," the woman cried. "What is this? First the animals; now this…"

"There was an eruption," April said as she stared at the television.

"We are now getting reports," said the reporter on the television, "that all of Southeastern Asia is under a cloud of super-heated gas and ash," the reporter paused. "Millions upon millions…," the reporter paused again sounding distraught. "Now, we will not know the full extent of the damages for some time but we do know that the damages are catastrophic to say the least. I don't think that there is any other word that can describe what is going on. Now, in Colorado, again, catastrophe is the word that we would use as we are now getting satellite images that show that about twenty percent of the country is under a cloud of ash and smoke which is growing and moving eastward. This all occurred at 1:00am as the first eruption in Indonesia went off and then at approximately 40 minutes after, Colorado. Now, in a few minutes, the president will address the country again. But, for now, citizens are being told to stay indoors. That means all citizens from coast to coast, as these massive eruptions are affecting us all. After the presidential address, we will be going to our *weather center* team to discuss how this is going to affect our weather.

This is an unprecedented catastrophe," the reporter paused. "You may have already heard some people call this an 'extinction level event.' However, we insist that it does not have to be, so please stay calm and remain indoors until further notice."

"How can they tell us to stay calm if they are calling it an extinction level event?" the old woman cried.

"I don't believe it." April said. "It's happening. I knew it would come but I didn't think it would feel like this."

"What?" The woman asked in fear.

April turned to the woman and said, "Everything is going to change. Everything we have ever known will change forever."

Suddenly the reporter on the television sounding even more distraught than before began to speak again.

"My goodness," she said. "This just in ladies and gentlemen... I don't believe this," she said as she was apparently trying to hold in her emotion. "We have just received confirmation that the President has just been killed while being transferred to a secure shelter. This is…"

"Oh my goodness!" the old woman exclaimed as she and April could hear their neighbors loud reactions from outside.

The young girl who was with the older woman was startled by the woman's reaction and began to cry.

"Baby, please," the woman said. "Please don't cry."

April walked to the little girl and asked, "What's your name?"

"Anayah," the girl cried. "My brother's name is Namir."

"Anayah," April said. "It's ok for you and Namir to be scared. I'm not going to tell you to not be scared because… Well, this is a scary thing that's happening, right?"

Anayah nodded.

"But you are safe," April said. "Your grand mom and I won't let anything happen to you."

"You're not scared?" Anayah asked.

"I *am*," April answered. "I don't think there's anyone who is not scared. But you have to understand," April carefully explained. "There is a difference between being scared and weak and being scared and staying strong. Do you understand?"

The girl nodded.

"If we stay strong, we will be safe. Ok?" April said. Anayah nodded.

"Now, you stay strong for your little brother like your grand mom is being strong for you," April said.

Then, Angel, April's dog came over to Anayah and began to lick her and play with her.

The older woman, staring at the dog said, "And these animals… What do you think they're all about?"

April looked at Angel and said, "I think they are here to protect us. I think they realize that they need us as much as we need them and that the time has come…"

The night passed as the ground trembled. More people came to April's house. They told April that they felt a strong sense of security coming from her home. No one slept except the children. By morning, there were several families in April's home. Animals surrounded the home by the dozens.

Morning came but the light that usually came with the dawn was not there. Instead, the sky was an eerie crimson. That morning, April found out that the gunshot she heard was indeed a suicide. She also found out that the bright light that appeared in the sky had caused some people to have seizures.

Through the night April and the old woman heard two more gunshots before the morning came- both were suicides as well. People were horrified and did not know what to do.

"After all that our people have been through," the woman said as April listened. "…Slavery, murder, our women and children taken from us, raped and God knows what else… You'd think we'd be stronger than this. Committing suicide without even knowing what's next," she chuckled. "Heh, it's not like we haven't been doing it for years already anyway," she looked at April. "Killing each other…? We've been doing it to ourselves for years."

April stared and pondered for a moment. "Are we really to blame though?" she asked. "Just like today; the fear and confusion; hopelessness. Not knowing what's next; the feeling of our world ending… Is there really a difference? " April asked. "Whether it's with mother nature or dealing with oppressors… When will we have say over our own destiny? When?"

The people in the house stared at April.

"I mean, I don't want to sound… Cliché…" April then stops not knowing what to say next as if she lost confidence in what she was saying. She then turned the television on.

"… As the National Guard make their way through the residential neighborhoods,"

The voice of the news reporter was heard saying. "Again, we are in a state of Public *Emergency* which means state Governors may use the National Guard as the state's police. This is not Marshall Law although many people are labeling in as such. In a few minutes we will have an expert in this scenario give us a clear explanation of how this works.

Once again, just hours after the President's death, the Vice President and Congress members are declared missing. Attorney General…"

"Oh my God…" the older woman said as she held her grandson. "Oh my goodness, oh my goodness," she repeated as she became more and more scared. "If they can't even keep *them* protected how in the world."

"Please stay calm Mrs. Pittway," a woman said to the old woman. "They said that the National Guard is on their way."

"They just got done saying that most of Eastern Asia is destroyed," a man watching the television said.

People began to weep.

"…Indonesia, the Philippines, Singapore, Papua/ New Guinea, Cambodia, Malaysia, Vietnam… All under water. Billions are dead. Millions in Australia and China are dead. And they're expecting millions more to die within the next hour from the clouds of ash and hot air," the man continued, as his face expressed fear and sadness.

But what about us?" a young man asked. "Wasn't there an eruption in Colorado or something too?"

The man pondered for a moment and answered, "Colorado, Utah and New Mexico… destroyed almost immediately. It was a huge eruption. It… It was a super volcano, they said," the man stuttered.

The people in the room gasped.

"They're not giving numbers of deaths because… I think they're just stalling with that so that people won't get scared and act stupid. But they say that it's going to affect the whole continent in a 'catastrophic' way. The reporter said…" the man paused. "That between the Colorado eruption and Indonesia, it's an extinction level event. The reporters are now starting to use that term a lot."

"She said that last night," Mrs. Pittway said.

"Yeah so much for trying not to scare us…" another woman said.

"Oh my God!" another woman sobbed.

During the conversations, April sat quietly as she pet Angel and watched the children sleep. She then glanced outside and watched the animals as they sat vigilantly in front of her house.

"Well, I think we should go get as much food and warm blankets and clothes as we can," a woman said.

"There is that new store down the street," a man said.

The people in the house disagreed with the man's suggestion of breaking into the store and the group decided to go to their homes and retrieve their own valuables, clothing and food.

"I heard that everyone is going to the school," a young woman said. "Maybe we should go there."

The group agreed. April did not say anything.

When everyone left April's home, she thought for a moment. She did not want to become overzealous and try to be a leader too soon. She knew that with her strength, she can provide protection for them. She decided to do only that- protect, but quietly and only when it was needed.

"They have to find their own strengths first," She thought to herself. "They seem to be doing fine. I will just follow."

April then looked out the window. She saw the people begin to make their way to the school. April grabbed two large carrying bags and filled them with some clothes, sheets and food for herself and Angel. She then went outside and followed the crowd. Angel followed her. As she walked, April looked back and saw some of the animals follow the crowd as well in a very protective manner. However, many of the animals stayed in front of April's house. She did not understand why.

April looked at Angel and asked, "What's that about?"

Angel looked at April then continued to walk by her side.

When the group of people got to the school, they found another group of neighbors. The school was locked. It was winter time and, although the event made the air much warmer than normal people stood outside of the school with heavy coats on. Some of the people became mad and began to kick the doors.

Across the street, a man began to call the group. He was the owner of the take-out Chinese food restaurant. He seemed very scared. The people barely understood him, for his English was not very understandable.

"I have food," he said. "Please come. Please." He then fell to his knees, put his hands on his face and began to weep.

Two women from the group ran towards him to help him up.

"My God!" Ms. Pittway said. "Poor Mr. Chen. I just spoke to him two days ago. His wife just went to visit their daughter in college out in Hong Kong."

People began to cry as they felt sorry for the old man.

"Come Mr. Chen. Come," A woman said as she helped the poor man up.

As some people attended to Mr. Chen, others continued to try to break into the school building. Eventually, one of the doors was broken open and people began to make their way into the school.

"Wait," one of the women said. "What if the police come?"

"Ha!" A young man exclaimed. "I haven't seen a police car come pass all night!"

"Their probably in the other neighborhoods helping them *other* folks," another guy said. "I don't think they're gonna be comin' 'round here to help *our* folk… Just like that national guard."

"Nah," an older man interrupted. "They're not in no other neighborhoods."

"Oh yeah? Where're they at then?" the young man asked.

"Home with their families," the older man answered.

The young man paused to think for a moment. He then said, "Yeah right," he laughed. "They'll be around soon. You know they're gonna wanna look for some of us folks lootin' and stuff. They want an excuse to beat on some of us. Especially now…"

"Nah, son," the man interrupted. "I'm pretty sure they're with their families."

"How do you know, old head?" the young man asked. "And why are you…"

"Because I'm their Chief, and I sent them home," the man said as he pulled his badge out from his back pocket. "I sent them home to be with their families."

Everyone turned to the man and became surprised.

"Heh," he chuckled. "No one recognized me, huh?"

"I did," a man stuttered. "But when you didn't say anything when people were kickin' the school doors, I thought maybe I was wrong. Why didn't you…?"

The old man looked at the group of people and said, "I'm not the chief of police now. I'm a just an ordinary citizen now. My men are with their families; the National Guard is now in charge… It's not what they are telling you, folks…" He rambled. "They're not going to tell you," he paused to think. "Police, the government… They think they know what to do until the time comes. The second the event took place, their words, their plans… Everything… Everything became worthless. We are alone. We are not on the list to be saved, folks."

A sudden gasp spread through the group.

"After the years of being on television, fighting crime and having a high profile- being the face of the department… In one short moment, I was reminded of who I really was," the older man concluded in a depressed tone.

Without a response from the group, the older man then made his way into the school building. The people saw that he had no one with him.

Meanwhile, Mr. Chen was being held by Mrs. Pittway. He had no one either. He and his wife owned a Chinese food restaurant in the neighborhood. One week prior to the event, Mr. Chen's wife left to Hong Kong to visit their daughter who was in college. Mr. Chen is sure that they are dead. He was overwhelmed with grief.

"Such a shame the way he and his family get treated around here," the old woman said. "Now, we're all he's got. The way he reached out to us…" Mrs. Pittway then began to cry.

Anayah and her brother held their grandmother.

As the people walked through the school to find a comfortable, safe place, the animals stood outside the doors appearing to guard the school.

"Where's everyone else?" Anayah asked.

"What do you mean, sweetie?" her grandmother asked.

"Well, this isn't everyone from the neighborhood," she answered. "There's not even a hundred people here. Where did everyone else go?"

"They're probably in their houses," the woman said. "Too scared to come out."

People walked the hallways of the dark, cold school and began to make their way into the cafeteria. Then, the man who spoke at April's house about the losses in Asia brought in a large world map and hung it on the wall. He then hung up a map of the United States. Pointing at the east coast of the United States he said, "We are here."

He then pointed to Colorado. "This is where the eruption happened," he said. "All of this destroyed…" He then, in detail, explained how the cloud was going to travel across the country and affect their area as it was explained on the news.

"If this happened all the way down there, how come we're feeling it here?" a younger man asked.

"That's how massive it is," the man replied. "A super volcano… A hundred times bigger than a regular one…"

The people stared in awe.

"In two, three days, we can expect a lot of ash and… It's going to get unhealthy and cold. We should find a strong building 'cause once the ash starts falling… It's going to be heavy; weighing down on the roofs and stuff. I'm not sure how safe it is to be in this old building…." He paused with fear. "We need to get masks too. We can't breathe in that air either… I don't…"

April looked on as she knew all of this.

"How do you know all of this?" a young woman asked the man.

"I… I'm a science teacher," he answered.

"Here? At this school?" the woman asked.

"No," he replied. "At… At a school in the suburbs. Plus, I watch the science channels a lot and they always have programs about this stuff," he stuttered. "I'm telling you, the atmosphere is… I'm surprised we're not… We have to get masks and… And…"

"This is Asia…" Anayah said as she pointed to the continent where the mass destruction took place.

The man stopped babbling and walked over to the world map where Anayah was standing.

"Yes," he said remorsefully. Then, circling the area where the destruction took place- Indonesia, Southeastern Asia, Australia,

Papua/New Guinea and the surrounding areas, he softly said, "all of this is gone. And I'm sure that there is a much bigger cloud coming out of there,"

As everyone walked away from the maps in tears to get settled, Mr. Chen walked over to the world map, placed his hand over where China was and began to sob.

That night, although someone was able to get the power and lights on in the school, power in the area kept going on and off. People brought flashlights and blankets. Some people brought power generators from their homes which was helpful to keep heaters and lights on.

Through the evening, people learned each other's names. The Chief of police's name was Ernest Monroe. The science teacher who knew a lot of information was Rafael Rivera. The young woman who helped Mr. Chen and asked Mr. Rivera how he knew so much was named Iris Gutierrez. Eve Walker was the name of the other young lady in the group. Another young man in the group who asked Mr. Rivera about the eruption was named Alkys Mohammed. They, along with April, Mr. Chen, Mrs. Pittway, her grandchildren and a few others stayed close to one another throughout the night.

They were all very helpful to one another. Mr. Chen had a large stock of food at his store and brought it to the school. The people in the school decided to stock all of the food together and distribute it evenly until the National Guard came.

Chief Monroe told the people that he knew where to get gas masks. Alkys had, in his home, two oxygen tanks for his grandmother who had recently passed away. Coincidentally, Iris and Eve were both paramedics and said that they had emergency equipment in their homes such as medicine, antibiotics, heart defibrillators, bandages and other utensils needed for emergencies.

Although April did not have much to provide, if anything, the people felt very comfortable around her. Everyone throughout the evening kept checking up on April. She would be asked if and her dog were alright; she would be offered food before everyone else. Everyone would also always make sure she was warm and comfortable. April could not understand the people's actions towards her. She felt strange. She also felt bad because, although she knew how she could protect the group, she could not tell them how she could help. She felt that she appeared helpless or useless to the group. Still, the people treated her as she was valuable. She did not know why.

The next morning, it was very cold.

"It's snowing," one of the children said.

"It must be the ash," Mr. Rivera responded. "It's not snow."

"No," one of the older women said.

"I'm sure it's the ash," said Mr. Rivera as he walked towards the door.

"It's snow," said Alkys.

When Mr. Rivera stepped outside, he put his hand out. When a flake fell on his hand, he saw that the flake was white. Another white flake fell on his hand. He placed his tongue on the flake to taste it.

"It is snow," he said.

He sniffed the air. The air was clear and smelled normal. Rivera, although happy, he was surprised that the air was clear and that it was snowing.

The streets were empty and no one understood why. The only people around were those in the school.

"I don't understand this," Eve said. "Where did everyone go?"

About to respond, April looked in the sky and said, "Is it just me or have there been no birds around?"

Both April and Eve looked around. They realized that they were both right. There have been no birds in the skies nor have there been many people walking around. Eve expected more people to be about. With the many people who lived in the neighborhood, there should have been many more people out in the streets. There were less than 100 people staying at the school.

As for the birds, no one could explain their disappearance. April also noticed that she hadn't seen any insects either. It was very strange. It scared April. And when she spoke to the people about it, it scared them as well.

"We are going to get gas masks," said Chief Monroe as he and Alkys entered a white van.

"Where?" asked Eve. "Can we come?"

"We don't know what or who is out there. For all we know, there could be mass chaos out there," said the Chief. "There may not even be masks. The place may already be ransacked. I think you'd be safe here."

The men then drove off. As they made their way to the police headquarters, Alkys expected the worst. He was convinced that they were going to encounter trouble. Still, Chief Monroe was more optimistic about his community. He tried to help Alkys have faith by telling him that things aren't always how the media portrays them.

"You'd be surprised how we really react when there is adversity," Monroe said. "You have to understand, son, there has never been a time like today. There have been disasters; but we've never been told that we are close to extinction. Now, I know things are gonna get crazy but I think people are thinking now. I mean, really thinking. People are probably in their homes really trying to understand what they need to do next; getting closer to their families; getting closer to their God."

"Do you believe in God?" Alkys asked.

"I do," Monroe answered. "You?"

Alkys thought for a moment. He then said, "I'm supposed to, right? I mean, it'd be a sin if I didn't, right?"

Monroe thought about what Alkys was trying to say. He knew that what was occurring was testing Alkys's faith.

"Look," Monroe said. "I'm not the most religious person. As a cop, I've seen things that made me question religion all together. But then I think that I am here today because I'm not dead. And that's religious in its own way."

Alkys looked at Monroe not understanding what he meant.

"What I'm saying is," Monroe continued. "I don't know why we struggle or why other people suffer and die. All I know is that *I'm* not dead and that I won't know all I need to know until I die. And I wouldn't have known what I know if it weren't for what I saw other people go through. Now, they say 'what doesn't kill you makes you stronger.' But, at the same time, what kills others make you stronger as well. It makes you smarter. And I view that as God teaching me how to live for what he has next for *me*," he paused. "Now, I don't know why he took those millions of people… And I might not ever know until I join them, if I join them. But I do know that I am not with them. I am with you and the people at that school. Heh, for all we know, we may be soldiers for the battle of Armageddon and those millions of people may have been the enemies. Shoot, or even vice versa. We might be the bad guys, I don't know…"

"Yeah right, I'm not the bad guy," Alkys said as he laughed.

"… Yeah, I know," Monroe laughed. "I don't know if any of this made sense. I think I was just trying to calm myself. What I'm trying to say is that we shouldn't question life, faith, religion or God. Not because it's a sin; but for many other reasons. We may just not like the answers…"

The men drove as they both pondered. They did not know answers. But, they did know that they were both afraid. Still, the conversation made them feel more at ease. As they drove, they saw no one on the streets.

"Where are they?" Alkys asked.

"I told you," replied Monroe. "They are probably in their homes with their families trying to figure things out."

"Come on," Alkys said in a frustrated tone. "Millions of people? After what happened, shouldn't there be someone out here? Homeless people? Someone looking for answers, food, something??"

"Look a news van," Monroe pointed out.

Alkys blew the van's horn to get the other van's attention. Both vans pulled over. A man with a camera and a news reporter, a woman, exited the van.

"Chief Monroe?" asked the woman as she realized who he was when she approached. "What are you doing?"

"Ms. Kanniki," Monroe said recognizing the reporter. "Where is everyone?"

"Haven't you heard?" she responded. "The National Guard is evacuating the City. They sent a message out on the radio. They are having every one go east towards the coast. Southeast really... They are saying that as the clouds approach, it will be safe... Something about coastal winds making it safer... The highways are backed up.

"But what about the people who don't drive?" Monroe asked.

Looking surprised that Monroe did not know, the reporter answered, "Public buses and trains from all surrounding cities have been picking people up. Buses are all you really see on the highways.

"Here," the camera man showed Monroe on a small television. It was an aerial view of the highways headed towards the east coast shorelines. Buses lined up on the highways, and crowds of people trying to evacuate, headed east.

Out of breathe from his surprise, Monroe said, "I don't understand… How come we didn't know about this? We haven't seen a bus, truck or National Guard all night in our area."

Dumbfounded, the reporter shrugged her shoulders and said nothing.

"I'm sure there were people who decided not to go… And what are you doing?" Monroe said.

"They told people to go to the sports' complex. Some people are at college stadiums too. I'm just going around surveying and documenting as much as possible," the woman said. "We are leaving on the next helicopter to DC in a half hour. Chief…" she paused with sadness. "After what happened to the president, something happened," she paused again.

Monroe waited for her to continue.

"I'm sure you realize that they are not going to save everyone when this thing gets worse," she said.
Somewhat understanding what she meant, the chief asked for clarity. "What do you mean?" he asked.

"The suburbs; the upper class areas; they are the ones who are getting the help for the most part. But, even some people in those areas are being neglected. And because there's no direct devastation here… I mean, because people aren't really in trouble here… People aren't really noticing. It's not like there is a reason for people to call out for help or to stand on their rooftops. So, no one is noticing this. They are only protecting certain people. The broadcast stations are shut down and they are only transmitting what they want to whom they want," she explained. "Chief, you've got to get out."

"But we have about a hundred people on the north side," Monroe said. "We…"

"We have to go," The man interrupted as he pulled the news reporter back to the van.

"Don't go to the stadiums," she shouted to the chief. "Go to a strong building and try to wait it out. Get food and water from wherever you can. They are saying it's going to last years. But you have to survive the clouds first."

"How do we do that?" the chief asked.

The woman answered as they drove away. But Monroe could not hear her.

As they got back into their vehicle, Monroe said, "Lets' go get those masks."

As they drove closer to the police headquarters, Monroe and Alkys noticed a group of people outside of the building. As they got closer, they realized that what they saw was a violent confrontation. A group of ten to twenty white and black American young adults were savagely attacking a small family that appeared Middle Eastern American. The oldest man of the family already looked dead.

Abruptly, Alkys, who was driving the van, began to drive fast towards the crowd causing the group to disperse.

"What are you doing?" yelled Monroe.

"I see little children in the middle of that group," Alkys responded. "I'm not about to let those people hurt those kids."

Then, Alkys got out of the van and ran to the family's aid.

"What the hell are you doing?" He yelled to the crowd.

"Didn't you hear?" one person yelled from the crowd as the rest didn't even bother explaining.

One person hit Alkys to the ground. Then, Monroe ran in between the group and Alkys.

Quickly, Alkys remembered that, before they left the school, he saw Monroe tuck something in back. Hoping it was a gun; Alkys grabbed Monroe and pulled whatever it was tucked in the small of his back. It was a gun and Alkys quickly pointed it to the crowd.

"What are you doing?" Monroe asked with fear.

"Getting answers," Alkys said as he held the group at gunpoint. "Now, what is going on?" he asked.

Some people in the group ran. Some stayed. Out of the group, a man asked, "You didn't hear?" Pointing to the family, he then said, "They're the ones who killed our president."

"*They* killed the president?" Alkys asked sarcastically as he pointed to the crying family.

"You know what I mean…"

"No! I don't know what you mean!" Alkys exclaimed as he pointed the gun closer to the man. "What are you talking about?"

"On the news," the man explained. "They said that a group of *'Islamist extremists'* men attacked and killed the president…"

How is that possible?" Chief Monroe said. "All the security the President is supposed to have…?"

"They said that the US is responsible for all of this," the man said.

"That's crazy…" Monroe exclaimed.

"That's enough," Alkys said as he pointed the gun. "I'm so sick of people like you. Did those children kill anyone?" he asked as he pointed to the crying children behind him. "I'm so tired of people like you. And I guess I'm a terrorist because of my name, right? Right!?" he yelled as he gripped the gun tighter. He then went to shoot the gun in the air but it did not go off. The gun was locked.

Quickly, Monroe grabbed the gun from Alkys's hand. The group that was left was about to attack but Monroe quickly unlocked the gun as he fired it into the air.

"Get out of here," he yelled.

The group scattered.

Alkys and Monroe then helped the family into the van and took them with them. The man that appeared dead was still alive but needed help.

With everyone in the van, Monroe drove around the building and entered a secured area. Luckily, Monroe was able to use his security card to enter the underground drive way. The building still had power. He told everyone in the van to remain in the van as he went into the building. Monroe walked through many security doors and went up and down many floors until he found what he was looking for. Finally, when he reached a lower floor, he found a large custodial cart. He somehow fit it through another security door that led to an area where they stored Police S.W.A.T. gear. In this room, there were bullet proof vests, helmets, and gas masks. In a secured, fenced in, small room there were high powered guns. He also, found oxygen tanks and first aid kits. He filled the cart first with gas masks. There were at least a hundred of them. He knew he had to be quick. As Alkys and the family waited, Monroe made three trips back and forth from the building to the van. When he returned to the van, he handed the family the first aid kit to help the older man. The woman took it and began to aid him.

When Monroe returned from his final trip, Alkys saw that Monroe did not bring guns.

"No guns?" Alkys asked.

"No guns," the Chief responded.

"Don't you think we'll need them?" Alkys asked.

"Why? So we can help nature take its course quicker?" Monroe asked sardonically. "I'm not about to put deadly weapons in the hands of people who have no hope; people who are only going to get angrier when they realize that the government abandoned them... again."

Understanding Monroe and sympathizing, Alkys stood silent but then said, "But we don't have to put them in their hands. I mean, what about the other people we haven't seen yet who might get angry and want to do something stupid? How will we protect the people from them? I mean, you never know."

Monroe thought for a moment. He looked at the family and thought of the violent people they had just encountered. He then thought about what the news reporter told him about them not being protected. *"They are only protecting certain people,"* she said.

Monroe then turned around and went back to the building.

"Where are you going?" Alkys asked.

"To get two or three rifles and some ammunition," Monroe answered. "But that's it!"

On their way home, Alkys and Monroe began to see few people in the streets. They saw animals as well walking with the people- dogs, big cats and even bears.

"How come there were no animals? Alkys thought out loud.

"What?" Monroe asked.

"The animals," Alkys said. "I thought they were protecting everyone. Where were they when the family was being attacked?"

Before Alkys could finish, the young girl with the family softly said, "The guards; the army."

"The National Guard?" Monroe asked. "What about them?"

"They killed them," the girl said in a grief-stricken tone. "They killed them all."

Shocked, Monroe and Alkys asked, "How? Why?"

"They just started shooting them," the girl explained. "The animals did not even fight back. Some of them tried to take away the weapons but they were all killed."

"Did you see all of this?" Alkys asked

As tears began to come out of the child's eyes, she answered, "Yes."

When Monroe and Alkys made their way back to the school, there was about an inch of snow on the ground and, because there were no trucks clearing the roads, the roads were slippery. Still, they made it back to the school safely.

When they returned, the people were happy to see them. At the same time, Iris and Eve were driving up to the school in an ambulance. They had medicine, oxygen tanks and mattresses.

As the family exited the van, Iris and Eve quickly went to aid them. They saw that they were hurt; especially the older man. Monroe then explained everything. From what the reported told him to the incident with the group; he told the people at the school everything.

Afterwards, he, Alkys and a few others helped bring out the materials from both the van and the ambulance. Hidden in a storage compartment in the van, were the guns. Monroe and Alkys decided not to tell anyone about the guns.

"Food?" Monroe asked. "Did anyone bring food?"

"We brought in the last bags of rice and water from Mr. Chen's store," someone said.

"But we need more," added Mrs. Pittway. "I think it's time we made a moral decision."

Monroe thought for a moment. "With everyone gone, I don't think it would be considered looting anymore," he said. "It's surviving."

"How many stores are in the area?" April asked.

"Two supermarkets, a few convenience stores, corner stores; and that new store with pretty much everything from electronics to clothes to food," Alkys answered.

"We should focus on food right now," April said.

"And when that runs out, it's not like we can't drive somewhere else to get stuff. We should look around," Alkys said.

"No," April asserted. "We need to stay here for now. As you and Chief Monroe pointed out, people are starting to come out and we don't want to take away from what they may need. Right now, I think the safest thing to do is stay with our community. Not because we want to stay separated but because we don't know if the other neighborhoods are ready to come together. Plus, we don't want anyone thinking that they are being invaded by outsiders. Let's stock up what we have here before the clouds come and then see what's next."

"The girl is right," said Monroe. "We don't have time to be risky and drive around. Let's just focus on us and what we have here for now."

"We should put as much food in the school's freezer and stock up on as much food as possible," April said. "Fresh foods and meats will start to go bad soon…"

Several hours passed and the people worked together to get food into the school's freezer and canned goods and other materials into closets and classrooms. It had stopped snowing which made it easier for the people to work.

Suddenly, as April, Iris and Eve carried the last bags out of the van, Angel approached April and began to whine and push April.

"What's the matter Angel?" April asked.

"What's going on?" asked Eve.

"I don't know," April responded.

The animals then began to run faster and faster towards the people in front of the school. The people began to scream in fear and run into the building. As the people ran into the building, the animals- dogs, cats, raccoons and all other animals found in the area began to coerce the people up the stairs of the building. Some of the animals began to grab materials and food and run up the stairs with them. There was chaos as people were afraid, trying to understand what was going on.

April stood in the middle of the street waiting to see what was coming as Angel kept barking and pulling her. Then, April noticed a loud sound coming closer to the building.

From the third floor of the building, Mr. Rivera opened the window and yelled, "April get in. Oh my God get in!"

The ground shook and the noise became louder and louder and April could no longer hear Rivera. She could only see him pointing to the other end of the street.

April looked and saw nothing. Then, she felt something cold hit her feet.

Angel was pulling and pulling but April stared.

When she looked down, April saw water covering her feet. Then, as she heard crashing and an explosion up the street, she saw a wall of water rushing toward her. April quickly began to run. When she entered the building, she ran up the stairs. She did not look back and ran as quickly as possible.

The water filled the first floor; then the second. Some water made it to the third floor but everyone was safe. However, the vans, much of the materials, the freezer and the food were under water. Some of the generators were on the fourth floor, safe. Also, because there was no room for them in the lower floors, Monroe stocked the gas masks and first aid kits on the fourth floor as well.

"What in the world…?" cried Mrs. Pittway as she held her two grandchildren close and tight.

Everyone else cried.

It would be a whole day before the people could go to try to salvage what they could. For, after a day, the water began to recede. The streets flooded more than once, but after a day, the waters receded.

Trying to figure out what had just occurred, Rivera turned on the radio. But, sadly, there was no frequency. People felt scared and alone. They cried about their loss- their houses, property, cars and their neighborhood. They thought the worst. Some suggested and most agreed that it was a tsunami that hit the city.

"We are about 60 to 70 miles from the shore," said Mr. Rivera sadly, "It must have been… I mean, the whole east coast."

"All of those people," said Monroe. "They thought that they would be safe…. So many people."

"It is the end of the world. Oh my God!" cried a man.

Looking at the world map and placing his hand where the Caribbean Sea is, Rivera said softly and sorrowfully, "Puerto Rico, Dominican Republic, Haiti, Jamaica, Cuba… All of the Caribbean, washed away," he cried as he slid his hand across the islands on the map. He then took his hand and dragged it down the map along the eastern coast of North and South America.

"What now?" a woman asked in a disheartened tone.

"We wait…?" Alkys responded.

"For what?" the woman asked. "To be saved or to die?"

"We are not going to die." Monroe replied.

"Well, nobody is going to save us," the woman argued. "No one…"

"I am going to my house…" interrupted April. "The animals are walking in the street now so it looks safe. I'm going to see how damaged my house is and I'm going to see what I can salvage. I suggest you all go do the same. We cannot lose focus on us. If there is anyone out there coming to save us, it may take them a while to get to us. There are many of us who are healthy here. There are also many of us who are hurt- physically," April said as she pointed to the hurt family and some of the people who were hurt by the flood. "And emotionally," she said as she pointed to Mr. Chen and Mrs. Pittway who sat with her grandchildren appearing horrified. "If someone *is* coming to help us, we need to make sure that we are alive to *be* helped," April asserted. "So, if you are not hurt, please, help those who are. Otherwise, there'll be no one to save."

"She's right," said Monroe. "Let's secure the area and get as much food in here as possible. Who knows…? This might be our home for a long while. Mr. Rivera, I need you to get a few people together and make plans for this cloud that is coming our way. How bad do you think it's going to get? How can we survive this? We will all meet here in three hours and go over it. Ok?"

Rivera nodded as everyone began to go to the street to survey the damages.

Before everyone began to leave, April mentioned one more thing. "The animals!" she said.

"What?" Monroe asked.

"We need to feed the animals too," April said.

Monroe nodded in compliance.

As the people walked past April, they looked at her with confidence and pride. A couple of people even hugged her for her words of encouragement. April then left.

As April began to walk towards her home with Angel, she heard someone call her name.

"April!" called Anayah as she ran towards April. "Can I come with you?"

She began to walk with her. As they walked, Anayah kept looking at April with in admiration.

"What?" April asked as she chuckled.

Anayah laughed and said, "I wish I was like you. You're smart and you're not afraid anything."

April smiled and said, "Now, what makes you think I'm not afraid of anything? I'm afraid. I told you; it's…"

"I know it's about staying strong… Or something like that." Anayah interrupted as she smiled. "But you were just telling *me* that 'cause *I* was scared. But you're really not scared, are you?"

"I am, Anayah," April answered sincerely.

"Of what?" Anayah asked.

"The same things you are scared of," April replied. "Not knowing what's really going on. Not knowing what's next. Dying… A lot of things."

"But you don't look scared," Anayah said. "I just think you're so cool. I've never met a girl like you. You look so young but you seem so mature and strong."

"I'm still scared," April replied. "I want you to remember that it really is ok to be scared."

"It's all about how you handle yourself…" Anayah said.

April smiled and said, "Right!"

As April and Anayah walked towards April's house, they saw debris scattered all throughout the street. Large vehicles were crashed into houses. Large rocks, sea weed and sand littered the streets. Some houses were torn to shreds.

April was very careful looking for electrical wires and dangerous objects and made sure that she and Anayah steered clear of them and remained safe although electrical power was shut down throughout the area. Surprised, she saw that there were no dead bodies around.

But, what surprised April and Anayah even more was that, as they walked closer to her home, they found it intact.

The air was cold and, as they walked closer to April's house, they noticed snow beginning to fall again.

"We should be quick," April said. "All of this water is going to freeze over."

They approached the house and saw some of the windows broken. April opened the door and found the inside of her home soaked and destroyed. She looked around the house. There were not many things of high value in her house. There was a safe upstairs full of money but April wondered what good money was at this point. Still, she went to the safe and took a lot of the money with her without Anayah noticing. Then, she looked around some more. She had no pictures; nothing with much sentimental value. April just stood and looked around, thinking; remembering her time with Eugenio Martinez. She really missed him. Still, she needed to think of the present time. That was her way of remaining strong.

"There's something I want to show you April," Anayah then said sounding secretive.

"What is it, Anayah?" April asked, still pondering.

"Look," Anayah said as she extended her hands to her side. She then stopped and said, "Wait! I need to open the windows." She then went to all of the unbroken windows of the house and opened them.

After opening the windows, Anayah went back to her original position and extended her arms and hands again.

Realizing what Anayah was about to do, April said, "Wait! What are you about to do? I don't think you should…" She then saw that Anayah was not listening and focusing on what she was about to do.

Then, as Anayah held her hands out to her side, a very warm air began to build inside the house; wind began to blow through the house. The wind was very warm. It made April sweat. The wind was strong as it made its way through the house. April was amazed that such a young child could have such control over such power. April watched in awe.

Suddenly, April felt a strong pressure in her ears and heard a roar. She then saw what was beginning to look like a small funnel in her living room. Immediately, Anayah stopped.

April looked at Anayah and noticed that she looked scared.

"Oh no!" Anayah said, "Oh no! Please no. Please stop," Anayah yelled, "Stop!"

"What's happening?" April yelled as the wind grew stronger and louder.

Anayah said nothing. She just looked at the small funnel in fear. Just then, the funnel disappeared and the wind died down.

Anayah sighed and with a tear falling from her eye, she said, "Thank God!"

"What *was* that??" April asked.

"I'm sorry!" Anayah cried. "I was just trying to help. I didn't know…"

"It's ok, girl," April said as she went to hug the young child. "It's ok."

Realizing that Anayah was manipulating warm air April said, "You have to be careful with that. Warm air combined with cold air can create a tornado." She then laughed.

Anayah, touched by April's understanding and calm manner, began to cry and laugh at the same time.

Suddenly, a loud roar came from the sky. April and Anayah ran outside. When they looked up in the sky, they saw three military jets fly across. The jets were really low. They were so low that the ground shook and the noise was deafening.

April and Anayah began to run back towards the school. As they ran towards the school, they saw other people running from their homes back to the school. They saw Eve.

"What is that," Eve asked.

"It looked like jets," Anayah answered.

"Jets?" Eve asked. "I mean, I know. But why? Are they coming to save us or what?

Suddenly, in a distance, there was a loud explosion. The explosion made everyone immediately stop and duck. It scared everyone.

Thinking of the people in the stadiums that Monroe and Alkys told the people about, April said, "Oh no! You don't think…?"

Eve looked at April with an angry yet terrified look. They all then began to run to the school. As they ran into the school to meet up with everyone, they saw people run up the stairs towards the roof of the school. On the roof, they saw Rivera.

"The explosion came from over there," he said, pointing towards a cloud of smoke south of where they were. "With the snow, I couldn't see clearly but…"

"Did the jets bomb something?" Eve asked.

Out of breath from the excitement, Rivera answered, "The stadium… It's a few miles south from here, in that direction." He pointed.

The people gasped in disbelief.

"Why would they do that?" Anayah asked.

No one answered.

"Why would they do that?" Anayah asked again with fear in her voice. "April, why would they do that?"

"I don't know Anayah," April answered quietly. "I don't know."

"We should get off the roof," Monroe stated. "Who knows what or who they'll bomb next?"

Scared, the people began to evacuate the roof.

Later that evening, everyone attempted to get as comfortable as possible. No one really slept. Scared of the unknown, everyone slept on the 4th floor.

April lay near Anayah and her family.

"Why warm air?" April asked quietly as they lay down.

"Huh?" said Anayah.

"I was just wondering, why warm air?" April responded. "You know... Your gift."

"It actually gets very hot," Anayah replied. "It's actually a lot stronger than my grand mom's."

"What about Namir?" April asked.

Anayah thought quietly for a moment and said, "He's normal. He don't got no powers."

April thought for a moment and said, "Oh." She then asked, "What happened to your parents?"

"I don't remember," Anayah whispered.

"What do you mean? You don't remember *them* or you don't remember *what happened?*

"Oh, I remember them... Well, I remember what they look like," Anayah told. "I just don't remember what happened. One day I'm with them playing in the park; next thing I know, I'm waking up in my Grandmom's house and I got a baby brother."

April looked perplexed and did not know what to say.

"They said I had amnesia," Anayah said. "It happened almost three years ago. My Grandmom don't really talk about it, because she said she don't want to upset me. I think she don't want to upset herself, so I don't talk about it."

"Are your parents… dead?" April asked.

"I don't know. I mean, I thought they were, but I don't know now," Anayah answered.

"What do you mean?" April asked, again looking puzzled as she lay on her stomach with her head turned towards Anayah.

"I mean, it's like a feeling. I don't know. I feel like, I would know if my parents were dead. I would feel it. And I don't feel it."

April did not say anything. Anayah's words made her think deeply. Although she was not sure what happened to her mother, April *felt* the physical absence. Still, April felt her mother was with her in her heart. But, at the same time, she felt the absence that Anayah spoke of- the absence Anayah did not feel. The thought brought a tear to April's eye.

"Tell me about your gift," April regressed. "You said it's stronger that your grandmom's…?"

"Why do you call it a gift?" Anayah asked.

April thought for a moment. She then answered, "I don't know. I guess because the word 'power' sounds like a bad thing nowadays. Presidents have 'power' and they misuse it. Police have 'power' and they sometimes misuse it. And you saw what the military did with *their* power. I mean, the worst kind of people can have 'power' and they can use it in the worst way. I say 'gift' because… I don't know. I guess because… A gift is always a good thing. Right?"

Anayah smiled and said, "Yeah."

April and Anayah were silent for a moment. Anayah then explained, "My Grandmom can move the air around like me. And it does get warm but it's not as strong as mine. It's warm because… Well, my Grandmom says that she thinks it's from the friction of the par…ti…cles… in the air. She said that if it got any stronger, it'd turn into fire. There are enough flammable gases in the air that, if there was enough friction it could catch fire."

"All you need is oxygen to create fire," April said.

"Yeah?" Anayah asked and then pondered. "Well, when I get older, I'm gonna do some research," Anayah said attempting to sound mature.

"You should," April said with a smile. "You're pretty smart already."

April felt close to Anayah. She wanted to mentor her. She also wanted to tell Anayah her story. But, April was not ready to open up to anyone; not even an innocent child.

Meanwhile, as April and Anayah were falling asleep; Rivera and Alkys were still attending to the family that was attacked. They were all asleep except for the youngest girl. She was about 15 years old.

Quietly, Alkys said, "It's a shame how closed-minded people are. I can't believe they would do this," he paused. "How long have ya'll been in the states?" he then asked.

The little girl smiled and, somewhat confused by the question, she answered, "I was born here. My mommy and daddy were born here. My grandfather was born here. My other grandfather and grandmother moved to New York from Iran and the moved to Philly when they were older just before my mom was born.

"So, you guys are Iranian, huh?" Alkys asked.

The girl was silent for a moment, and then answered, "We are American."

Understanding that his thinking was like that of the people he spoke of, Alkys apologized then asked, "What is your name?"

"Laila," she answered.

"Laila…," Alkys said. "Can you tell me about what happened with the animals?"

Laila was quiet. She pondered for a moment, and then explained, "My dog and my cat were killed last. They were trying to protect us. But they… They just killed them. The Army… They killed them. It all started when the sky lit up. The ground shook and all… The animals were all around the neighborhood already and the people were going crazy. We were scared, but me and my family somehow knew that the animals would protect us. But, some people were paranoid. They didn't understand…" she stopped herself for a moment, then continued. "The army was there quick. I don't know why… I don't know why, but the animals started becoming really… I don't want to say 'crazy,' but… They started being really… active. They started pulling the people into their houses. And then the people started being scared and fighting with the animals. But, the animals weren't fighting back. Some people even beat their own pets to death… But the animals didn't fight back. It wasn't until the army men started helping the people fight the animals when the animals started fighting back. They weren't even really fighting; they were growling and roaring and hissing at the army. Then, they stared shooting them. The soldiers started shooting the animals. Even the smaller animals that could have escaped were killed. They didn't run away… It was like they were standing their ground for the people… My pets weren't even doing anything. The army men just walked up to them… When they came closer, my dog started growling, but… They just shot them. The next day, someone heard that the people who killed the President were Middle Eastern or something. My neighbors were killed. Some of our other neighbors knew us and knew that we were American, and they did nothing when people started to attack us… Why?" She began to cry. "Why attack a whole group of people for what one or two people did? Especially after what happened… Don't they realize…?" Laila cried more.

"I guess the people who killed the president thought that the government was involved with what happened," Alkys suggested. He then thought for a moment, staring at Laila as he felt sorry for her. "I'm so sorry you and your family had to go through that. I know that things aren't that much better here but, just know that you will be safer here."

The older man that was severely beaten, lying on the table, turned to Alkys and, with a weak voice, he said, "Thank you."

The following morning, as everyone was getting up from a restless night, someone announced that it was snowing again.

Later that morning, Monroe and Rivera called for everyone to meet in the cafeteria of the school to go over safety procedures. They spoke about how to use the gas masks and oxygen tanks; some people were given a quick course in First Aid and Cardiopulmonary resuscitation. Others were given roles like evacuation leaders, food dividers, maintenance, animal caretakers, and monitors to look out for any trouble. To keep a low profile, April volunteered to take care of the animals.

Some people did nothing but walk back and forth from their houses. Some of them were still in denial of what was going on; some felt bitter about it all; some were just emotionally distressed and did not want to socialize with anyone.

As the meeting went on, April went to walk outside to check on the animals. The animals seemed restless. April just stood at the doorway to think. She felt a bit sad. She also felt guilty. With everything that was going on, she felt that she was not thinking enough of her mother and now Martinez. It was almost like she felt that she owed it to them to at least think of them. Just then, April felt a warm breeze hit her from behind. April turned around and saw Anayah.

"Hey, April," Anayah said. "What are you doing?"

Realizing that Anayah had just used her gift, April said, "You know you should be careful. You don't want everyone to know about your gift."

April then noticed that Anayah was a bit bothered by what she had just said.

"Why not?" Anayah asked. "I think it's cool." She then paused for a moment. She then asked, "So, what are you doing?"

"I'm just thinking" April said.

"About what?" Anayah asked.

"My mom," April answered.

"You miss her?" the young girl asked.

"Yeah," April responded.

Anayah thought for a moment and then asked, "What happened to her?"

Suddenly, the animals began to get loud. The wolves began to howl; the dogs began to bark. The other animals made noises as well.

"What's going on?" Anayah asked.

April looked around trying to figure out what was causing the animals to act that way. She then saw Angel looking to the sky. April then looked up. She then noticed the sky beginning to look darker. She saw that along with the white snowflakes falling to the ground were grey and dark colored flakes. First there were few. But in moments, more and more started to fall. The sky and the air began to darken quickly.

"Oh no," April said. She then ran to the people inside the building. April went over to Rivera and Monroe. "You should come outside," April said.

At the same time, others began to run in, afraid and acting frantic.

"What is it?" Rivera asked as they walked to the door.

They then looked and stood quietly as if their worst fears had just been realized.

"Ash!" Rivera said.

"I was actually beginning to think that it would not come," said Monroe.

"Are we fully stocked?" Rivera asked with a blank stare. "I mean, do we have everything; enough to last...?"

"I'm not exactly sure if it's enough. But we did stock as much as we could," Monroe answered.

"Good," Rivera said quietly; still with a blank look on his face. "We should get everyone inside. We should close all of the windows. We cannot breathe this stuff in."

"Let's gather everyone in the cafeteria," Monroe said to Rivera. "I think you should explain to everyone what is going on."

Rivera nodded.

Minutes later, everyone was gathered in the gym.

"This is it folks," Rivera said. "The ash has finally come."

"... Yeah, I think it's time that we realize that we are going to be on our own for a long while," Monroe stated. "Does everyone know what is expected them? I mean, do we know our duties; does everyone know where the food is, the masks, bedding...? Are we clear that we cannot breathe this ash and...? Look," he paused. "Things are going to get hectic. This ash, as Mr. Rivera pointed out is going to create havoc so, we really need organization. Now, I suggest, for organization and safety's sake, that we put together some sort of political system."

"You mean, like a democracy or something?" Iris asked. "You're saying we should elect... 'Leaders' or something?"

"Yeah," Chief Monroe replied, "What I'm saying is, we need to start thinking and behaving like we are going to be here for a long while. And to keep things organized we need, well, to put together some sort of body."

"Yeah, like a county…?" Eve asked. "Do we really need to get into politics now? People are scared," she said sounding concerned that it may lead to complications.

"Yeah, like our *'great'* country, right Chief?" Alkys said sarcastically. "How about we appoint some slaves too, *Boss?*"

During the discussion, April stood in the back of the cafeteria wondering if she should intervene. She did not feel that it was the right time to speak so she stood quietly.

"Now, look," Monroe interrupted. "This is not the time to dwell on the past… On something a kid like you probably knows nothing about. You don't appreciate…"

"Appreciate what?" Alkys interrupted. "This great country of ours? You don't know me, sir! You don't know what I appreciate. You don't know what I know. I know about this country. I know about democracy. What I'm saying is it doesn't always work… *Didn't* always work. Maybe we should think of another model… At least try something until we can think clearly. If you haven't noticed, it's the end of the world."

"That's exactly why we need to organize this. And it *does* work!" Monroe said. "It's worked for this country before and we need to…"

"Why not elders?" Mrs. Pittway said unexpectedly.

"Excuse me?" Monroe said.

"Elders," she repeated. "Like our ancestors."

"Like whose ancestors?" Monroe asked

"Your ancestors, Sir!" Alkys exclaimed.

"Why are you talking to me like this?" Monroe asked Alkys.

"Because you are acting like once you became chief of police, it was like you lost…"

"Stop it!" Mrs. Pittway said. "Our ancestors used to run their villages by having their wisest people, their elders make the decisions."

"Yeah?" Monroe asked. "Where are these villages now?"

Alkys and a few others became upset by Monroe's question.

Peacefully and calmly, Mrs. Pittway answered, "Well, many of these small villages became rich cities; cities that thrived in peace for hundreds of years. We're not trying to build a country and go to war, are we?"

"Have any of these primitive villages ever been in a situation like this?" Monroe asked with a snobbish tone.

"Well, they have been around for a very long time..." Mrs. Pittway answered. "Has this country ever been in a situation like this?"

"Look, putting all of the resentment we may have towards this country..." Frustrated, Monroe paused. He then continued, "We should use it as a model. We need to survive! And the only way we can do that is..."

"...By following in the masta's footsteps, right?" Alkys interrupted.

"Look kid there ain't been masters in almost two centuries and there damn sure ain't no slaves in here!"

Alkys then continues to argue, "Oh! '*Ain't?*' We getting a little...?"

As April was about to interrupt the argument to bring some sense to the meeting, an unexpected voice was heard.

"Stop it. Just Stop!" the voice called. It was Anayah walking from the back of the cafeteria. "You all have been acting like children. I'm a child and I'm disgusted over what I'm hearing," she yelled. "I agree with my grandma. I mean, even though I'm acting more mature that some of you right now, I still value and respect the opinions of my elders and I think all of the elders in this room have something valuable to offer this, this 'community' to keep us safe."

"Look, kid…" Monroe began.

"I think we should listen to her," April called from the crowd, interrupting Monroe.

April, by this point, had earned the respect of everyone in the room. There was a quiet mutter throughout the crowd as the people agreed with April.

"Ok…" Chief Monroe said.

Anayah looked at April with a smile that showed great appreciation. April smiled back as she leaned against the wall, waiting to see the wisdom that the young child had to offer.

Anayah went on to express her agreement with her grandmother and stressed that it was important to establish respect amongst the group before anything.

"Without respect there can be no organization," she said. "If we try the politics, we will be divided… I think."

Monroe obviously disagreed; he was set in his ways and did not want to agree with Anayah. Quietly, to himself, but with the people able to hear him, he said, "Talk about slaves and masters… That's the slave mentality if you ask me."

Anayah felt a bit hurt by Monroe's comment.

April, having heard Monroe and seeing that Anayah was discouraged by Monroe's statement then said, "With all due respect Mr. Monroe, the one who follows in the master's footsteps is simply a loyal slave."

A gasp moved through the crowd.

"What did you say?" Monroe asked as he became insulted. "Are you calling me…?"

"I'm not calling you anything, Mr. Monroe." April said. "I'm just simply stating that we have to understand the mentality of the people in this room. Once again, there is a strong sense of abandonment. For years we have tried it 'their' way… We have tried to assimilate and be a part of a world that doesn't want us. We even had a president who, although he was successful, he was reminded every day that *he* was not *their* president; we were still reminded of who we were during and after his presidency. We were reminded of that once again this week. Don't you think we ought to give *us* a chance now? All of us come from worlds viewed as primitive, but what do we get when we try to be what they call modern…? Besides… What do we have to lose?"

Monroe sat quietly as he pondered. He then looked around as the people looked for his response and said, "Why is everyone looking at me?"

April then walked to Monroe, put her hand in his shoulder and said, "We are waiting for the permission of one of our elders to move forward."

Monroe looked down and thought for a moment. He then smiled, looked up and said, "We may move forward!"

A light cheer moved through the crowd.

Monroe then stood up and said to April, "I'm not that old, you know."

April smiled and said, "I know Mr. Monroe. Let's just say that you are one of our 'wisest.'"

Monroe laughed, put his hand on April's shoulders and said, "thank you, April."

"Don't thank me," April said as they walked to Anayah. "Thank Anayah."

Anayah then smiled.

Days passed. There had been some deaths at the school since the ash began to fall. By this period in time, there had been cures found for many diseases including asthma and other respiratory illnesses. Sadly, however, because there was no way to get to these remedies; some children and elderly people passed away from the vulnerable conditions. In some cases, the ash was to blame. In others, it was the large amount of dust from the old school and lack of important resources that led to the unfortunate deaths of some. Some, becoming paranoid, left the building without anyone knowing and never returned. Unfortunately, while outside, they succumbed to a horrifying death from breathing in the ash that would turn to mud in the person's lungs.

After some time, people became comfortable as they tried their hardest to live freely, given their circumstances. Some were eve able to obtain sports equipment to use in the school's gym.

One day, to try to keep their minds off the fear of the world around them, many people gathered in the gym to play a sports tournament. Tragedy then struck, bringing the people's fears back to the forefront.

As people smiled and seemed to forget their troubles for a moment, noise began to come from the ceiling. Suddenly, the ceiling collapsed and fell on the people. As some played in the middle of the gym and others watched from the stands, ash weighing on the old and dilapidated roof of the gym caused the ceiling to fall. Many were trapped under the debris. Ms. Pittway and others ran for masks and oxygen tanks. They then ran to the aid of those in the gym. Several people were killed.

As they continued to try to help and evacuate the gym, the ash continued to quickly pour in. There was chaos. There were too many people to help but too little time. With the fear that the rest of the building would collapse, people moved as quickly as possible.

April, trying to think of something quickly, was helping to get people out of the gym. As people cried hysterically and as disorganization set it, it became harder to gain control over the situation.

Monroe, Rivera and the others who attempted to help were losing patience and energy. They looked at April with discouraged looks. Then, April called for everyone's attention.

When the people heard April's voice, they stopped and looked at her.

"If you are not hurt, you must help," she called. "If you are too distraught to help, you must leave. We must focus and not be in the way of help. We must get everyone... Mr. Rivera, where would you say is the strongest place in this building?" April asked.

Stuttering and coughing, Rivera struggled to think, "U... Under the stairs... at the main entrance... everyone should go under the stairs. At... At the main entrance, and under the door ways on the first floor.

Rivera then began to cough. The air quality was becoming more dangerous.

April began to direct everyone. Things gradually began to run smoothly as the people listened to April. Her voice commanded respect and the people listened to her.

Suddenly, April felt a warm breeze come from behind her. April then noticed the ash flying around in a funnel and out of the gym. The people in the gym became scared and confused. They did not know what was going on. April turned around and saw Anayah. Anayah had her hands out and her eyes closed. Using her gift, the young girl was moving the ash out of the building.

As the people calmed their emotions, they noticed what was going on. They noticed that Anayah was controlling the air. People yelled in fear. Others stared in awe as they tried to grasp an understanding of how the young girl was able to do what she was doing.

"No!" April exclaimed quietly but with slight irritation. She knew that once people realized what was going on, things would change in the community. She knew that there would be much misunderstanding and prejudice. Many people would not understand. April knew that everything was going to change for Anayah. However, things would not change for Anayah in the ways that Anayah hoped for.

"What is this?" Monroe asked in more anger than fear.

Confused, people were not moving fast enough.

"Later!" April yelled over the sound of the wind. "Everyone must be moved out."

After the gym was quickly cleared and those who were hurt were treated, the gym was sealed off. Several people were killed by the collapsing ceiling. Others died a few hours later from breathing in the ash during the commotion. They had not retrieved oxygen masks before running to help.

After everyone was under the stairs at the main entrance, the main worry was whether the whole building would collapse. Dozens of people squeezed under the stairs and wondered if this was the time of their deaths. Others lay dead in the gym. Others roamed the building, checking the stability of the building. Others lost hope, accepting their fate.

Worried about the building, Monroe looked at Anayah. He thought about what she did and what she could do.

"How did you do that?" He asked Anayah.

April became concerned, realizing the potential problems that may arise now that people had witnessed someone with gifts.

Anayah looked at Monroe with a look of pride on her face. She felt strong and important. April was aware of Anayah's feelings and became concerned.

"I have a gift," Anayah said. She then looked at April and smiled because she said the word "gift" like April said.

"Do you think you can get the ash off of the roof of this building?" Monroe asked.

"Sure!" Anayah said enthusiastically.

"Anayah," April interrupted. "I don't know about this. She's just a child ..."

"No I'm not!" Anayah said frustrated. "I *can* do it."

"Anayah…" April said, but Anayah interrupted.

"No, April!" She said. "This is my power. Not yours. You don't know what I can and can't do. You don't know anything about me."

"What are you talking about, Anayah?" April asked, as she tried to speak to her privately. "Listen… Let me talk to you for a second."

"No!" Anayah exclaimed as she pulled away from April.

April, trying to calm Anayah down, attempted to pull her aside but Anayah stubbornly pulled away once more. April became agitated but did not want to make a scene.

"Please, Anayah…" April said.

"And I ain't no child neither!" Anayah exclaimed.

"You don't understand…" April said, attempting to get Anayah to listen.

"I understand," Anayah argued. "You're jealous. When you told me not to use my power around everybody… It was 'cause you were jealous."

April tried to remain calm. "Anayah," she said. Then she pondered for a moment. "I'm not going to argue with you about jealousy. I'm trying to look out for you."

"What is going on here?" Ms. Pittway said as she approached April and Anayah. Realizing what the conversation was about by the expression on Anayah's face, Ms. Pittway said, "Nayah, you didn't!"

"Ms. Pittway, "April said. "You have to speak with her. She…"

"Grandma, I can do it," Anayah said.

"Do what?" her grandmother asked with a fearful tone.

"Ms. Pittway," Monroe said. "We need Anayah to use her gift to help us. It's important that we clear the ash from the roof of the school before the whole building collapses. The ash has become heavy for the old roof."

"I understand," the old woman said.

"Ms. Pittway," April interrupted.

"April!" Monroe said loudly, silencing her. "If we don't get the ash off of the roof of the school, its weight will bring the building down.

"He's right," Rivera said as he entered the conversation. "It may look like dirty snow but it's not snow," he explained. "With the moisture in the air, once it starts to pile on, it can be as heavy as cement."

"So, if we don't do something, we could all be buried," Monroe said.

Ms. Pittway looked at Anayah with a disappointed expression. She did not like the fact that everyone found out about her gift. However, she felt pressured by Monroe and Rivera, and the severity of the situation.

"How do you suggest she do it?" The grandmother asked.

Anayah's face lit up with enthusiasm.

"Well," Rivera began to explain. "She cannot go out there without a mask. If she breathes in that air, she will suffocate.

Ms. Pittway pondered for a moment. "Okay," she said hesitantly.

Anayah became excited as a child would as Rivera and Monroe took her to get prepared. When they took her to get the gas masks and talk to her about what she needed to do, she focused hard. She was quite nervous because she knew that she still had not gained full control of her gift. She thought of how sometimes she had lost control and she did not want to hurt or kill anyone. But, Anayah did not want to say anything. For one, she did not want to alarm anyone. Second, still having a childish mentality, she felt that this was the opportunity to show everyone her great power and become popular among the group.

While Anayah was preparing, April stayed with Ms. Pittway. She knew the importance of getting the ash off of the building. Still, she was concerned about Anayah. Could she handle the position in which she had been put?

"There has to be another way to get the ash off of this building," April said quietly, unable to keep her thoughts to herself.

"You don't think she can do it, do you?" Ms. Pittway asked.

April turned to the old woman and said, "Ms. Pittway, I think your granddaughter has an extraordinary gift. She is an extraordinary child. But that's exactly what she is- a child. She needs more time to develop. I've seen her gift and she still needs to learn control."

Ms. Pittway sighed and said, "I know. Do you think that what she's doing is dangerous?"

"Very," April said. "If she loses control, she could kill herself and many others."

Ms. Pittway became hesitant and indecisive on what to do next. By the time they had made up their minds to stop Anayah, she, Rivera, and Monroe were already outside. Ms. Pittway and April ran to get the masks to go out after them.

As they ran towards Anayah, she had already had her arms out ready to use her gift. The wind began to pick up. From the friction in the air, thunder began to roll and lightning began to strike. Slowly, the wind began to push the ash off of the building. But the wind became warmer and faster.

April stopped running and called out to Anayah, but she could not be heard over the noise. Suddenly, a loud thunder startled Anayah and forced her to strengthen the wind. As the wind grew stronger and warmer, it mixed with the cool air in the atmosphere.

Tears began to pour from Anayah's eyes from fear of losing control.

April began to run closer. As April grew tenser, the energy around her began to intensify. The electricity within and around April grew stronger. Suddenly, April saw a funnel cloud begin to emerge.

Anayah cried but tried her hardest to control the winds. Then, another funnel cloud emerged. Monroe and Rivera were terrified as they did not know what was going on. They began to step back.

Then, Ms. Pittway, using as much of her own power as she could, pushed a gust of wind towards one funnel in attempts to break it apart. As it did break the one funnel apart, the other grew stronger, pulling apart some pieces of the building. As the tornado roared towards the building, screams could be heard from inside.

Monroe screamed, "That's enough Anayah. You must stop."

Anayah cried but did not say a word, nor did she look at anyone. She could not. She tried to stop and pull away but could not.

April, preparing to use her gift, in hopes that the electricity would break the winds apart, noticed Ms. Pittway collapse from exhaustion. Suddenly, as the energy built around April, it attracted static from the clouds above her. Then, a loud explosion came from the clouds and, "BOOM!" April was struck.

All of the sudden, the winds stopped. But, as April lost consciousness, she heard a section of the school building collapse. She also, heard people scream for their lives as the building fell on them. April then blacked out.

▲

Going in and out of consciousness, April saw three people with masks and thick white suits. They picked April up and carried her to what appeared to be a futuristic ambulance. The vessel had no wheels and hovered silently, without any noise coming from it. Opening her eyes intermittently, April noticed that she was being transported away from the school.

When they arrived at their destination, the three people moved April into a building that she recognized as the Museum of Anthropology in Philadelphia; the museum she once visited. Drowsy, yet conscious, April was carried on a stretcher. She was then placed on a bed, where she was unable to move. Her body was too weak, as if it were under the influence of something beyond her control.

April looked around as her body was covered by a golden fleece like fabric that she had never seen or felt before. The fabric was cold and silky but so light that she could barely feel it. Having this fabric covering her from her bare toes to her neck made April unusually relaxed.

The room she was in was very odd. The walls appeared to be gold or brass, but they were shaped like wooden panels that leaned into the room. There was a spherical object next to

April's bed that glowed with a strange light blue color whenever she took a breath. The room was eerily quiet. April could clearly hear herself breathe.

As the three strangers walked around, now changed in thin indigo-colored suits covering their entire bodies and faces, April attempted to speak but could not.

Then, in her mind, she heard, "Relax, April. You do not need to speak."

April looked over to the woman and thought, "Can you hear my thoughts?"

"Yes, April. We all can." She responded.

"Who are you?" April asked in her mind. "And why am I here?"

"We are your friends, April," the woman responded. "We are here to prepare for your return."

"Return?" April asked. "Am I going back…?"

"Yes," the woman responded.

"Will I be traveling through time?"

"No April," She responded. "This way is safer."

"What way?" April asked.

"Sleep," The woman replied

"Sleep?" April thought.

"Yes, April," April heard in her thoughts. It was a male communicating with her this time. He sounded familiar to April, but April was so entranced that she could not figure out who it was.

"You are going to sleep for a very long time," the voice said. "You will not age. You will be protected in this room. It is free of contaminates. It will be pressurized until it is time for you to awake."

April began to feel drowsier and weaker. Breathlessly she asked, "How?" She took a deep breath then asked, "Why…?"

As she heard the voices in her mind, the world was already beginning to change; time was beginning to elapse. It was as if the voices became dreams in an endless sleep.

As April heard the voices in her dreams, her three friends left the room, boarded the ambulance, and hovered away. They left April in the room inside the large edifice that April knew as the Museum of Anthropology in Philadelphia.

As she dreamt, explosions occurred around the building where she slept. Then, snow piled up all around. Winter lasted for years. Mountains of snow covered the building. As time passed, more explosions occurred; missiles flew in the skies. Tornadoes blew with great ferocity where April and the other survivors had stayed. Eventually, the winds and storms spread throughout the lands. The skies remained grey through the years with a burst of fiery red and orange flashing every once and again.

"Your name will be spoken and remembered, April," a voice said in April's head. "Those whose lives you touched will remember your words, inspiration and actions."

Sleeping through time as she dreamt, April spoke with the voice. "How can I lead if I am asleep?" she asked.

None of the voices answered, and April then fell into a deep sleep.

Suddenly, a massive explosion occurred a great distance away from the building where April slept. Although the explosion was far away, it was so massive that it could be seen and felt from where April slept. Then, a huge wall of heated smoke and debris rushed through the city blowing and tearing away almost every structure that stood in its path.

The building in which April slept still stood, but it was significantly damaged. The city was in ruins. Then, as time passed, immense snows, storms, and floods engulfed the city. As time continued to elapse, the waters dried away and the dust began to blow in from as far as the Sahara across the Atlantic Ocean. The world that April knew had now changed.

As her time was nearing, what April knew as an urban landscape was now a desert. Most of the buildings that once stood were now dust, sand, and memories. April now lay in a triangular golden shack awaiting her moment. The skies, now clear and bright, made the sands glow a golden color. In the distance, as time continued to elapse, strange and wonderful buildings were erected. Domes and pyramid-like structures rose; majestic objects flew in the skies. It appeared that the people were flourishing.

In the distance, opposite to where April lay, an abrupt flash of light then appeared in the sky. Out of the flash, a large object fell and crashed to the ground.

Seconds later, closer to the new city, another much smaller object fell as well. Smoke bellowed from both objects. Out of the smaller object that crashed near the city, a person appearing to be a young girl crawled out. Stumbling, she walked out of the wreckage and towards the city. Suddenly, after a few yards, she screamed and collapsed. Moments later, the girl gained strength and continued to stumble toward the city. Although she fell several times, the young girl managed to make it to the city alive.

As the young girl entered the city, she and the wreckage slowly began to disappear as if it was all an illusion; as if it did not really occur at all. Still, the wreckage that crashed in the shadows of the mountains, opposite to where April lay remained.

Years passed and the skies began to cloud once more. The desert sand no longer glimmered a golden reflection. In the distance, near where the city still stood, a rectangular structure was raised. Suddenly, a flash of light exploded in the sky just above the structure.

Time slowed down. Above the structure appeared what looked like a bubble or sphere. The sphere floated above the city and remained there for some time. Days passed and the sphere remained. Then, people and animals began to run from the city in a mad panic. The people began to run towards the mountain on the other side from where April rested. As they passed April's resting place, as if it were on purpose, no one looked at the golden pyramid. Some even ran passed the shack-like structure turning their heads or covering their eyes as if there were ashamed to look at it. Nevertheless, they ran past it towards the hills and away from the city that was once their home. Some others ran towards other directions.

A canyon where a river once flowed was nearby. Many ran towards the other side of that. There were also objects appearing to have passengers flying in other directions. The event was chaotic.

Time passed and the strange sphere remained in the sky. On the outskirts of the city, a barrier made of strange looking trees was created. It was miles long.

Then, with no warning at all, the sphere in the sky let out a silent energy and blue light that destroyed the city. The sphere then disappeared and the daytime skies became dark. Clouds grew above the destroyed city. Lightning flashed violently. As animals walked towards the city, they were scared away by the massive explosion created by the lighting.

Then, back where April slept, a quick sudden burst of steam blew out of the structure. It appeared as if the structure was depressurizing. Suddenly, there was another loud explosion from the lightning. The thunder was so great that April felt the ground shake, waking her from her long deep sleep.

Having lost some of her memory, April noticed that she was in was very dark and damp room. She quickly sat up. April was confused and frightened. Suddenly, there was another loud explosion.

April screamed.

"Where am I," she yelled. "Amisi!" she called.

No one answered.

She yelled louder, "Amisi! Anybody!"

Anxiously, she examined the room in which she was. April did not recognize where she was. The room's walls looked like they were made of old copper and there were no windows. She saw an old odd shaped door. As the ground continued to quake, April ran towards the door and pushed it open. Breathing heavily and trembling, April felt lost. She entered another room similar to the one she was just in. She ran towards another door and pushed it open. When April pushed the door open, she tripped down a step onto hard ground. April scraped her knee and the back of her right hand as she tried to break her fall.

Her knee was not too badly hurt. However, her hand was bleeding profusely. She looked at her hand in pain. Still, the site in front of her took her attention.

April stood up and stared. In front of her was a desert of grey sand with grey skies. She looked to see where the explosion came from. Suddenly, lightning struck a lone dried-up tree about 30 meters in front of her. As the explosion shook the ground, April jumped backwards, tripped over the step and through the door behind her. Confused, shaking and with tears in her eyes, April sat on the step and stared.

Far away, April noticed smoke. April also noticed that the lighting had died down and she began to walk. She looked back and curiously looked at the pyramid-like structure from which she came. Still a bit disoriented, she continued to walk toward the smoke without noticing the blood dripping from her hand. Leaving a trail of blood as she continued to walk, April continued to tremble and breathe heavily. All she wanted was to find someone. April was very scared. Nothing made sense to her.

Then, four wild dogs appeared from behind the triangular shack behind April in the distance. April did not notice them. She was too focused on what was in front of her. In the distance, April began to see flashing lights over the horizon. As the lights flashed in the eerie grey sky, the ground trembled softly. Still, behind her, the dogs followed. The dogs growled. April, almost in a daze, continued walking without noticing.

Trees then began to appear over the horizon. The trees were odd. As April walked closer, the trees looked more like giant bushes with purple leaves. They were spread out with a few meters in between each of them. The giant bushes ran for miles from both the right and the left as if to fence off the other side. As April fearfully walked closer to the odd shrubbery, the dogs ran faster towards her. By this point, it appeared as if the wild dogs were intending to harm April. Exhausted and ready to submit to the pain in body, heart and mind; April stumbled to the ground. When April fell, she noticed the dogs behind her. They were growling and running fast towards her.

April gasped. She gathered all the energy she had left in her, pushed herself up off of the ground and, confused, she began to run. April ran with fury in her eyes. After passing the row of bushes, she stumbled and fell to the ground. Suddenly, just as the dogs were about to pounce on April, a giant creature leaped out of the giant bushes. It was Balhib.

Letting out a giant roar, Balhib swatted one dog, stepped on another and roared loudly at the other two. The dogs bowed in fear, as if they were pleading for their lives.

"Leave these grounds!" Balhib yelled with a roaring voice.

The dogs continued to bow, howled and walked off.

The ground continued to quake.

Balhib turned to April and softly asked, "April, are you alright? Your hand…"

Balhib rubbed his mane on the scrape, wiping the blood away. He then had April climb onto his back.

"Where are we? What happened? Why was I…?" April asked exhaustedly.

"Things are not the way they were April." Balhib answered.

Balhib began to walk quickly towards the light over the horizon.

"Rest, April," Balhib said. "You need time to gain your strength."

After some hours of resting on Balhib's back, trying to recover, April kept falling in and out of sleep. April then awoke from a dream that reminded her of most of the things that she had experienced.

"Balhib," April said.

"Yes, April," he replied.

"How did you come to this…?" April stumbled in her words, not really knowing what questions to ask or how to ask them. "I mean, how is it that you are…? Where did you come from, Balhib?" She asked.

"April, it is not really important where I came from or how I was created." Balhib responded. "I *was* created, April, so to speak. But, all that I am going to tell you is this: Imagine a people who were so intelligent and, at the same time, in such pain and in such a state of abandonment and resentment; hopelessness and in need of a reminder of where they came from. And, after over a hundred years, they used their intelligence and need for this reminder to push through; to survive... With their intelligence, newfound resources and partnerships with animals and nature; they created this 'symbol'- a symbol of protection and of the greatness from which they came. I suppose that you can say that I am a product of this."

April pondered.

Balhib then continued, "Thousands of years ago, April, a people were given this Earth. In fact, they were given the privilege to reign over this Earth. Now, they were definitely not perfect... Not in the beginning and, most certainly, not throughout their reign. This people needed constant reminders from their '*Giver.*' They needed redirection quite often, for they were far from perfect and in need of discipline. Nevertheless, the Earth was given to them. But, as a loving parent would do for his children, their 'Giver'- a much higher being- sent Himself down often to repair damages, provide redirection, guidance and sometimes discipline. I am sure you have heard these stories, April."

April listened carefully, as Balhib continued.

"And the people reigned, April. They created and built. They created languages and arithmetic; agriculture, arts and sciences. They built structures, cities and societies. And, while they made mistakes throughout their reign, they reigned nonetheless.

But... They were invaded. They were attacked. They were attacked by a..." Balhib chose his words carefully. He then shook his head. "I cannot find a word that can fully describe what they were. They implanted themselves into this Earth and strategically began to take the people and their culture; their stories and creations… They gave these stories new faces and new names; made them their own. And, the invaders did this to '*humanize*' themselves… To make it easier to connect with those they wanted to oppress. This made the invasion easier.

The 'Giver' saw this and attempted to intervene. But, many of his children did not recognize him due to the extent of this invasion. But, he managed to remain recognizable to enough of his children to keep the invasion from being completely successful."

Balhib then became quiet.

April, expecting more to the story, asked more questions.

"Why? Why and how did animals get involved?" she asked.

Balhib answered. "Well, this is their Earth as well, April. It was gifted to them as well. And they serve an important role on Earth just as the people do. They have always shared this gift and so, they must share the responsibility in its protection.

"But what about the one's that tried to kill me?" April asked.

Balhib chuckled, "many of our animals were corrupted just as many of our people were. Just like the people did not recognize their *Giver*, those animals did not recognize you."

There was a silence.

"There was a strong relationship once between the people and the animals. Humans argue that they themselves have evolved far more advanced than other animals on this planet. But, the fact is that all living creatures have evolved appropriately and all creatures are 'advanced' in their own right. Tell me, can a human survive naked in a tropical forest as a gorilla would? Would he survive in the ocean as a dolphin would? Humans understood this one. There was an understanding between all creatures. They all understood their niche and there was a strong relationship. But, after the invasion, the understanding dissipated and the relationship faded. Animals gradually drifted back into their environments, leaving the humans to themselves. Some relationships remained in the manner that you saw in your world- pets and such. But, that was due to the niches that were created throughout time- humans needing companionship, those companions needing food and shelter; humans needing food and so on."

There was a long moment of silence, as April thought about everything that she was just told.

April sighed and asked more about the story. "Then what happened?? What happened to the people?"

"Their reign did not truly end, April. It was simply interrupted," Balhib answered. "Thousands of years of greatness, cannot be erased with a few hundred years of corruption."

"So... Then, what?" April asked. "How do the people rebuild themselves?"

"The 'Giver' sent himself to the Earth to repair damages?" Balhib asked. "He came often, either as His own son or as a messenger. The stories are many but few are told, and they are altered..."

"Yes!" April exclaimed. "This is all starting to make sense! My life! The people... Those who are gifted- me, Anayah, Eugenio, Amisi and her people! And, so many others... And," April paused, elated and laughing. "I... We... We have been preparing to fight with you. This is what I have been preparing for... You! You are Him, Balhib!

Balhib smiled and remained silent for a moment.

They then, approached the city.

Seeing a half-destroyed pyramid like structure, April was surprised. She was perplexed.

It was a city in ruins. People roamed the streets appearing to be depressed and paranoid. Animals, behaving completely different from the way they behaved the last time April was in this world. The animals were fighting and growling at each other over scraps of food found on the ground. The city that April once found to be magical now appeared to be in shambles.

"No!" Balhib responded. His image then began to fade, and his voice began to echo away. "Not me."

Suddenly, the memories in Aprils mind changed. The children jumping on Balhib's paw changed to children jumping with joy because they knew of his presence. The memory of Amisi greeting Balhib changed to her taking a moment to pray with April before they went on their way to the festival. And, at the festival, when Balhib entered the room; that memory changed to the people taking a moment to pray before they commenced.

And the dogs; April was the one who fought them off. When she fell, she felt an energy surge through her that made her fight and scare those dogs off with her gift.

"I knew that you were the 'Giver' who sent Himself down for his people..." April said, seeming confused. "But, you also said that you were created…"

"April," Balhib replied. "I am often 'created' and recreated. I am often given a name, a face, and an image. The people often found themselves needing comfort and, in those times, I am recreated for them."

"So, I *am* here to fight with you!" April stated, seeming to have found her answer."

Balhib, his face nearly faded away, smiled. "April, I sent you here *as* me."

Balhib then disappeared.

"But, I was thinking that it was through science or something," April argued. "Not like… Wait! But why am I *here*? Why here? Why this time?"

As his face completely faded and his voice echoed away, Balhib said, "To see."

Suddenly, there was an explosion. April was knocked to the ground due to the blast. April found herself back in front of the shack like pyramid structure from where she awoke. April looked up and, over the horizon saw a large group of people. It appeared to be two groups of people in conflict. Explosions, death and destruction consumed April's surrounding. All of the sudden, the conflicts closely surrounded April.

April watched in dismay as people- the people who she came to know as her people- were destroying themselves. She looked over and saw a young girl fighting.

"Amisi!?"April called.

When the girl turned, April saw Amisi for a moment. Then her face changed. The person who she was fighting with caught April's attention.

"Anayah!?" April called.

At that moment, April felt someone approach her from behind. April then quickly turned and, before she could react, she was grasped by the throat. As April struggled for air, so much that she could barely open her eyes, she looked at the man holding her. She saw the face that she had seen twice before- once in the hospital in Puerto Rico and again in Anthony's home.

"You did this!" the pale-faced man said to April with a chilling voice.

April, without thinking; and with all of her emotion, let out a burst of electric energy that jerked her body and flashed into the man.

The pale-skinned man smiled and, with a thick accent, he said, "Look around you April."

"Who are you?" April asked, as she struggled to catch her breath.

"I am your past April," the man grunted as he gripped tighter to April's neck. He smiled sadistically and said, "I am your future." He then chuckled, "You think killing me will help? That is, if you think you could actually kill me."

Then, as her eyes began to water from struggling, the skies became darker than they already were. The clouds became thick and the crackle of the thunder echoed in the skies.

"You are not my past... I don't know you." April struggled to say as tears fell from her eyes due to her struggle to breathe.

"Of course you know me April!" the man laughed

April was deeply afraid. She wondered what type of gift this man had.

"Gifts?" the man asked as he laughed.

April grew more afraid as she realized that he had just read her mind.

"You think that I have 'gifts'?" the evil man asked. "You think that what I have is man-made? That I *evolved* into this?" He laughed. "You know nothing of what I have! I am much more than that, little girl. I am much more than you and your race. And I am tired of you, your people; your 'world.' You will now die."

Suddenly, Balhib, as if he appeared out of the dust in the air, jumped towards April and the man holding her and pounced on the man. Just as Balhib was about to bite the man's head off, the man turned into flames and disappeared. Balhid then ran into the crowd of people and disappeared.

April was dumbfounded. But, she took no time to think of the situation and continued to look at the people fighting. Feeling somewhat responsible for what was going on around her; April began screaming at the people to stop fighting. But no one stopped. They could not hear her. No one paid April any attention. Then, a large flame burst out of the ground and a man, different from the man she just struggled with, jumped from out of the flame. With fiery red eyes, light skin and no hair, the man began to run towards April with fury. His hands began to flame. Without hesitation but with fear, April quickly shot a burst of electric energy towards her attacker. The man disintegrated. Then, another man jumped out of another burst of flames and ran towards her. Once again, April disintegrated him. Then another, and another. They continued to come after her.

At that moment, the people's attention began to turn towards April. Just then, April realized that the people battling around her had nothing to do with her fight with the men who were attacking her. She realized this because, as the people noticed her fighting these men, the people stopped fighting one another and started showing concern for this person they've never seen before but somehow recognized- April.

The men ran at her one after another, knocking her to the ground. April had blood coming from her mouth and nose. The evil men did not appear to want to kill April immediately. It was as if they were tormenting her. Then the first pale-skinned man appeared again out of nowhere. He quickly grasped her throat. April struggled to breathe as she gurgled the blood that was in her mouth.

She struggled to speak, "Why…"

"Who do you think you are to ask me anything, little girl?" the man roared. He then threw April.

The man could easily kill her and everyone around her but he did not. April realized how powerful he was. Still, in fear, she attempted to shoot him with her gift. But the man put his hand up. With his sudden movement, April was without power.

"I was to reign!" the man yelled at April with anger. He then walked to April and said, "This," he pointed around. "This is… This was to be mine." He then picked April up by her hair. "But you and your followers had to screw it all up for me," he said. "This earth is mine."

April looked at him confused.

"You still don't know?" He asked April angrily.

As he spoke, men jumped from the flames with spears and what appeared to be branding sticks. The men began to attack the people burning marks on any exposed body parts.

April, with blood covering her face, stared at this evil being unafraid, but weak.

"How could you not know about me?" the man asked arrogantly. "My story is told in English, Latin, Arabic and Hebrew and every other language in this *'God-forsaken'* world…" He paused. "God-forsaken." He laughed.

April, struggling to remain conscious asked, "Are you the devil?"

The evil being responded, "Devil, Shaytan, Satan…" He laughed. He then mocked, "I am that I am. *I*," he stressed as he pulled April's face closer to his. "…am that I am!" He then threw April to the ground and watched the people be ravaged by his soldiers. "It could have been much easier for you and your people," He said with a deep dark tone. "It was to be so that you all had a choice. Either accept me and be allowed to live in this world with me, or suffer. But then you were born." He ran to April and picked her up by her hair again and yelled, "Who the hell are you?" He then threw her to the ground once again sending her skidding several feet away. "You are not a God! You are not a 'Messiah!' You are a little girl." He then quickly threw a flame at April. But with the little power she still had, April put up an electric shield and blocked it."

He then ran to her and picked her up again.

"You think those *'powers'* are any match against me, little girl?" he asked while burning her arms with his grip.

April screamed in pain. She turned to look at the people. They were no longer fighting each other. They were running in fear as the evil army of monstrous men chased them to either cut their heads off or brand their skin.

April cried. She looked around and, with an exhausted whisper she called, "Balhib!"

"April," She heard in her thoughts. "You are not just a girl. You were never just a girl." It was the voice of Balhib. "Your story was written, April. It was written and re-written in all of the languages as well. Your coming was written. The story was changed throughout the centuries. It was combined with myths and truth. You have lived what has never before been lived. You have not lived a life. You have lived lessons. Lessons preparing you for what you must now face. You are the *Giver* and the *Given.*"

April's eyes widened, as she finally got what Balhib has been trying to tell her. April felt a sense of enlightenment and empowerment. Suddenly, April was alone.

▲ Chapter 7
Nekhtet

April awoke. First she heard beeping and a hissing sound. Then, she heard voices.

A voice gasped. "I can't believe it!" The voice said excitedly.

Two other voices sounded cheerful as April began to move her body.

She was in a bed in a very bright room. She was in a hospital.

"Ms. Lewis? Ms. Lewis," A woman called. She had a thick accent.

April turned slowly and looked for the voice. Her eyes hurt as if she had not used them for some time. Her vision was blurry. She could barely see. She then turned to the voice.

With very little strength, April felt surprised. But, due to her lack of strength, April was unable to express her emotions. She saw a nurse. The woman who called April's name looked like the nurse from the hospital in Puerto Rico, Mayet. But, because she was so weak, April could not express what she was feeling. April felt that she had been asleep for a very long time. She kept falling in and out of consciousness. However, she noticed people in her room show happiness as if it was a very good and miraculous thing for her to be awake.

Days passed, and April lay in her bed. She had gained little strength. Yet she was able to sit up at times, with the help of her inclining bed, and ponder. Gradually, April began to believe that it had all may have been a dream. She could not remember much except what she had grown to believe was a dream—the desert, the beautiful city; her life with her mother and Eugenio Martinez… In her heart, she felt love, sadness and longing for them. But, she could not help but feel that it was not real.

The people who continued to enter her room had very familiar faces. She saw the doctor who looked like Dupri, the nurse who looked like Mayet; another doctor who looked like Saini. But, she did not see Amisi, Anayah, Martinez, or Khai. Still, she paid that fact no mind for she was almost convinced that it was all a long lifelike dream.

Her hospital room, where it was apparent that she had been in for some time, was decorated with an abundance of flowers, letters, stuffed animals and children's drawings. There were pictures of flowers and animals. Then, April saw pictures of pyramids and people in ancient Egyptian garb. She then saw a drawing that captivated her. Unable to speak and move much, April grew excited. What she saw was a drawing of a great sphinx. At the bottom of the drawing was a short note.

The note said, *"Ms. Lewis, thank you so much for being there for me. You have saved my life in many ways. You have been like the Great Sphinx you taught us about watching over me. I will never forget you. Love, Balhib Shahid."*

After reading the note, April was practically convinced that what she had felt to be real maybe was not. She began to feel that she now needed to come to terms with her present situation. She needed to start remembering what had brought her to where she sat.

There was excitement around her. "She's awake. She's awake!" April would hear people say.

As people would come into her room, they would hug her. Sadly, April did not remember who they were. Some faces, she would recognize. But many she could not place. As they came and left her room, interestingly to April, they would walk to her window, look outside and smile. People would say very little. They knew, as they were told by doctors, that if they said too much to April, it may be too overwhelming for her. So those who visited said little. They would sit by her bedside, hold her hand and smile.

While being visited, someone turned the television on in April's room. The evening news was on.

"In other news," the reporter said. "The government is calling for calm in the streets as great excitement continues to build in the '*Enhoods*' communities over the awakening of…" Suddenly the television was turned off.

"She should not be watching this," the nurse said as she unplugged the television. "Not yet."

April turned her head and showed no care.

For some time, April sat. She was too far from the window to look out. But April would often hear helicopters and jet planes fly across the sky. She wondered about what was going on in this world that she suddenly awoke to.

Then, April was surprised by her visitor one morning. It was early in the morning. Still unable to speak or show much emotion, when she saw who walk in, April felt shocked. It was Anayah. Or at least it looked like her; only a bit older

April stared, as Anayah walked over to her bed.

"Is this Anayah?" April wondered. "Is her name Anayah?"

"Hey Sis," the young woman said with much excitement. She then kissed April on the forehead. "I came by the other day. But you were asleep." Tears began to build in the girl's eyes. "They tell me that I shouldn't say much…" she became choked up. "…Because it might 'overwhelm' you."

April stared at the girl.

"Do you remember who I am, April?" the girl asked. "It's me, Anayah. Your best friend"

April suddenly felt a sense of relief and happiness. Tears began to fall from her eyes. She then smiled. With the little strength she had, April nodded.

Anayah then leaned towards April and gave her a big hug.

Anayah then turned around and looked towards the door. She then whispered, "Do you remember anything?"

With tears still in her eyes, April shook her head no.

"…Seven months ago, April" Anayah said. "The two people who saved you were heroes. Their names were Eve Walker and Iris Gutierrez."

April stared and appeared confused. April, finding strength to speak asked breathlessly, "Heroes…?"

"Well, they were able to keep you alive and get you through the crowds to get to this hospital. You could have ended up in one of the outside hospitals and they would have surely let you die."

Anayah realized that April did not understand. She hesitated but asked, "Can you walk, April?"

April thought for a moment. She then nodded.

Anayah then grabbed April by the hand and helped her up. She then began to walk April towards the window.

As April made her way towards the window, she looked at the golden sky. She noticed that they were on the fourth or fifth floor. As she walked closer, April noticed something beyond her belief. She became breathless from what she saw. Suddenly, voices began to scream with excitement as April stood at the window. She saw what must have been thousands of people standing outside the hospital. April was overwhelmed. She saw her picture and name portrayed on banners. Anayah unlocked the thick glass windows while holding on to April as if she were an older woman and pushed the windows open.

Then, as more and more people noticed that it was April who was standing at the window, a loud roar began to spread. Excited and filled with joy, people began to scream and cry. The roar spread for a long distance. It echoed throughout skies. April noticed people reaching for her with tears in their eyes. Signs that read, "You are queen," were scattered throughout the crowd.

Startled by the noise, the nurses and doctors ran into the room about to yell at Anayah. But they stopped and watched as April took in the joy. They watched in awe and with pride.

April, weak and overwhelmed, turned to Anayah. "How…? Why…?" April asked breathlessly.

Anayah smiled at April and explained, "It started with one student," She paused to laugh. "I was your first. Then a dozen. You taught them not only their history but also their future. You taught them to not settle for contentment. You taught them to reach for happiness; to fight for happiness if they had to. They did... They even had to fight their own, sadly." She paused to cry for a moment. "It took a while. But…" Anayah paused again. "You touched their lives. Don't you remember? …Your lectures, classes, and marches? …Your books?"

"Books?" April whispered.

"Yes, April!" Anayah exclaimed. "Everything from social justice to the pros and cons of time travel to genetics… You told them about possibilities. April, you are a genius."

"Time travel? Genetics?" April asked.

"Yes!" Anayah answered. "Anti- matter; time- space manipulation."

April continued to struggle to speak but continued. She pointed to the crowd. "This, for studies? For books?" She asked.

Anayah stared at April and looked puzzled because April did not understand.

"No, April," she answered. "Because you gave back. It was for us… April, understand that it was more than your research and writings. It was more that your teachings. You are tough. You made them see what they didn't always want to see. You hurt their feelings when they needed to be hurt. Showed them… Showed us… Love when we didn't deserve to be shown love…"

April began to drift away into her thoughts. It now made sense to her. She came to the realization that it may all indeed have been a dream. It made so much sense. Her books on time travel, history, and genetics. She understood that she was a teacher, which may explain the school; the drawings on the wall. It all came together like a puzzle. She was finally beginning to accept that it was all a dream. But what about her mother, she thought. What about Amisi? What about Khai? What about the man she loved and the man who tried to tear them apart? What about going back and forth from time to time and place to place? As the years passed, they felt so real. But, she thought again. What about her mother? And what about Amisi?

"… And then came that day," Anayah continued. "…The day you put yourself in front of the bullet."

April became perplexed. She then reached her hand to the upper part of her chest and felt it. It was a scar. April began to shed tears. It was the scar she looked for when she was with Martinez. Another clue.

"They had enough of you and your following. They sent the National Guard to put a stop to your…" Anayah paused and sighed. "You weren't even concerned with them. All you were doing was trying to fight and strengthen your own. You weren't even fighting them or protesting them. You weren't even thinking about them. It was all about you and your people,"

Anayah stressed as she pounded her right fist onto the palm of her left hand. "But they still felt threatened. They put a warrant out for your arrest for breaking fabricated laws...," She paused again then continued. "You were snuck on an airplane to leave the city to go to a gathering in New York. The National Guard found out and came to the airport to halt the plane... There must have been over a thousand people there. As the crowd was disbursing because they realized that they drew too much attention, some guardsmen began to provoke some of the people. As you were coming down the stairs of the airplane peacefully, one of the guards screamed 'gun,' you jumped in the middle and you were shot. The people fought to get you medical attention but the guard wouldn't let them. Eve Walker and Iris Gutierrez were guards. They turned around, pointed their guns on their own men and had you escorted to an ambulance. They made sure you were brought here safely. Out of fear of 'retaliation,' as they say, neighborhoods were enclosed by the army. People were sicking their pets on the soldiers. Then, many animals were killed." Anayah laughed from frustration. "I would come to your bedside every day and tell you what was going on. I cried when I told you about the animals. It was the saddest thing."

The story that Anayah was telling April explained a lot. April understood now the correlation between what she was being told and what she had now been convinced to have been a dream. But one thing that was not a dream, was her following.

"But, April," Anayah said cautiously. "That's not all. The government was attacked. The president and most of his cabinet were killed. Many people in the government turned on each other. There is now a president with very little power and the military now practically runs itself. They have our neighborhoods enclosed."

April loses focus once more. She became overwhelmed. She could not take in so much information. It was too much for her.

"Stop," She said as loudly as possible. "My mother?" she asked.

"Miss Amisi?" Anayah responded.

April paused in shock. She did not understand. She became confused. She wanted to ask about Amisi. But she was more concerned with her mother.

"My mother?" April asked again as she sat on the bed.

"Your mother, Miss Amisi was…"

Suddenly, April entered into a state of thought so deep that Anayah's voice became distant and practically mute. April understood now that Amisi was the name of her mother. That was the final piece of the story that she needed. April was now convinced. She no longer felt the need to wonder. Whether her mother was dead or alive; whether she was there or away. None of it mattered. She now knew that Amisi was her mother.

Then, as Anayah and April sat silently for a brief moment, they heard something. They listened closely as the crowd outside quieted down. The sound came closer and closer. The sound echoed across the sky like drum beating its way through the clouds. April struggled to get up. Anayah helped her up and they both walked to the window. As they watched, the nurses and doctors on the floor ran to April's room. One nurse placed her hand over her mouth as she gasped in disbelief.

"They are actually going to go through with it," a doctor said.

"No. It can't be." Anayah said.

April turned to Anayah with a puzzled look on her face.

"They have come to kill us April." Anayah said.

April did not understand. She wondered how she and her supporters, students and followers could be such a threat that the military would send helicopters to kill them.

"All we want is change April," Anayah said. "All we want is change."

April still did not understand the severity of the situation. She looked down at the people. As she examined the crowd, she noticed a man who looked like Mr. Chen surrounded by young students who looked like they may have been his students. Some of the children hugged his waist in fear. He consoled them. In the crowd nearby, there stood two men who looked like Alkys and Mr. Rivera. They also were surrounded by a group of students. The children cried as they appeared to know what was about to happen.

Just a few yards away, April saw an older man in a security guard uniform. The man looked like Chief Monroe. He turned and, with tears in his eyes, looked up at where April stood. When he made eye contact with April, he smiled then turned.

"We wanted to be free," Anayah said. "Free from things as simple as propaganda and media control. But then it got bigger. It got so much bigger."

"We then learned that there was so much more," a doctor said. "We learned about the changed history; the falsified history books, laws, doctrines. How this country came about and how others were destroyed... How peoples were conquered and destroyed and how it was covered up."

April's dream conclusively came together.

Anayah turned to April and said. "You made us aware, April. You led us to…" Anayah paused to look fearfully at the helicopters as they approached. "You," she said almost breathlessly, "you taught us to be strong enough to ask, search, and contest."

"And now they've come to end it," A nurse said.

"BOOM!" the first missile exploded near the crowd. Then another missile was released.

April felt great terror and an overwhelming sense of anxiety.

The nurses and doctors screamed in horror.

Anayah held April in fear.

Emotions ran rampant within April. Fear overtook her heart and spirit. But then, a split second of clarity came unexpectedly to April.

"My gift…" April then heard within her. "My gift," said the voice of Balhib.

Suddenly, as if she was overtaken by a great energy, she felt great strength.

She looked at the crowd as they scattered looking for shelter; crying in fear. April quickly looked around as if to analyze the moment. She looked in the sky and, behind the helicopters; she saw a massive airplane headed towards them. When she had realized what that airplane may be bringing, April thought no more.

Without hesitation, April raised her hands and felt an immense power burst from her body. As she aimed at the helicopters, they exploded. Then, she aimed at the approaching airplane. A giant ball of energy surrounded the airplane. Then, electricity within the ball struck the vehicle causing it to implode. The nuclear bomb that it carried detonated, causing the ball of energy to blast and send a massive force of energy throughout the sky. The force of that energy was so great, that all of the electricity in that part of the world was lost. Seconds later, it began to rain.

*"**nekhtet**" (nekh-TET) or "VICTORY!" The perfect Kemetic word for situations where you feel you have overcome something, or you wish to extend praise to another person or situation that deserves praise; equivalent to the English custom of shouting "Hooray!" Some Kemetic Orthodox liturgies and prayers include the repeating (or shouting) of "Nekhtet!" in a litany.*

Mark Martinez is a writer of poetry, short stories, novels and fictional narratives. He is a servant leader in the city of Philadelphia, where he is passionate about the education and advancement of children of color.

Mark is a father of three girls and he is avid about creating literature that illustrate characters that they can relate to. His writings address social issues such as education, Civil Rights, African/Indigenous & Latino/Caribbean history and culture.

www.ingramcontent.com/pod-product-compliance
Lightning Source LLC
Chambersburg PA
CBHW031304170626

46807CB00001B/310